precious bones

precious bones

Mika Ashley-Hollinger

A Yearling Book

All rights reserved. Published in the United States by Yearling, an imprint of Random House Children's Books, a division of Random House, Inc., New York. Originally published in hardcover in the United States by Delacorte Press, an imprint of Random House Children's Books, New York, in 2012.

Yearling and the jumping horse design are registered trademarks of Random House, Inc.

Visit us on the Web! randomhouse.com/kids

Educators and librarians, for a variety of teaching tools, visit us at RHTeachersLibrarians.com

The Library of Congress has cataloged the hardcover edition of this work as follows:
Ashley-Hollinger, Mika.
Precious Bones / Mika Ashley-Hollinger. — 1st ed.
p. cm.
Summary: In 1949 in the Florida Everglades, a ten-year-old girl called Bones, whose father is part Miccosukee Indian, tries to discover what really happened when he is accused of two murders and sent to jail.
ISBN 978-0-385-74219-1 (hc) — ISBN 978-0-307-97421-1 (ebook) —
ISBN 978-0-375-99046-5 (glb) [1. Country life—Florida—Everglades—Fiction.
2. Fathers—Fiction. 3. Mikasuki Indians—Fiction. 4. Indians of North America—
Florida—Fiction. 5. Everglades (Fla.)—History—20th century—Fiction.] I. Title.
PZ7.A8266Pr 2012
[Fic]—dc23
2011028581

ISBN 978-0-307-93070-5 (pbk.)

Printed in the United States of America

10 9 8 7 6 5 4 3 2 1

First Yearling Edition 2013

This is dedicated to my mom,
who did not have the opportunity to write this story,
but without whose help I never would have been able to.

And to my dad,
for having the courage to walk on the wild side.

the storm

The sweltering month of July was gradually melting into August. Baby alligators were busy pecking their way out of their eggs when the biggest storm of the summer of 1949 blew into our lives. I was standing in the middle of our living room floor, cool brown water swirling over my feet and reaching nearly to the tops of my skinny ten-year-old ankles. The morning sun was just peeking in through our picture window, painting shiny rainbows across the water's dull surface.

My daddy, Nolay, paced slowly from one end of the room to the other. He was just as barefooted as me because there was no reason to be wearing shoes inside your house when it was full of water. Each small step sent ripples of coffee-colored water circling around the legs of what pieces of furniture we hadn't stacked on top of each other. Nolay solemnly raised his arms in the air and declared, "We live in the womb of the world! It's the womb of the world. Any fool can see it's God's womb of the world!"

Like a contented cat, Mama was curled up on the couch.

I don't think she was really that contented, she just didn't have any choice but to sit there. Her slender arms wrapped around her legs and hugged them close to her body. Her head rested on her knees; only her eyes moved back and forth as she watched my daddy's every move.

Out of the corner of my eye I saw something dark and shiny slither along the side of the wall right behind the couch. I kept my mouth shut, because if there was one thing Mama didn't like, especially inside her house, it was snakes.

I was not quite sure what a womb was, but if Nolay said we lived in one, then it must be true. My daddy was about the smartest man I ever did know. I hadn't met very many men, but of the ones I had, he was about the smartest. He was a true man of vision.

He'd had the vision to nestle our house between a glorious Florida swamp and a long stretch of sandy scrub palmetto laced with majestic old pines. Although Mama often pointed out that his vision blurred when it came to the exact location. "If you had put this house a hundred yards closer to the county road we would have electricity. We would have a icebox and a sewing machine," Mama would say.

Nolay would shake his shaggy black curls and reply, "Lori, Honey Girl, you know I don't want to be any closer to that dang county road!"

Honey Girl was my daddy's nickname for Mama because her blond hair dripped down her back and around her shoulders like golden honey.

"If I could, I would have put us on a float right out in the middle of the swamp. But don't you fret, one day I'll buy my own durn electric poles and stick 'em in the ground myself."

But Mama couldn't deny that Nolay had had the vision to build our house on a strip of land at least a foot above water level. It only flooded when the heavy summer rains came. It really wasn't that bad; sometimes the water just seeped in and covered our floor with a fine, shiny mist.

Our house also had a flat tar-paper roof because, as Nolay had explained, "No matter how big a storm comes through, this roof will stay put. You go puttin' one of those pointed roofs on and sure as shootin' the first hurricane will take it off. Same thing goes for puttin' your house up on stilts." Yes, sir, Nolay was a true man of vision.

At any rate, all the excitement had started the day before. Me and Mama had just returned from a Saturday trip to town and were inside the house putting away groceries when Nolay called us.

"Honey Girl, Bones, y'all come on out here and take a look at this." He was standing in the yard looking east. That was where the Atlantic Ocean lived, and most of our storms came from that direction.

What I saw filled up the horizon. It looked like a massive black jellyfish. The cloud floated just above the ground and moved with fierce intent, heading directly toward us. The three of us stood like fence posts until Nolay said, "That's a mighty big storm coming our way. Y'all get the animals inside the house."

Me and Mama sprang to life, called the dogs, and looked for the cats. Half an hour later I made a final count: three dogs, five cats, one raccoon, one pig, and one goat, everyone accounted for. As I ran out the door I yelled over my shoulder, "Mama, I'm goin' out to help Nolay."

Nolay had just closed the door to the chicken coop. Old Ikibob Rooster sensed something was up and already had his brood cornered in one end of the coop. By the time we headed for the house, that jellyfish cloud was nearly on top of us. It hungrily gobbled up the silver-blue day and turned it into gloomy darkness.

As it hovered above us, it looked as if God reached his long pointy-finger down from heaven and ripped a huge gash in the stomach of that jellyfish. Gray sheets of water fell furiously to the ground. Cannonballs of thunder crashed and rolled angrily over the swamps. Like gigantic knives, silver streaks of lightning sliced through the darkness and stabbed the earth.

Me and all the animals were wide-eyed and looking for something to crawl under. Except for the flashes of lightning and the soft flicker of our kerosene lamps, our house was as black as the inside of a cow. I had never been inside a cow, but I imagined this was how totally dark it would be.

Our summer storms usually dumped a ton of water in the swamps. Water was precious to swamps; they needed it to stay alive. Sometimes a thin layer of water would run through our house, but this storm was big, and it was angry. The swamp quickly filled and began to leak out over its shallow edges. The little sliver of land our house sat on was soaked up like a dirty dishrag. Swamp water, along with some of its inhabitants, seeped under doorways and through cracks and crannies.

Water came from every direction; it slid down the sides of our walls and dripped from the ceiling in endless streams.

Nolay began to bark out instructions. "Stack up them chairs, put a quilt on the table and get the cats up there, put the dogs in our bed, get the pig and goat into the washtub! Bones, do something with that dang crazy raccoon!"

When the three of us sat huddled together on the couch, Nolay murmured, "Don't worry about nothing, it's just a little water. It's just a storm, a big storm, but it's not a hurricane. The roof will stay on."

It was too wet and too dark for us to make it to a bedroom, so we decided it was best to just stay put right there on the couch. Nestled between the two of them, I fell asleep with the assurance that Nolay knew about hurricanes. The one in 1935 had blown his family home clear down to the ground. That house sat not ten feet away from the very spot we were at right now. About the only thing left was a pile of bricks where the chimney had stood, the artesian well that we still got our water from, and a mammoth mango tree.

On occasion, when things would get out of hand, like they were right now, Mama would look over to Nolay and say, "Why did you build our house next to one that blew down in a storm? You could have put us on higher ground."

But my daddy, with his vision and truthfulness, would reply, "Because this is where my home is and always will be. Don't worry, Honey Girl, I guarantee this house ain't gonna blow down."

Nolay's real name was Seminole, but no one ever called him that. His daddy, who was Miccosukee Indian, named him in honor of their kindred tribe. Nolay lived up to the true meaning of his name, which was "runaway; wild one."

All night long that storm pounded us with huge fists of water. At the break of dawn, as we waded through our living room, the first words out of Nolay's mouth were "Well, am I right or am I right? I said the dang roof would stay on, and it did!"

Nolay was right about the roof staying on, and it wouldn't be a concern any longer. Our real troubles would be coming all too soon.

saving the day

Mama refused to get off the couch, even after Nolay offered her a piggyback ride. She hugged her legs close to her body and kept her chin on her knees. She was not about to stick her feet in that dirty brown water. Just as Mama turned her head sideways, a little black snake wriggled along the side of the wall. She pointed and said, "My goodness, what is that? Is that a snake inside our house?"

I quickly waded over to it. "It's only a baby. It's scared and it's just trying to find its way back outside."

Mama groaned. "And I want it to go back outside." She looked at Nolay. "What else has the womb of the world dumped inside our house?"

"Lori, that's just a little ol' baby, it squeezed in through a crack. Don't worry; they ain't nothing in here but some harmless water."

I crept behind the couch and gingerly picked the snake up by its slippery little tail. I turned to Mama and said, "Look, Mama, it ain't much bigger than a fat old fishin' worm. It's probably one of Old Blackie's babies. I'll just take it outside where it belongs." Blackie was our resident blacksnake. She lived in the giant mango tree in our backyard.

Armed with Crisco cans and mason jars, I was ready to go outside and catch the bounty of tadpoles, minnows, and whatever else the swamp had spilled out on our driveway. Or what we called our driveway; it was actually a two-rut dirt road with ditches cut in on both sides. After every big summer rain I took it on myself to go out and catch as many living things as I could and dump them into the pond in our front yard. Of course, a fair amount of the creatures I would be picking up that day came from the pond in our front yard, but I felt it was my duty to save as many as I could.

With a great display of authority I dropped the pathetic little snake in my Crisco can and made my way to the front door. I whistled, and our three dogs, Nippy the raccoon, and Pearl the pig almost knocked me down as they clambered toward the door. Harry the goat had made himself quite comfortable in the washtub, his head hung over the rim and his big glassy eyes looking forlornly in my direction.

I strapped my trusty Roy Rogers cap pistols around my waist and opened the front door. I was getting too old to still be playing with cap pistols, but they just felt like a couple of friends hanging out with me. Nolay called out, "Bones, you watch out for snakes. Take a hoe or machete with you. They bound to be lookin' for dry land. And keep your eye on those dang dogs; the fools will stick their nose right on top of a snake."

"Yes, sir, Nolay, I'll look out for 'em."

Outside, the road was spotted with mud puddles full of minnows and tadpoles. Barefooted, I waded very gingerly through the brown water, just in case there was a snake laying around. The thirsty Florida sun had already begun to suck up huge amounts of precious water. As the puddles dried, the helpless little creatures were left to die a slow death in the heat.

I found the perfect spot and started building sand dams to reroute the water and trap the critters. Nippy ran happily from puddle to puddle and snatched up minnows and tadpoles. She would squat down on her haunches and with her little humanlike hands devour the critters like pieces of candy. I knew I couldn't interfere. Nolay had told me, "That's the way God set up nature; one day you're sittin' at the dinner table and the next day you might be on it."

Pearl dug a mudhole by some twisted palmetto roots and the dogs romped through the tangled scrub pines. I had nearly filled a whole Crisco can with squirmy things ready to be set loose in our big front pond, when I heard a gunshot ring out from the direction of our house.

I turned and ran as fast as I could back to the house. The dogs followed in hot pursuit. One of the dogs, Paddlefoot, smashed through my dams and sent cans and jars full of saved creatures wriggling out over the dry sand.

Breathlessly, I opened the door and stepped inside our living room. Mama stood on top of the couch, her little pearl-handled .32 revolver in her hand. Nolay was in front of her, a dead cottonmouth moccasin laying on the floor between them. He picked it up and held it by its tail. Part of the snake's body still curled on the floor; a trickle of blood flowed from its head and swirled out into the glossy brown water.

Nolay looked the body up and down and calmly said, "Well, I got to admit, that is a mighty big snake. Bigger than me, gotta be over six feet."

Mama stood still as a stone on the couch, the pistol pointed in the direction of the snake and Nolay.

Nolay said, "Honey Girl, you are one dead-eyed shot. Look at this, right through the head." He cleared his throat. "You might want to put that gun down. This snake cain't get no more deader than it is right now."

Mama moved her eyes from the snake to the gun; a look of puzzlement crossed her face. She slowly sat back down on the couch and placed the gun by her side.

Nolay glanced at me, then back to Mama. "I tell you what, Honey Girl, I'll go bring ol' Ikibob inside the house. I guarantee if there's any snakes left in here, he'll hunt 'em down. If there's one thing that ol' rooster don't like, it's a snake." He turned and walked out of the house, dragging the dead snake behind him. "Bones, you stay here with your mama."

I looked at Mama curled up on the couch. "Mama, if it's all right, I gotta get back outside. Paddlefoot knocked over all my cans and everything is out there drying up to death."

Mama stared at the hole in the floor where the bullet had dug in. "You go on back, Bones, I'll be just fine."

Mama may have come from the red-dirt farmlands of Georgia, but when her and Nolay settled down in the swamps, Nolay made sure she knew how to use a gun. Everyone in these parts had guns in their houses. They were for hunting and protection, not for hurting anything.

Outside, the animals were waiting on me. They followed me back down the road. Both Nippy and Pearl began to gobble up the helpless tadpoles and minnows flopping on the dry sand. I grabbed my Crisco can and tried to outrace them to the little bodies.

By noon dinnertime, the sun had lapped up the last drops of water. I had saved everything I could. I whistled, signaling the animals it was time to go home. The three dogs—Silver, Paddlefoot, and Mr. Jones—ran past me and bolted up the sandy road. Silver and Mr. Jones skirted around the muddy holes, but Paddlefoot ran right through them, splashing muddy water all over hisself and anything else close by.

Paddlefoot wasn't the brightest of the dogs, but he was one of the most lovable. He was golden Labrador and maybe Great Dane. His feet were nearly as big as his head. Nolay had saved him from a sure death by his first owner, Jakey Toms. Jakey was a hunter; his yard was filled with an assortment of coon dogs, hog dogs, and rabbit dogs, but no pettin' dogs. His dogs were for workin', not lovin'. Jakey said Paddlefoot was too dumb and clumsy to train. He was getting ready to put a bullet in his head when Nolay intervened and brought him home. Paddlefoot wasn't dumb; he just didn't want to work. He wanted to be loved.

Nippy and Pearl walked along by my side. Harry the goat was standing out in the yard. When he saw Pearl, he began his stiff-legged dance in our direction. He went directly to

Pearl and placed his little wet nose on Pearl's snout. Pearl grunted contentedly.

I entered the kitchen with Nippy under one arm and Pearl waddling by my side. Pearl was a gift from Nolay. He came home from a hunting trip with a sackful of smoked pork and a squealing baby pig. When she was young, her skin was as soft as a baby's. As she matured, wild-pig bristles covered her body like the combed-back spines of a porcupine. When she was a piglet, she had a little box in my room that she slept in, but where she really liked to sleep was in my bed with me. Now that she was grown, she and Harry the goat shared a pen outside. But often as possible, I would quietly hold our front door open and she would sneak in and climb into my bed.

Mama let out a deep sigh. "Bones, take Pearl outside. She's just too big to come in the house."

"But Mama, she's cleaner than the dogs, and you gotta admit she's very well-mannered." As if to prove my point, Pearl shuffled up to Mama, sniffed her hand, and grunted in reassurance.

Mama turned to me. "Bones, I don't know if you have noticed, but Pearl is not a little piglet anymore, she's a hundred-pound bristleback sow."

Just then a cockroach the size of a hummingbird flew across the room. It went straight in front of Mama's face and landed on the wall. I grabbed a rag and knocked it to the floor; in one quick motion, Pearl devoured that cockroach and snorted for more.

"Did you see that, Mama? Not only is she a good pet, she's useful, too."

"Good Lord, what next. A houseful of snakes, cockroaches, and a pig."

"Mama, do you know that there are twenty-seven different kinds of cockroaches in Florida?"

"Bones, where on earth did you hear such a thing?"

"Mr. Speed told me. He said there are really over forty different kinds that live here, but only twenty-seven belong here. I guess the rest of 'em are kinda like Yankees, they just came down for the weather."

Mama shook her head. "That is depressing news. Bones, do you believe everything Mr. Speed tells you?"

"Mama, I swear, he knows something about nearly everything. It would do you a world of good to sit a spell with Mr. Speed. He has more information in his head than ten of those ol' cycopedas."

"I believe it's called an encyclopedia. And maybe if he knows so much about cockroaches, he can tell me how to get rid of them."

"Mama, you should just go talk to him sometime. Besides Nolay, Mr. Speed is about the smartest person I ever did meet. Other than Little Man, I consider Mr. Speed my best friend. Not only is he smart, but he's real nice to be with, too."

I wasn't sure why, but Mama turned away from me as a smile started spreading across her face. She said, "I will certainly try to do that."

I walked back into the living room. The bullet hole in the floor was a small jagged crack filled with shiny dark water. Nolay and Mama had swept nearly all the water out. There were just a couple of shimmering rainbows left where the water had flowed. As usual, after a few days of sunshine, the musky smell of dampness would disappear.

Mama's pistol was still sitting on the couch. There would be another time when I would see her holding her little pearl-handled .32. Only, she wouldn't be shooting at a snake.

yankees

Along with the flood, summer's gentle rains were quickly replenishing the swamp's precious water, turning last winter's dry drabness into a rich blend of greens and golds. Two days after that big storm blew in, we were still cleaning up the mess it left in our yard.

It was a hot, soggy afternoon; I was outside with Nolay, swabbing our window screens with DDT to keep the mosquitoes out. The pungent smell of the liquid filled my nose and brought tears to my eyes. I swabbed a patch across a screen and said, "This stuff sure makes pretty rainbows, don't it, Nolay?" Before he could answer, the dogs started to bark.

We watched as a strange-looking car drove slowly up our bumpy driveway. It was a big, cumbersome thing, so low to the ground that its bumpers dug into the sandy top of the road. It looked like a fat black cat slinking up to our house.

Nolay and I put our DDT rags in a bucket and went to see who these unknown visitors were. I looked back at the house and saw Mama come to our big picture window and peek out around the curtains. Even Old Ikibob stopped scratching in the dirt and stuck his head up, blinking one eye like an orange caution light.

As the car pulled up to our house, I could make out the silhouettes of two men in the front seat. The man on the passenger side rolled his window down. He leaned his arm on the open window and stuck his head out. "How do, mister. Do those dogs bite?"

Nolay stuck his hands in his pockets and stared straight back into that window. "Only Yankees."

The man chuckled and brought his arm back inside the window. He continued, "Well, sir, we're not from around these parts. My name is Decker and this is my partner, Mr. Fowler. We were just out driving in these lovely backwoods and happened on this quaint little road. Decided to see where it led. I take it you are the gentleman of the house?"

Nolay cocked his head a little sideways, like Old Ikibob did when he stalked something, and replied, "If you mean do I own this land, you are correct."

Fascinated by this unusual car and its passengers, I decided to take a closer look. Accompanied by the dogs, who promptly wet on all the tires, I ran my fingers over the fancy chrome hood ornament. As I walked around the side, the man sitting in the driver's seat gave me a wordless glance. I went around the back and saw the license plate with Dade County, Florida, as its place of origin. I didn't pay much attention to what Nolay and the men talked about. But suddenly I heard Nolay yell, "Lori, Honey Girl, bring me my gun.

I'm gonna shoot me a couple of low-down land-grabbin' Yankees!"

The dogs immediately came to attention. Silver, our half-wolf shepherd, ran around to the open window of the passenger side and lunged in. She grabbed a mouthful of Decker's shirtsleeve and ripped if off, exposing a gold watch that dangled loosely around his wrist. Decker began to scream and roll up the window.

Paddlefoot and Mr. Jones raced around the car and growled and bit at the tires. Excited by all the commotion, Old Ikibob, who was always ready for a good fight, leaped on top of the hood and began to attack the windshield. He pecked and flapped his huge wings against the glass. His long claws scraped the metal and left deep raw gouges in the shiny black paint.

Mama ran out of the house with a shotgun in her hand. Nolay grabbed the gun, looked at it, and said, "That ain't the one I wanted. I wanted a rifle, but this'll do."

The two men in the car wrestled with each other as they tried to get the car started. We could hear their muffled voices through the closed windows. I couldn't see who, but one of the men yelled, "You crazy backwoods cracker, I'll have the sheriff out here on you. See if I don't!"

The car's big engine roared to life; the tires dug into the soft sand and sped around the pond and out toward the driveway. Nolay fired a couple of well-aimed shots into the sky and off to the side of the car. The acrid smell of gunpowder filled the air and ran up our noses.

We watched as the heavy car bounced over the deep ruts and potholes. Through the back window we could see the two men as they were thrown up nearly to the roof. One time the car came down so hard that the back bumper broke and hung lopsided, leaving a dark snail's trail down our sandy driveway.

Nolay laughed so hard tears streamed down his face. The dogs' pink tongues lolled happily out the sides of their mouths as they panted and rubbed up against us. Ikibob strutted around the yard, flapped his wings, and crowed in triumph. There was so much commotion in the yard that Pearl got up from her favorite nap hole under a big cabbage palm and waddled over, with Harry close on her heels.

Nolay finally managed to choke out between tears and laughter, "I hope those dang Yankees got the message that this land ain't for sale."

Everyone seemed to enjoy the moment except Mama. She stood with both hands on her hips, her eyes cold as lime Popsicles. "Nolay, that was a purely foolish thing for you to do. We are civilized people. You cannot just pick up a gun and shoot at people."

"Wadn't no harm done, Honey Girl, I was just having a little fun."

"That was not fun for those poor men. You scared them half to death."

"They were on my land uninvited; I had every right to run 'em off."

"You could have just asked them to leave. Nolay, one day some of your foolishness might come back to haunt you."

Nolay shook his head and said, "I ain't scared of being haunted. And I sure as heck ain't gonna let nobody, especially a Yankee, come on my land uninvited."

I looked up at Nolay and said, "When that man said you were a backwoods cracker, it didn't sound like he was saying it in a very nice way. He made it sound like a insult or something."

Nolay leaned back on his heels and winked at me. "Bones, without knowing it, that Yankee man paid me a compliment. I've always told you, I'm mighty proud to be a cracker, and you should be, too. We come from a long line of people living here in Florida. Them fellas will never have that privilege."

"Yes, sir, I'll remember that."

All too soon those Yankees would be back on our land, but they wouldn't be trying to buy it.

reems brothers

The day after that incident in our front yard, me and Nolay went out to the back of our scrubland to check on our rabbit traps. I didn't like killing rabbits, but they sure were good to eat. Nolay said a rabbit was a smart creature, and if it went inside our box trap it was because it wanted to be caught, it was ready to let its spirit go. It would be an insult to the rabbit if we didn't kill and eat it.

When we got to our trap, Nolay bent over and slid the little wooden door open to check inside the box. "Yep, there's one inside." Out of the corner of my eye I thought I saw a movement at the edge of a row of scrub pines. "Nolay, what's that over yonder?"

He stood up and squinted in the direction I pointed to. "Looks like a group of men. Dressed kinda funny-like for being out here." He set the trap down, with the rabbit still inside, and started to walk toward the men. "Let's go see who it is."

As we got closer, it was easy to make out the forms of the

Reems brothers; they looked like fat possums wearing overalls. The two Yankee men, Decker and Fowler, stood alongside them. They were dressed in gray slacks and heavy button-down shirts.

Little dark smiles of sweat sat under their armpits. One of them kept bending down to brush specks of dirt off his shiny white shoes.

Nolay's face darkened as he recognized the men. He muttered under his breath, "Gol-durn Whackerstacker Joe and Peckerhead Willy. I shoulda known."

When the two Yankees saw Nolay, they both took a couple of steps back.

Nolay went straight for the Reems brothers. "Peckerhead, what in blazes are you doing out here?"

"Just showin' these fellers around," Peckerhead said.

"Showin' 'em what? I threw those low-down land-grabbin' Yankees off my land just yesterday."

Peckerhead stuck his thumbs in his overall straps, spit a glob of tobacco juice toward Nolay's feet, and replied, "Ain't none a your bizzness what I'm showin' 'em. This here is my land, and I'll do what I dang well please."

"Listen, you rat-brained polecat, you're on my land! You see that row of slash pine over yonder? My family planted that. Like I told you before, that's the official boundary between our two properties. Now you and these Yankees get off my land before I turn you all into buzzard bait!"

Peckerhead spat out another glob of tobacco juice. "Why don't you go back and live on the reservation, where you belong? Maybe you got it wrong, maybe you're standing on *my* land."

Nolay held his rifle down by his right side; I could see his knuckles whiten as he gripped it, one finger wrapped around the trigger. He took a step toward Peckerhead, his voice soft and clear. "Just because it says you own this land on a piece of white paper don't mean you do. My people owned all this land. My family was living here when yours was still digging its way out of pig slop!"

Nolay moved in even closer and took a deep breath. "Like I just said, you see that row of slash pine over yonder? That's the beginning of my land and the end of yours. Now get off my land."

I saw Whackerstacker's and Peckerhead's hulking frames both move toward Nolay. I stepped in front of Nolay's right arm, keeping the rifle barrel pointed to the ground, and said, "Nolay, it's gettin' late. We should be headin' back before dark."

The Reems brothers looked at me and stopped. The Yankee with the shiny white shoes stepped forward, placed a shaky hand on Peckerhead's arm, and said, "It's okay, Willy, we don't want any trouble. We can conduct our business elsewhere. The kid's right, we should all be going. It's getting late."

Peckerhead glared in our direction, spat out another brown stream of tobacco juice, and sneered, "I'll be seein' you again, dirty monkey."

Nolay took a step forward. I wrapped both hands around

his right arm. "Nolay, let's get back home." He looked down at me, and I could see the anger floating in his eyes. I could sure see that being called a dirty monkey was definitely not a compliment or something to be proud of.

Peckerhead turned and began walking away. We stood and watched as the four of them disappeared into the scrub pines. Nolay turned abruptly and started to walk back toward the house. I ran after him and called out, "What about the rabbit? It's still in the trap."

Without breaking his stride he said, "Let it loose."

"But—"

Before another word tumbled out of my mouth, he turned and said, "Bones, I told you to let it go. Now do what I say. I'll see you back at the house."

I watched as he vanished into the shadows of dusk. When I got back to the trap, the door was still open and the rabbit sat at the other end of the box, patiently waiting for its death. Usually, Nolay would reach in, grab it by its ears, and pull it out. With one swift punch to the back of its small neck, its life would be ended.

I looked into its glossy black eyes and whispered, "Sorry, fella, I know this is wrong, but I gotta let you go. I reckon it just ain't your time."

As I lifted the back of the trap to release the rabbit, I was surrounded by a sudden and piercing quiet. Every night creature had become silent, the sign that something larger and more powerful was close by. My hands froze; the hair on the nape of my neck stood up. I stared into the tangle of scrub pines and shadows. I felt the presence of something, or some-one, staring back at me. A musky smell filled the air.

I dropped the trap. The rabbit dashed out and was swal-lowed up by the darkness. I turned and ran as fast as I could in the opposite direction. I pounded my feet on the trail to alert any living thing in front of me that I was coming, so get out of the way.

Like that little trapped rabbit, I was breathing in short gasps. My ears filled with the sound of my breath and the pounding of my feet. I was too scared to look back, but I was sure there was something behind me.

When I reached our house, Nolay had just walked up to the front door. "Good Lord, Bones, what on earth got after you?"

Breathless, I bent over and panted out, "I'm not sure, No-lay, but I think it was Soap Sally. I think she was in the dark, staring right at me."

"Now, Bones, why would ol' Sally be out there after you?"

"'Cause it was wrong of me to let that rabbit go. I dis-respected it, and I think she was out to get me."

"Naw, ol' Sally ain't gonna turn you into soap over a rab-bit. You gotta do worse than that."

"I don't know, I just don't like thinking about her out there. Next time I'm taking the dogs with me. Nolay, does she turn dogs into soap, too?"

"Naw, she just likes bad little kids, they make the best kind of soap." Nolay smiled at me. "Why, you haven't done anything bad, have you, Bones?"

"No, sir, I sure have not."

He wrapped his arm around my shoulders. "Come on, Bones. We best be getting cleaned up for supper."

As we walked into the house, I turned and stared into the darkness. Something was out there, looking back at me. I couldn't see it, but I could feel it.

night songs

That evening, as twilight began to lay its soft gray veil over our house, I helped Nolay light the kerosene lamps. The wicks flickered to life and slowly filled each room with a dim yellow glow.

Mama was in the kitchen when Nolay ambled in. He put his arms around her waist and said something that made her giggle like a schoolgirl. It was a humid evening and Nolay was stripped to the waist. His thick chest, as hairless as a turtle's, gleamed like bronze in the dim light. He turned his sky-blue eyes in my direction and said, "Bones, let's you and me go do a night check on the critters."

Outside, the night symphony had just started up. Fireflies darted around, flashing their secret codes to each other. Like ghostly shadows, bullbats swooped down out of the darkness and scooped up mosquitoes and gnats by the mouthful.

The dogs accompanied us as we checked on Ikibob and his brood. Ikibob was a huge Rhode Island Red. He stood over two feet tall, with spurs the size of small railroad spikes and an attitude between a Brahman bull and an Arabian sultan. According to Mama, Ikibob was the result of one of Nolay's many blurred visions.

One day Mama had said, "It sure would be nice to have a rooster and a couple of chickens so we could have fresh eggs." Not long after that statement, Nolay pulled up in our old blue pickup truck with the bed stacked with chicken crates. There were five, to be exact; one hundred biddies in each crate. Where he got those crates remained a mystery. There were some things me and Mama just did not inquire about.

Those five hundred fluffy yellow biddies quickly grew into chickens that crowed, squawked, and scratched all day and all night. They turned our life in the swamps into a chicken coop.

The end came the day a flock of them invaded Mama's kitchen. She had just set aside a mound of fresh biscuit dough to rise when she went out to check on something. While she was gone, some chickens broke through the screen door and went on a rampage. They pecked, scratched, and messed on everything in sight. Mama's immaculate kitchen looked like a dozen pillows filled with chicken feathers and flour had exploded.

That night when Nolay came home, she met him at the door. She placed both hands on her hips and said, "The chickens or me."

"Now, Honey Girl, you know how durn important a chicken is. I cain't just get rid of 'em like that."

"Then share them around with our neighbors. Are you saying that a chicken is more important than me?"

Nolay had raised an eyebrow as if to ponder her question. He wrapped both hands around her waist and said, "Honey Girl, a chicken couldn't measure up to a clippin' off your fingernail."

He turned to me. "Bones, in the morning you pick out ten of your favorite hens and that danged rooster that's twice the size of all the others. Lock 'em up on the back porch. I got me an idea. Tomorrow I'm goin' vistin'." The next day he came home and informed us, "This Saturday we're going to the beach, and our neighbors are coming out here for a chicken hunt."

Saturday morning we locked up the chosen chickens. Mama packed us a lunch that could have fed a Boy Scout troop, and off we went. When we returned there was nothing left of the chickens but a few feathers. Nolay surveyed the yard, put his hands in his pockets, rocked back on his heels and said, "Well, am I right or am I right?"

From that day on, Ikibob was lord and master of our yard. He not only bossed his hens around but the dogs and us as well.

That evening, by the time me and Nolay reached the coop, Ikibob already had his brood put up for the night; all we had to do was close the door to the chicken house.

Pearl and Harry shared a pen together next to the hen-house. Mama flat refused to let the two of them sleep in the house at night. Pearl was stretched out in her favorite hole and Harry was curled up right underneath her plump belly.

Nolay shook his head. "Look at them two. I swear that pig thinks that goat is her baby. Or maybe the goat thinks the pig is his mama. Any way you look at it, them two is the best of friends."

After we secured the animals, Nolay said, "Let's walk the boundaries." This was something we tried to do every week or so, walk the edges of our clearing and have the dogs mark their territory. Their scent, along with our human tracks, was a silent message to wild animals to keep out.

Like an inky black umbrella, the night slowly closed in around us. The sky filled with stars that twinkled and dripped down to the edge of Florida's flat horizon.

"Look up there, Nolay," I said, "God's angels are busy spilling out bushel baskets of stars. Did you know that every star is someone's miracle?"

"How you figure that?"

"Mr. Speed told me. He said that miracles happen around us every day; we just have to look for 'em. A miracle is a special gift from God. Every time there's a miracle, he puts a little piece of a star in a jar, and when they add up big enough, you get your very own star."

I let that information sink in and then continued. "My miracle today was a baby gopher. I found it turned upside down in a puddle; it was craning its little neck up above the water to keep from drowning. I dried it off, set it in a dry spot, and it crawled away."

Out of the darkness Nolay replied, "Well, I reckon Speed

would know about miracles, 'cause it's pretty much a miracle he's able to sit on that bench every day. Bones, you stop by and talk with him nearly every day, don't you?"

"Yes, sir, as often as I can. He's so full of information, and I really enjoy his company. If I ask him a question and he don't know the answer, next time I'm with him he'll have figured it out."

"Speed always was a bright fella. Him and me go a long way back. He's about five years younger than me, but we did attend the same school together."

"I didn't know that."

"You know how he got his nickname, Speed?"

"No, sir. I never have asked him that. I thought that was his real name."

"Well, back when we was kids, that boy was just about the fastest runner in the whole state of Florida. He actually raced against a horse one time and nearly outrun 'im.

"He was sharp as a tack, everyone thought he had a bright future. But then the war started up and he joined the army. And I guess the rest is history."

"Yes, sir. I guess it is."

"But now, let me get this straight. It was a miracle that you saved that gopher, so you earned a little piece of a star?"

"Well, I reckon me and that gopher will divvy up a piece of star. It was a miracle for both of us."

In the dimness I could see Nolay's shadow as he shook his halo of black curls back and forth. I couldn't see his face, but I could feel his smile.

As we headed back to the house, the kerosene lanterns flickered and spilled out a soft orange glow through the windows. At night our house came alive, like it had a heartbeat all its own. Mama's silhouette moved around in the kitchen window as she fixed our supper.

When we walked inside, Nippy the raccoon scurried across the floor and made little chirping noises to let me know she was hungry.

The kitchen filled with the aroma of frying slabs of fatback. Mama deftly picked up a heavy cast-iron frying pan and poured the sizzling grease into the grease jar that she kept on top of the stove. She called it her secret seasoning, but it wasn't much of a secret; everyone I knew had a grease jar on their stove.

As we sat down for supper I looked over at Nolay and said, "You know I can't help but to keep thinkin' about what happened when we were out huntin' rabbits today."

"What exactly are you referring to?"

"About when we met up with the Reems brothers and how they acted toward you."

"Bones, them men ain't worth takin' the time to think about. Neither one of 'em could find their tail with both hands and a flashlight."

"Well, it's really not about how smart or stupid they are, it's more about how mean they are. Like today when ol' Peckerhead called you a dirty monkey, why did he do that?"

Mama's eyes snapped up and shot across at me. "Bones, you will not be repeating insults to your daddy. And remember your manners. That would be Mister Peckerhead to you. You are much too young to be calling an adult by his first name."

"Yes, ma'am, I'll remember that. But Mama, it's the truth, that's what he said to Nolay today. And their kids, those Reems boys, are even worse; every time one of them sees me they call me names. They'll say things like, 'You're no better than a dirty monkey,' or they call me squaw or something else mean. Or at least they do any time Little Man isn't around."

Mama's eyes softened as she looked at me and said, "I'm sorry to hear that, Bones. Some people just enjoy hurting other people. But it's only words. They can't hurt you unless you let them. Just let them roll off you like drops of water."

Nolay put his fork down, leaned back in his chair and said, "Now, Honey Girl, you know that words can hurt a lot more than some water splattering on you. They can burn clean through your skin and right down to the bone. I can attest to that firsthand. And that Reems family is a bunch of no-account lowlifes. And I tell you what, I don't feel good about them or them durn Yankees prowling around on my land. I don't like it one bit. Next time I see 'em I just might do something about it."

Nolay looked directly at me. "Bones, they call us dirty monkeys because when the Spaniards first arrived here on our shores my people lived in huts built of palms fronds and mud. Back then, takin' a bath wasn't so important as it is nowadays. Matter of fact, a little dirt and smoke smell helped to keep the skeeters away, so most of 'em were pretty muddied up. So the Spaniards called them *mico sucio*, which means 'dirty monkey' in Spanish. Later on that name grew into Miccosukee, which is what my people are called today. It's a strong name. A proud name. But it sure didn't start out that way."

Nolay leaned forward, picked up his fork, and took a bite of food. A frosty blanket of silence fell over the three of us. I looked over at Mama, but she was staring down at her plate.

I took a sip of my tea, sucked in a deep breath, and said, "Nolay, when you were little, did Soap Sally ever get after you?"

My words sliced into the blanket and split it open. It spilled down around us in invisible threads.

Nolay looked up and said, "She sure did. But as you can see, she never caught me."

"Do you know any kids she did catch?"

Nolay leaned in toward me and whispered, "Bones, you been hearing these stories all your life. You know ol' Sally's been in these swamps a long time. Every now and then a kid would go missin'."

I felt my eyes widen. I whispered back, "Have you ever seen her? Do you know what she looks like?"

"She looks like any ol' witch does. When I was little, sometimes at night, I would hear her prowling around, lookin' for a kid to snatch up. When she passed by my window, I could smell her. She smelled like smoke and lye soap. She spends a lot of time bent over a big ol' black pot, stirring up kid-soap."

I sat, almost too stunned to speak, and looked from Nolay to Mama and back again. Finally I blurted out, "That's what I smelled out there today when I let the rabbit go! And I've smelled it before. I know I have!"

Mama put her fork down and said, "Bones, your eyes look like they are going to pop out of your head." She turned to Nolay. "Why on earth do you keep telling such stories? You know there is no such thing."

Nolay shrugged. "How do you know she ain't out there?"

"Because I have never seen a witch. They don't exist."

"You believe in the devil, don't you? And you ain't never seen him."

"That is totally beside the point. You should stop telling scary stories to Bones. Or any child, for that matter."

"I ain't trying to scare Bones or anyone else. I just think kids should be on the lookout for things like that."

Mama looked across at me. "Bones, you have nothing to be scared of. Soap Sally is just an old swamp legend. She does not exist." Mama shook her head, let out a little sigh, and turned the conversation to another subject: electricity. For the hundredth time, she said, "It sure would be nice to have a icebox."

Nolay leveled his cool blue eyes in her direction and replied, for the hundredth time, "Honey Girl, we are only five telephone poles away from electricity. Before you know it, I'll have you a big white shiny icebox sitting right there in that corner." He flashed her one of his dazzling smiles, then looked across the table at me and winked.

Mama wrinkled up her nose, and a smile slowly slid across her face. "How many times have I heard you say that?"

As Nolay and Mama went back and forth, I sat there thinking about Soap Sally and some of the places I had smelled that peculiar scent. I wasn't about to open my mouth and say so out loud, but I was almost certain I had smelled that exact scent out at Miss Eunice's house. For me to say such a thing about an old woman's house would surely end up in my ear getting a good pulling.

Nearly every evening, after supper, it was story time. Sometimes Mama and me would sit captivated as Nolay spun tales of his childhood in the swamps. He told of times when alligators were so plentiful you could walk clear across the water on top of them. Of nights filled with the haunting screams of panthers as they prowled and stalked their prey.

Of course there were the stories about Soap Sally and what a slippery old witch she was. If you were good, you didn't have anything to worry about. But if you were bad, that was another story altogether. Problem was, I didn't quite know how bad you had to be to be turned into soap. Mama would nearly always interrupt Nolay with something like "You stop telling scary stories, especially at night. You'll give us all nightmares."

I was mesmerized by his story of Sandy Claws. She was a black bear that had a taste for his mama's pies and would steal them right off the window ledge as they sat out to cool. Nolay would shake his head. "That bear was quite a character. She started coming around our house when she was just a cub following behind her mama. Then one day she showed up by herself. That's when mama's pies started goin' missin'. We would go outside, and sure enough, there would be her foot-prints with them big ol' claws diggin' into the sand. Mama's pie pan would be laying there licked clean as a mirror."

Other nights it would be Mama's turn to read us stories from her collection of *Saturday Evening Post* magazines. Me, Nippy, and a couple of cats would crawl in bed between her and Nolay. Mama didn't mind Nippy sleeping in bed with me. She was a real clean critter, not much bigger than a cat, and she made the sweetest purring sounds you ever did hear.

The orange glow of our kerosene lamp danced around the corners of the room as Mama's melodic voice mingled with the songs of the night. In the distance the muffled bellow of a bull gator looking for a friend blended in with chirping crickets and croaking frogs. Lulled by the sweet sound of swamp and family, I drifted off to sleep. In the morning I would wake up in my own bed, surrounded by an assortment of animals.

friends

Thursday morning I woke up bright and early. Right after breakfast, Nolay asked if I wanted to go with him to the Grant Fish House. "I want to find out when Ironhead plans on going net fishing again."

"Yes, sir, can I bring Nippy with me?" I always enjoyed summer break because I got to spend a lot more time with Nolay than during schooltime.

"I guess, but you gotta keep her on a leash. That dang coon is overcurious."

When we pulled up to the Fish House, a small group of men were milling around by the entrance to the docks. Ironhead saw us drive up and walked over to the truck. He was a young man with a body shaped like a beer keg. His thick arms and legs jutted straight out, as if he didn't have any elbows or knees. His head sat directly on his shoulders with no visible neck. Sometimes when a ray of sunshine crossed his red hair just right, it looked like his head was a blazing fire.

Ironhead leaned one hand on the side of the truck and

said, "I tell you what, hit's been a-rainin' bullfrogs. I been meanin' to come out y'all's house and see if y'all done floated away."

"You're sure right about that; it's been a dang wet week. But it's a good thing, 'cause the swamps always need a healthy dose of summer rain."

Ironhead let out a little sniffling grunt, signaling he had some important news to tell us. He considered himself a verbal newspaper in our community. "The sheriff stopped by here this morning and tolt us he was looking for a missin' Yankee man. Sheriff said the Yankee man's partner reported him missin' yesterday. His partner said the two of 'em was out by the Reems place, where it butts up against your swamp, and they got separated. Durn strange if you ask me."

Before Nolay could answer, Ironhead took a couple more sniffles and continued, "Two fellas come nosing around two, three days ago. Well, hit was one of them. You seen anything out your way?"

"I reckon a couple of fellas stopped by our place, but I didn't pay much attention."

I was just ready to open my mouth when Nolay's eyes turned in my direction and put a lock on my lips. I don't know why he didn't mention seeing those Yankee men a second time.

Nolay set up a time with Ironhead to go net fishing the following week, and we headed back home.

• • •

On the ride back I looked over at Nolay and the words tumbled out of my mouth. "Nolay, don't you remember them two Yankees that come out to our house? You scared 'em so bad, they broke their car getting out of the driveway."

"Yeah, I remember them two fellas, but I don't know if it's the same two Ironhead is talking about. There's more than a couple of Yankees nosing around these days."

I could see by the way Nolay cocked his chin a little to one side that he was through talking. But I was certain it was the same ones Ironhead was talking about, because they were the only Yankees I had seen around here.

When we pulled up to our driveway, I saw my best friend, Little Man, standing by the front door. He had a croker sack slung over one shoulder and a four-prong gig over the other. He was a full year older than me, and I couldn't remember ever not having Little Man as my best friend. We sat together every day on the school bus; we shared our food, our thoughts, and our feelings about what a waste of time school was.

Little Man and his family were our closest neighbors; they lived about two miles away. Nolay and Little Man's daddy, Mr. Cotton, grew up together. Mr. Cotton was called Cotton because he had a headful of hair as white as a cotton ball. Nolay said Mr. Cotton was one of the best durn hunters in the entire county. And Little Man had a talent for worm fiddling. He could wiggle a stick in the ground and worms would just come dancing up to the top.

Little Man was a big boy, nearly as big as his older twin brothers, Earl and Ethan. They were six years older than him and had just graduated from school. His real name was Irvin, but only his mama ever called him that. His soft, doe-brown eyes were placed wide apart in his round face, which, like his entire body, was a mass of freckles. When he was curious about something, he had a way of scrunching up his face so a perfect question mark wiggled up right between his eyes. No matter how much grease he slapped on his wheat-colored hair, it sat on his head like a bird's nest.

I got out of the truck and walked up to him. "Hey, Little Man."

"Howdy, Bones, I'm goin' giggin' down at the river. You wanna come along?"

"Sure I do."

He held up the croker sack and said, "I got something for your mama."

"Come on inside. She's most likely in the kitchen."

Little Man walked in, set the croker sack on the kitchen table, and said, "Mornin', Miss Lori. This here is a mess of fresh-picked mustard greens and butter beans."

"Why, thank you, Little Man, and how's your family doing?"

"Everyone's fine. Pa's grinding up a load of sugarcane, said to tell you he'd have a batch of sorghum syrup by the end of the week."

I broke into the conversation. "Mama, Little Man is going fish gigging down at the river. Can I go with him, please, Mama?"

"I don't see why not, just be careful and be home by noon dinnertime."

"We will, Mama, and with some fresh fish to fry."

Nolay had helped me make my fish gig, and I was mighty proud of it. The four-foot wooden shaft was made out of a straight cypress branch. Together we had scraped and polished it to a smooth finish. At the end Nolay had attached a four-pronged metal spear. It was in perfect balance for spearing fish, crabs, and frogs. I grabbed my gig and we headed down our driveway for the two-mile hike to the Indian River.

As we walked barefoot along the sandy road, I told Little Man the news. "Did you hear about that Yankee man that's gone missing?"

"I ain't heard about that. What happened?"

"Just this morning Ironhead told me and Nolay that the sheriff stopped by the Fish House and told them that a Yankee man had gone missing yesterday."

Little Man shook his head. "That don't make sense. How does someone go missin'?"

"I don't know. But Ironhead said that two of them were out on the Reemses' land, close by our swamp, and they got separated. And you know what else? I think that Yankee man came out to our house just last week."

"You sure?"

"Course I'm sure. It was a couple of days after that big storm blew in. There was two of 'em. But Nolay got a gun and chased 'em off our land."

"Mr. Nolay chased some Yankees off his land with a gun?"

"Yep. He didn't shoot directly at 'em or anything. But he sure scared 'em good."

Little Man shook his head again. "Mr. Nolay sure is something. But it just don't make sense why Yankees that don't know nothin' about the swamps would be out there."

I nodded in agreement. "You're right about that, it don't make sense. And you want to know something else? We saw those same two Yankees out on our property with the Reems brothers the very next day."

"What were they doin' out there with the Reemses?"

"I don't know. But Nolay sure did get upset with them. And he chased them off again, only this time he didn't shoot at them. And you want to know something else? I think I ran into Soap Sally out there."

"Soap Sally? Bones, you know there ain't no such thing. That's just an old swamp legend."

"Well, I'm not so sure. I mean, if legends ain't real, how do they get started in the first place?"

"I ain't sure about that. I've heard stories about Sally all my life, but I ain't never seen her."

"Have you ever smelled her?" I asked. "Because I think I have. A couple of times out by the swamp's edge I've smelled something musky like old dried-out lye soap or wet rags."

"Come to think of it, I have smelled something like that. But that could just about be anything in the swamps. There's always something dying or decaying out there."

We strolled over the railroad tracks, passed by the Last Chance General Store, and came to the two-lane paved highway, U.S. 1. I looked back at the Last Chance storefront and saw Mr. Speed sitting on his bench. I waved, and he slowly raised his hand in return.

We crossed over the highway and found our usual path down the bank of the Indian River. As we walked along the shoreline, swarms of fiddler crabs scuttled sideways across the sand, looking for a hole to duck into. They brandished their one large claw high in the air like a small sword. Hermit crabs dressed in every imaginable manner of shell marched together as one colony toward the water's edge.

The riverbank was pocked with large holes where land crabs lived. Several of them sat defiantly at the front of their holes. Perched on long spindly legs, they pointed their purple and orange claws in the air and clapped them together in a threatening gesture. That fearsome display was just show. If you touched one with a stick, it would fall apart.

As Little Man and I walked along the riverbank, I thought of the day about a year ago when I found a croker sack washed up on the sand. Inside a burlap bag, bunched together like soggy black socks, were the bodies of five tiny puppies. They were so young, their eyes were still sealed shut. Four were dead, but one wiggled with signs of life. I took him home, and me and Mama nursed him with a baby bottle. We named him Mr. Jones and watched as that soggy little sock grew a magnificent glossy black coat. His pensive eyes sat in his head like two golden coins. Mr. Jones was a mixture of so many things we couldn't tell for certain what he was. One thing for sure, he was a true and loyal friend.

We silently waded into the brackish water, soft, warm sand squishing up between our toes. Beds of turtle grass moved gently in the current, revealing small fish, river shrimp, and snails.

Little Man looked in my direction and said, "Bones, you look out for stingrays. Watch for two bumps in the sand. That'll be their eyes. We don't need no accidents happening."

"You tell me that every time."

"Well, sometimes I just got to repeat myself, that's all."

It was low tide, and the sharp edges of huge beds of oysters, sleeping through the summer months, peeked out above the water's surface. A couple of glossy ibis waded in the shallows, their strong curved beaks shoveling through the mud in search of worms and bugs.

Further out, a blue heron stood like a statue on one leg, its long neck arched and ready to strike at passing fish. A small family of grebes floated out in deeper water, a couple of babies catching a ride on their mama's back.

Little Man pointed to a spot that rippled on top of the water's flat surface. "There's a big school of mullet feedin'. You go around that side, and I'll take this side." We silently waded out to the school. We raised our gigs like Indian spears and plunged them into the water. We were each rewarded with a fat mullet wiggling at the end of the sharp prongs.

After a couple of hours Little Man held up our croker sack and said, "This here is enough mullet for the day, plus we got a couple of blue crabs. Best we be heading back."

We climbed back up the riverbank, crossed over U.S. 1, and headed for the Last Chance General Store. As we got nearer, sure enough, Mr. Speed was still sitting out there. He wore a clean pair of blue overalls and, perched sideways on his head, the green baseball cap that me and Little Man gave him last Christmas.

He was the only child of Mr. Ball and Miss Evelyn, who owned and operated the Last Chance. The pride and joy of his mama and daddy, when World War II broke out in 1942, he did his patriotic duty and enlisted in the army on his eighteenth birthday.

Shipped overseas to a place whose name no one could pronounce, he returned home two years later with half his head a shiny mass of scars and half his mind filled with fascinating information. Every morning one of his parents made sure he was comfortable on his bench, where he spent the day seeing things that no one else could and sharing his wealth of information with all who would listen.

Being that I was only three years old when Mr. Speed joined the army, I don't remember knowing him before that. But I will never forget the first time I met him. I was five years old and had gone to the Last Chance with Mama. When we walked around to the front entrance of the store I stopped dead in my tracks upon seeing a strange man with scars covering half his bald head sitting on the front bench. Mama reached over and took hold of my hand. She leaned down and quietly said, "Bones, there's nothing to be afraid of, he's a very nice man. He just met with a bad accident. Let's go over and say good morning to Mr. Speed. I'll introduce you to him."

I figured as long as Mama had ahold of my hand and she wasn't scared, it would be all right. We walked up to the bench, and Mr. Speed slowly turned his head in our direction. Mama said, "Good morning, Mr. Speed, I'm glad to see you back home. You remember my husband, Nolay? I want to introduce you to our daughter, Bones."

Mr. Speed looked directly at me. His eyes were brown speckled with gold. It was like looking into two glasses of cool sweet tea. A thin, lopsided smile spread halfway across his face. He said, "Bones. Good name. Bones."

The way he said my name brought an instant smile to my face. Whatever fear I had felt before flew away like leaves in a breeze. "Thank you, sir, and I like your name, too."

Mama looked at me and said, "Bones, if you want, you can sit out here and visit with Mr. Speed while I go get a few things inside."

Sounded like a good idea to me, because I sure was curious to get to know this new neighbor. I walked over and climbed up on the bench beside Mr. Speed. We didn't say to much to each other that first day, we just sat and enjoyed each other's company. From that day on he was one of my best friends.

"Good mornin', Mr. Speed," Little Man and I said in unison.

"We been down to the river," Little Man continued. "You want me to bring you an RC Cola?" Mr. Speed bobbed his head in affirmation as he continued to stare out into nothing.

Inside, with the soft light of the store, I recognized the silhouette of Mr. Ball behind the counter. He was a small, bald-headed man who resembled a turtle and moved at about the same pace, but he was kindhearted and never turned a customer away. Nearly everyone in the community had a running tab at the store. Being that the Last Chance had the only telephone within a ten-mile radius, Mr. Ball was known to take messages from friends and family and pass them on.

I caught a glimpse of Mr. Speed's mama, Miss Evelyn, sitting at her desk in a small room at the back of the store.

Little Man laid the croker sack on the worn wooden countertop, reached inside, and pulled out one of the blue crabs. "Howdy, Mr. Ball. You think we could trade this here for two RC Colas and a moon pie?"

"I think that would be a fair enough trade." Mr. Ball picked up a corner of the croker sack, peeked inside, and said, "Looks like y'all had a pretty good catch today."

"And Mr. Speed would like an RC, too. I can take it out to him," I added.

Outside, I handed one cola to Mr. Speed, and me and Little Man sat down on the front steps, next to the bench. We watched as cars glided by in both directions on U.S. 1. Being it was the only highway stretching from Jacksonville to Miami, just about every car coming or going had to pass by the Last Chance.

After an acceptable time of silence, Mr. Speed said, "Done counted 'leven Yankee cars passed by from this mornin'. Four New York, three Michigan, three New Jersey, and one Co-net-ti-cut, yes, sir, one Co-net-ti-cut." Sometimes Mr. Speed's memory got stuck together like the pages of an old wet book.

Little Man took a gulp of his RC. "You don't say, Mr. Speed. That's a tolerable lot of Yankees. Wonder where they're headed."

"Down Palm Beach, down Palm Beach, where all them coconut palms washed up on shore. People sure do love to see them palms, twenty thousand of 'em washed up and planted their selves right on the beach, yes, sir, twenty thousand of 'em."

"Twenty thousand," I said. "How did twenty thousand coconuts get washed up on the beach?"

"Shipwreck. About seventy-five years ago a ship wrecked in a storm and spilt all them coconuts on the beach. Some planted their selves and some was planted by people living there. Then they named it Palm Beach, yes, sir, Palm Beach."

Little Man shook his head. "Well now, that sure does make sense, don't it, Bones?"

"It sure does, and it's an interesting story, too." I took a sip of my icy-cold RC. It slid down my parched throat like liquid joy. "Mr. Speed, you should have seen the river today, it was just plumb full of schools of mullet, the busiest I've seen it in a while. Nearly every time we threw our gig in a school, it came out with a fat mullet on it."

Mr. Speed continued to bob his head and stare out into his private world. Then he replied, "Florida has seven hundred different kinds of fish, some so big they could swaller up a car and some so itty-bitty you can hold 'em on the tip of your finger, yes, sir, so itty-bitty you can hold 'em on the tip of your finger."

"Lordy, Mr. Speed, why, I reckon it would take about a lifetime to meet up with all of them," I said.

The three of us sat for a few minutes sipping our colas, me and Little Man nibbling our moon pies. Then I asked, "Mr.

Speed, you know anything about birds? There were all kinds of birds hunting on the river today."

He wagged his head up and down. "Got four hundred different kinds of birds, four hundred that live here, the rest of 'em just come down to visit. Some of 'em are right peculiar, like that big ol' pink flamingo. He don't start out pink, he just gets that way from being out in the sun. They don't roam around much, stay pretty much down in the South, down in the South."

"Come to think of it," I replied, "I never seen one of those birds in the river or the swamps, only pictures of 'em. Little Man, you ever seen a live flamingo?"

"Nope, can't say as I ever have seen one. We'll have to take a ride down Miami-way someday and see 'em. I hear there are flocks of 'em down there." Little Man stood up and let out a loud burp. "'Scuse me. Bones, it's gettin' late. We better be headin' back home if we're gonna make it before noon dinnertime."

"Yeah, I reckon so," I said. Little Man returned the three bottles to Mr. Ball. I gathered up our gigs and croker sack.

I turned and said, "It sure was nice talking with you, Mr. Speed. I enjoyed hearing about the birds and the fish and the coconuts, too. I'll be seeing you again real soon."

He bobbed his lopsided head and said, "Real soon, y'all come back real soon."

On the walk back home I said to Little Man, "I sure do enjoy talking with Mr. Speed. He pretty near knows something about everything. Where do you think he gets all that information?"

Little Man walked in silence for a while and then replied, "I reckon it comes from a place where you and me can't go, or a place we wouldn't really want to go. It's a place where just him and God sits together and talks with each other."

"Yeah, that makes sense. I do believe that Mr. Speed knows God as a personal friend; he's that kind of a person."

As we approached my house I turned and said, "Little Man, if you got time tomorrow, why don't you and me go out and see if we can find that missing Yankee man."

"Why would we want to do that? That's the sheriff's job."

"Well, you never know, he could be out there lost and scared and hungry. I could bring along the dogs to help us hunt."

"I got some mornin' chores to do, but I could come over later. If we're goin' out in the swamps, I'll be bringin' my gun and you should bring yours, too."

"Okay, I'll let Mama know, and I'll see you tomorrow."

Sure enough, there was something waiting out in the swamps, but it wasn't lost and it wasn't scared.

doubts

Pale sunlight had just begun to tap against my bedroom window when I was awakened by a warm nuzzling in my ear. I reached up to find the furry body of Nippy Raccoon resting on my shoulder. As I stroked her soft fur, her little humanlike hands began to knead my neck as she purred contentedly like a cat.

Nippy had been given to me by Little Man's daddy, Mr. Cotton. He found her along the highway next to her dead mother's body. She had the short, stubby tail of a female, not the long, elegant ones the males lost their lives for. Nippy was a born thief; anytime something bright and shiny went missing, it could usually be found tucked under her blanket in her small sleeping box in my room. But if you looked into her little bandit face, she stole your heart away.

I rubbed the sleep out of my eyes, picked up Nippy, and headed into the kitchen. Mama was sitting at the table with her usual morning cup of coffee, reading a *Saturday Evening Post*, but Nolay was nowhere to be seen. Mama looked up and said, "Bones, there's grits and scrambled eggs on the stove. Your daddy already ate and went out on some business. Just help yourself."

Nolay was mostly a commercial net fisherman. Him and Ironhead owned a boat together and kept it up at the Grant Fish House. But on occasion he went off on "business trips." I wasn't clear on what all he did on those trips. All I knew for sure was my daddy had a lot in common with a raccoon. He was intelligent, inquisitive, and mischievous. To hear him tell it, he never stole a thing in his life, but he sure borrowed a lot. Nolay often told me, "Bones, some people just got more stuff than they know what to do with. That just ain't right. Stuff shouldn't sit around idle."

After I got my breakfast, I sat down and said, "Mama, later on today me and Little Man are going out to the swamp for a while."

Mama put her magazine down and looked at me. "Why are you going out there?"

"Just to have a look around. You know how beautiful it is in the summer with all the birds and babies and stuff. And we just might find that lost Yankee man. He might be out there scared and hungry."

"What Yankee man are you talking about?"

"Don't you remember the story from last night? The one Ironhead told to me and Nolay about a Yankee man being reported missing to the sheriff? He was last seen out by our swamp."

Mama shook her head. "Yes, I remember that. But my goodness, Bones. Well, I guess it's all right. Just be careful and make sure you stay close to Little Man." Mama closed her magazine and stood up. "After breakfast I need you to help me with some chores in the garden."

Me and Mama were just about finished weeding when we saw Little Man strolling up our road. Mama said, "I'll finish up, Bones, you can go now."

"Thanks, Mama, we'll be home before dark."

I ran in the house and grabbed the single-shot .22 rifle Nolay gave me when I turned six years old. He said I could have an automatic when I turned ten, but I was still waiting on that one.

I ran out in the yard and whistled for the dogs. The three of them came bounding from all directions and surrounded me and Little Man.

Little Man had his .22 automatic rifle in his hand and a croker sack stuck in his belt. Pointing to the sack he said, "Just in case we run across something for dinner."

With the three dogs leading the way, we headed through the scrubland and toward the swamp. Silver stayed in front and zigzagged her way through the brush.

Silver was half German shepherd and half gray wolf. Nolay had brought her home as a puppy several years ago. She had a lanky body and penetrating blue-gray eyes. If something or someone strange entered our yard, she ran circles around our house to make sure the doors were protected. Sometimes at night she would sit alone, at the edge of our clearing, and howl in her haunting voice. She saw things the other dogs didn't; she was more wolf than shepherd.

As we walked, the underbrush came alive with the sounds

of small critters scampering for safer ground. Just as we came to the edge of the swamp, Silver stopped and pointed her nose at a thicket. The hair on her back raised and she let out a low growl. Little Man put his hand out to stop me from walking. Like an Indian hunter, he silently walked up to where Silver was. He slowly raised his gun and pointed it in the direction of the underbrush.

I watched as his head fell back and he rolled his big brown eyes up to the sky. "Good Lord, Bones, come over here and see what your dog found."

I walked up and peered into the thick growth. Laying on the ground was what looked like a small gray baseball. Little Man shook his head. "That ain't nothing but a little ol' armadillo your dog done scared half to death. When they get scared they curl up in a ball so nothing can hurt 'em. I knew we shoulda left these dogs at home. They ain't huntin' dogs. They just scare everything away."

I put my hands on my hips and said, "She found that armadillo, didn't she?"

Little Man shook his head again. "Come on, Bones, let's see what other critters these dogs can track down."

As we came closer to the swamp, we began to see the floodwater's path of destruction. Huge stands of saw grass and cattails were nearly flattened to the ground. The force of the water had cut deep ruts into the swamp's soft, mucky edge. The sun's reflection skimmed across the water's surface, turning it into an endless black-topped mirror. There were mounds of broken tree branches and dead logs scattered everywhere.

As I looked out over the debris, I turned to Little Man and said, "It sort of makes me sad to see the swamp hurt like this."

"It ain't hurt. This swamp has lived through hundreds of storms like this. It don't hurt it, it makes it better. You see all them piles of muck and rubbish. That there is mighty rich food for a swamp. It just helps it to grow bigger and stronger."

"I guess you're right, Little Man, it's been here forever and it will be here forever after. That does makes me feel better."

We picked our way along the pockmarked, muddy bark, and the dogs ventured further off, sniffing and smelling things only they could sense. As I squished along the muddy path, an angular object caught my eye. I reached down and pulled it out of the slippery earth. It was a hunting knife, like the one Nolay used to clean fish and game. Just as I turned to show it to Little Man, I saw Silver suddenly stop at a small mound of muck and broken branches. The hair along her back bristled, and she began to growl and slowly circle the mound.

Little Man laughed softly. "What's that dog got cornered now, a rat or maybe a big, bad ol' possum?"

Indignantly, I walked toward Silver. Seeing me approach, she squatted down on her hunches, pointed her nose toward the mound, and snarled. "What is it, girl?" I said. "What do you smell?" I followed her eyes to the top of the mound, which was littered with tangled branches and grass. Lying just underneath, covered with a slimy black coating of goo, was an unnatural form. The top half was jagged and wrinkled. The rest of it appeared to be matted with a layer of fine hair. As I got closer I saw something white and shiny peeking up through the pile of muck. Suddenly, like a firecracker exploding in my mind, I recognized the grisly shape. I turned around so fast I almost fell over my own feet. "Little Man, Little Man, quick, get over here!"

"What's she got now?"

"I ain't kiddin'! Get over here quick!"

Little Man sauntered over and stood beside me. I pointed.

Little Man's brown eyes almost popped out of his head. "Good Lord a-mercy! That there is a human leg!"

"I know it! And it's that Yankee man's leg!"

"How do know it's that Yankee's?"

"'Cause I could never forget those white shoes he was wearing," I said, pointing to the tip of the shiny white shoe poking out of the muck. "Them's the shoes he was wearing when me and Nolay saw them Yankees with the Reems brothers."

Little Man cautiously stepped forward for a closer look. "There ain't no body, just a leg from the knee down. Where's the rest of him?"

"I don't know and I don't care! Let's get out of here! We gotta get to the Last Chance and call the sheriff."

"You're right about that. But it'll be quicker if we go to your house and have your mama drive us down."

I handed the hunting knife to Little Man and said, "I found this. I think it might belong to Nolay."

"What's it doin' out here?"

"I don't know! Just put it in your croker sack and let's get out of here!"

56

Me and Little Man jogged back to the house fast as we could. I saw Mama just coming in from the garden carrying a basket full of vegetables. I ran toward her yelling, "Mama, we found that Yankee man's leg! He's out there dead! We got to go call the sheriff!"

Mama hugged the basket to her chest as if to shield herself from what she was hearing.

"Bones, what on earth are you talking about?"

Little Man stepped forward and answered, "It's true, Miss Lori, we done found a dead man's leg out there. And Bones says she knows whose it is, 'cause she recognizes the shoe he was wearing."

Mama looked at both of us. "Y'all get in the car. I'll get the keys."

On the drive to the Last Chance, Mama didn't say a word, but me and Little Man made up for it, talking to each other at the same time. We parked at the Last Chance. Mama went inside to phone the sheriff, and me and Little Man walked over to where Mr. Speed sat on his bench. His lopsided head slowly bobbed up and down as we told him our story.

After catching my breath I said, "Mr. Speed, what do you think happened? I think that man got lost and an alligator caught him and ate him. There's nothing left of him, just a leg." Recalling the grisly sight sent a shudder down my spine.

Mr. Speed shook his head. "Not the right time of year, not the right time. They're busy with their babies, with their babies."

Little Man said, "Now, see there, Bones, that's just what I told you. Why would a gator be eatin' someone this time of year? People ain't in their diet, and it's summertime—there's plenty of food in the swamps. All gators are interested in is marryin' up with each other and taking care of their eggs."

"But it just doesn't make sense. What was he doing out there?"

"You're right about that. It don't make sense."

Mama walked out the front door and came over to us. "The sheriff will be here in about a half hour. Little Man, are you all right waiting here for him? Someone has to show him where to find the . . . to find the . . . leg. I would rather Bones didn't go back out there right now. I'll drive out to your house and let your mama and daddy know where you are."

"But Mama—" I started.

"Yes, ma'am, I'm fine with that," Little Man interjected. "I'll just sit here with Mr. Speed and wait for 'im."

Little Man turned to me. "Bones, I'll try to stop by tomorrow and tell you what all happened."

"All right," I conceded. Then quietly to Little Man, "I'd go back out with you, but it's probably best that I stay with Mama. I think she's more upset than I am."

As I walked away, I looked back. Little Man and Mr. Speed sat side by side on the bench, the croker sack with the knife inside laying on the ground.

After me and Mama got back home, I helped her clean the vegetables. The two of us stood side by side over the kitchen sink. The noise of water splashing over the vegetables and sliding down the drain was the only sound in the room. Mama was quiet, and deep in thought. My mind was so full of questions I felt like they were going to dribble out my mouth. Finally I said, "Mama, why do you think that Yankee man was out there? I mean, that was one of the men Nolay chased off and said he'd do something about if he ever saw them on his land again."

Mama didn't look up, she just replied, "I don't know, Bones. It's a mystery, but I'm sure it will be cleared up soon enough."

"And Mama, I think I found Nolay's hunting knife out there where that leg was."

Mama stopped and turned to face me. "What are you talking about?"

"I found a knife, and it looks like Nolay's. How did it get out there?"

Mama turned back to the sink. "Bones, everyone out here has hunting knifes, and they mostly look about the same. It could belong to anyone."

"But if that man wasn't eaten by alligators, what could have happened? It was an awful sight to see. What happened to the rest of him?"

"If you don't know your way around the swamp, it can be an unforgiving place. There are so many things that could have happened to him. He shouldn't have been out there."

"Yes, ma'am, and I bet he wishes he hadn't been."

Answers to all my questions were laying right around the corner, but they wouldn't be the ones I wanted to hear.

stories

The next morning, I was up at the first crack of light. I got dressed faster than a flea jumping on a dog and headed for the kitchen. Mama hadn't even finished her first cup of coffee when I rushed in.

"Mama, can I go over and visit with Little Man?"

"Bones, the sun has hardly come up. You need to have some breakfast and do a few chores around the house. Little Man said he would come out and see you later today."

"But Mama, I want to go see him and find out what all happened yesterday with the sheriff."

"Well, at least go out and see that the animals are fed and watered. Then come in and get a bite to eat before you leave."

After I did all my chores, I ran back in, grabbed two sausage biscuits, then headed to Little Man's house. On my way out the door Mama stopped me in my tracks. "Bones, do not take any shortcuts in the swamp. You stay on the road out to Little Man's house."

"Yes, ma'am, I will." But she didn't have to tell me that, not after what I had seen laying out there yesterday.

When I came up to Little Man's house, I spotted him over by their big chicken coop.

"Hey, Little Man. So what all happened yesterday with you and the sheriff?"

I could tell by the way he puffed out his chest that it was going to be a good story. Together we walked over to his house and sat down on the front steps.

"Well, it wadn't long after y'all left that the sheriff drove up. He stopped by and let me ride up front with him in the police car. Bones, you should see what all he has inside that car. I tell you, that man is prepared for just about anything that could possibly happen."

"What kind of stuff does he have?"

"He has a sawed-off shotgun hung on the backseat and handcuffs and whistles and all kinds of books and papers. Up on the front dash he has a radio that he can use to speak to other police cars. And a great big ol' metal lunch box sitting on the floor. I swear, that man could just about live inside that car."

"Boy, I hope I get to see that someday."

"So anyways, me and Sheriff LeRoy took the lead and the hearse followed right behind us. The sheriff was real professional-like. He had his red lights flashing, but he didn't turn on his siren. We drove as close up to the swamp as we could, then we all got out and I walked 'em in to where we found the leg. Them hearse guys brought in a couple of bags of supplies and things. When I showed 'em the leg they took some pictures, then they got some funny-looking long pliers out and started picking in the mud around that leg."

"Why did they do that?"

"I ain't quite sure, but they was looking for something. Anyway, after they finished poking around in the mud, they used them pliers to pick the leg up real gentle-like and put it in a big plastic bag. All the time Sheriff LeRoy was walking in circles around the whole place. He looked like a old hound dog sniffing out a trail."

Little Man scrunched up his nose and scratched his bird's-nest-covered head. "Now, there was one interestin' thing. I watched as they pulled up that leg and I didn't see no gator bites or nothing on it. The top of it had been chewed up pretty good. But it didn't look like no gator bites."

"Did they find anything else?"

"Nothing that I could see. But I did hear something interestin'. Them hearse men were talking to the sheriff about the condition of that leg. They said that man had been dead for pert near three days. His partner reported him missin' only two days ago, but he had been out there longer than that."

A picture of that man laying dead out in the back of our swamp started roaming around inside my head. I shuddered. "That is an awful thought."

"I know what you mean. But that's what I heard. After them hearse men wrapped up that leg, they took it back to their car and headed out. Then me and the sheriff got back in his car and he drove me home." Little Man let out a laugh and shook his head. "The sheriff kept his flashing red lights on all the way out to the house. When he drove in our yard with them lights flashing, it nearly scared my mama half to death."

"Did you show the sheriff the knife I found?"

"No, I kept it in my croker sack. I wadn't sure if I should be giving that to him or not." Little Man looked over at me. "Maybe we should just keep it to ourselves for a while. I mean, we don't know for sure if it's Mr. Nolay's or how it got out there, but I think me and you should just think on it for a while."

"I already mentioned it to Mama. But she said it could belong to anybody. Nearly everyone out here has a hunting knife. Little Man, do you think Nolay was out there?"

"Of course he was out there. That there's his swamp. You know he goes out there all the time."

"Well, course I know that. But it still don't make sense why that Yankee man was out there in Nolay's swamp."

I was just about to question Little Man some more on his thoughts when Miss Melba walked up behind us. "Little Man, did you finish gathering the eggs?"

"No, ma'am, I'll go get 'em now."

Miss Melba looked at me. "How are you, Bones? How's your mama and daddy?"

"Everyone's fine, Miss Melba."

"Well, you give them my regards."

"Yes, ma'am, I will." I stood up and said, "I best be getting back. I still got chores to do."

On my walk home, the picture of that dead man's leg kept roaming around inside my mind, along with that knife and some of Little Man's thoughts.

the hands of god

Sunday afternoon me and Mama had just drove back from church services when I noticed the truck parked in the yard. Nolay had been away for a couple of days. We didn't go to church every Sunday, just on the ones that Mama had a calling to go. I wasn't clear on what exactly called Mama, but when it happened, we ended up sitting on a hard wooden pew at the Bethany Baptist Church. Little Man and his family also went to church there, and on the few occasions when there was an adult around who was willing and able to teach us kids, we would go outside and sit under the shade of a friendly oak tree and have Sunday school.

Nolay never had a calling to go to church. He said every day he walked on the earth he was in church.

Nolay was loading up his airboat with sacks of sugar and corn. I walked over to say hey, and he said, "Bones, I'm going out to check on some things in the swamp. You want to come along?"

"Yes, sir, Nolay."

"Go change your Sunday clothes, grab your rifle, and let's get."

I ran back to the house, took off my dress, hung it up, and put on my favorite pair of dungarees. They felt like being hugged by an old friend.

As I climbed into the airboat with Nolay, Mama ran out of the house and yelled, "Y'all wait." She handed Nolay a croker sack bulging with stuff. "Since you'll be out that way, would you stop by and give this to Miss Eunice? I canned up too much vegetables again." Nolay and I exchanged a knowing look. We both knew that was Mama's way of saying that this was not charity; it was just some more of God's abundance.

"Course I will," Nolay said, "and don't worry, we won't be gone long."

Mama said to me, "Bones, you should go in and pay your respects to Miss Eunice."

Nolay handed me the sack. "Put this up at the front." He reached inside his back pocket, pulled out his favorite red handkerchief, and tied it around his head. He grabbed a push pole and poled the boat away from the shore.

I looked up at Nolay and said, "There ain't no way I'm going in that house."

"Now, what makes you say that?"

" 'Cause it's haunted."

"Haunted? How do you figure that?"

"I just do. A couple of times when I was out there, I heard strange noises."

"That don't make it haunted." His blue eyes twinkled as

the hint of a smile spread across his face. "I won't make you, but you never know, you might get curious and want to."

"I don't think I'll get that curious."

Nolay sat on the top seat, and I sat on the one below him. He pressed the starter button and the engine roared to life. The huge airplane propeller mounted at the back of the boat pushed us along. Nolay glided the flat-bottom boat out over thick stands of saw grass. Soon as we hit open water, he pushed the throttle forward, and we went flying on top of the water, a huge liquid ducktail following behind us. Gasoline fumes mingled with the warm air and left a trail of smoky-gray fog over the water's surface.

The swamp was alive with rebirth. The late-afternoon sun burned down on the mirrored surface of the water, and the humid air wrapped around us like thin soup.

The airboat's noisy engine sent disturbing ripples of sound into the silent swamp. Snapping turtles, basking lazily in the warmth, slipped off their logs and into the still water. Two huge white herons rose leisurely into the air, their wings spread like billowing bedsheets across the clear blue sky. A pink-feathered spoonbill strolled along the shore, shoveling its flat beak into the mud. It turned and looked boldly in our direction.

We flew past tall stands of cattails and saw grass. At the base of a willow I spotted a familiar mound of mud and sticks. I looked up at Nolay and mouthed, "Is that Old Snaggle-tooth's nest?" He nodded. At one end of the nest, enjoying the heat of the day, several juvenile gators were stacked on top of each other like pieces of yellow-striped firewood.

I couldn't see her, but I knew the ever-watchful eyes of Old Snaggletooth, the reigning matriarch, were somewhere close by.

On the far side of the swamp, Nolay cut the engine and glided the flat-bottom hull around the back of a stand of cattails. In front of us, a huge tree lay sideways in the water. Nolay jumped down from his seat and grabbed the push pole. "Bones, lift up those bottom limbs." He pushed the boat under the limbs and we entered a small clearing, totally hidden from the entrance.

He moored the boat, and we walked through a tunnel of thick brush. We entered another small clearing, where Nolay lifted up some tree branches, and there it was, the thing he had come to check on: his moonshine still.

A small concrete-block structure, built of leftover supplies from our house, sat in the middle of the clearing. Like green snakes, copper pipes twisted up in the air and ran from the concrete tank into two five-gallon glass jugs.

"Looky there, Bones, perfect timing, that one jug is just about filled up. Go over there and grab me an empty one." After switching the jugs, Nolay placed the full one in a croker sack. He dumped the sack of corn and sugar into the concrete structure, then poured in a jug of swamp water. We picked up the empty sacks and walked back through the tunnel to the boat.

Nolay placed the jug under his seat and the two of us climbed back on board.

I looked down at the jug filled with shiny liquid. "Nolay, isn't moonshine against the law?"

"Well now, that would depend on how you interpret the law. The way I see it, there ain't nothing wrong with making a little extra money for your family. The only thing missing between shine and store-bought liquor is paying the government taxes. And Indians ain't required to pay taxes, so nobody's missing anything."

Now, that made perfect sense to me. My daddy had an explanation for everything he did.

Nolay poled the boat back out to open water and cranked up the engine, and once again we skimmed across the swamp water's smooth surface. On the other side of the swamp, Nolay cut the engine and pulled up to a small, sandy landing. There was just enough room to moor the boat. Past the clearing was a tangle of twisted oak trees and scrub palmettos. Nolay picked up the sack Mama had given him and asked, "Sure you don't want to come pay your respects to Miss Eunice?"

"No, sir. I'll just stay here and watch the boat so nothing happens to it."

"All right. Now, you stay put and I'll be back shortly."

I cradled my single-shot .22 rifle across my legs and watched as Nolay disappeared into the thick undergrowth. Alone on the boat, I felt the warm silence of the swamp wrap around me. The steady beating of my heart filled my ears.

I gazed over the edge of the boat and watched my reflection shimmer across the water's surface and stare back at me. My skin was a perfect blend of Mama's buttermilk and Nolay's light mahogany. My silver-blond hair hung like two curly tassels of corn silk halfway to my waist. The eyes staring up at me were the same piercing sky-blue as Nolay's. As I stuck my finger into the clear water, my image rippled and swirled across the surface.

I looked back to where Nolay had disappeared and thought back on some times I had been to Miss Eunice's house. Actually, I had never been inside that house. Usually me and Mama just drove up to the yard and she came out and met us. Or Mama would drop something off at the front porch. But on a couple of occasions I had heard some strange noises coming from an old shed by the side of that house. And there was a peculiar smell, sort of like something I had smelled out by our swamp. I couldn't put it all together, but it sure made me uncomfortable.

A sudden crash in the undergrowth jarred my senses. I jumped up and pointed my rifle in the direction of the noise. Out of the tangled brush, Nolay appeared. He threw up his arms in an exaggerated gesture and said, "Don't shoot, it's just me."

"Well, don't sneak up on me like that."

"Sneak up! I sounded like a dang wild Brahman bull coming through those woods. You must have been daydreamin' about something."

"I guess I was, but I kept watch over everything just the same."

He jumped into the boat and pushed us off the small landing.

"So everything was all right up there?" I asked.

He nodded. "Everything was fine. Miss Eunice was out

cooking something up in that big old pot of hers. I swear, for someone her age, she sure keeps busy."

A shiver ran down my spine. I looked back at Nolay to see what kind of expression he had on his face, but all I saw was the back of his head with its curly black hair.

Nolay climbed up on his seat. "We best be gettin' back, Bones, before your mama sends the game warden out after us."

He cranked up the engine; the noise from the huge propeller cracked the silence like an eggshell. Once again we flew out over the slick water.

As we neared the landing to our house, twilight was settling in. Nolay cut the engine and said, "Let's pole the rest of the way in. This here is my favorite time of the day, listening to the night wake up." The silence gave way to chirping, croaking, and grunts.

Softly, Nolay said, "Bones, you know people go to church 'cause they think that's where they can get close to God, but to me, this is the only church we need. This here is God talking to us. Now, I don't know if God is a man or a woman 'cause I ain't sure if a human can paint something as pretty as this. Just look around, Bones, look at the show God's lettin' us be a part of."

Suddenly, the silence was shattered by a bloodcurdling scream. The hair on my arms stood up, and I almost dropped the push pole. Nolay grinned and said, "That's a good sign. That ol' panther is lettin' us know he's still alive and king of the swamp." He pointed to a thick stand of saw grass and cattails at the edge of the swamp. "Bones, can you see him over there? He's looking right at us." I peered into the shadows and glimpsed the flicker of two bronze eyes. Slowly, the outline of a sleek cat's body unraveled itself from the shadows.

Soon as he recognized that we had seen him, he moved stealthily along the edge of the thicket and disappeared into the darkness. "He's letting us know that we live in his territory and he's the ruler here," Nolay said. "I been running into that ol' guy and his family, or what's left of 'em, since I was your age."

The sun had just kissed the day goodbye as we approached the landing to our house. The flat horizon looked as though someone had spilled a glass of fresh-squeezed orange juice across it. Clusters of orange dripped and melted into red and gold. Nolay and I sat bathed in a soft splendor as the colors reflected off the water's glassy black surface. The only sounds were our poles dipping gently in the water and the symphony of the swamp. Nolay leaned forward and whispered, "It's like we're being cradled in the hands of God, in the very hands of God. Can you feel it, Bones?"

I looked back into his crystal-blue eyes and replied, "Yes, sir, I sure can."

talks

When I got up Monday morning, Nolay was already gone. After I finished feeding the animals and ate breakfast, Mama asked if I would walk down to the Last Chance and pick up a can of lard and a pack of Lucky Strikes.

I always looked forward to a visit with Mr. Speed, but I was really eager to see him today. It seemed like so much had happened since the last time me and Little Man were with him.

When I arrived at the Last Chance, Mr. Speed was in his usual spot.

"Morning, Mr. Speed. I gotta buy a few things for my mama, then I'll come out and sit a spell with you. You want an RC Cola or anything? I know it's early morning, but I still think it would taste mighty good."

He wobbled his lopsided head in agreement.

When I walked inside the store, instead of Mr. Ball standing behind the counter, I found Mr. Speed's mama, Miss

Evelyn. I had never talked with her very much because she was usually sitting in the little office at the back of the store.

"Good morning, Miss Evelyn."

"How are you, Bones?"

"Just fine, thank you. If you don't mind, my mama needs a can of Crisco and a pack of Lucky Strikes. And she asked if you would put it on our tab."

"Of course." She turned to get the cigarettes and said, "You know where the Crisco is, just go back and get it."

On the way back to the counter, I stopped at the soda cooler and pulled out two bottles of RC Cola. I placed them on the counter and said, "This one is for me, so please put it on our tab, and this one I'm taking out to Mr. Speed."

Miss Evelyn smiled and said, "That's all right, Bones. The cola is on me. You just go out and enjoy your time with Speed."

"Thank you, ma'am."

I put the cigarettes on top of the Crisco can and wrapped my arm around it, then grabbed the two bottles. I went out and sat down beside Mr. Speed.

"How have you been, Mr. Speed?"

"Good, been good."

Together we sat and looked out over U.S. 1 and the glistening top of the Indian River.

Mr. Speed said, "They done made a tire that don't need no tube. It's called a tubeless—yes, sir—a tubeless tire."

"But Mr. Speed, how can that be? How can a tire hold air without a tube? And what will we float around on at the swimming hole? We need inner tubes to float on."

"They can make something to take its place; something will take its place."

"Yes, sir, I guess they will. Seems like someone is always making something new."

I wanted to talk with Mr. Speed about finding the Yankee man's leg and the knife, but those were not the sorts of things we shared with each other. He was full of information but not answers. I just enjoyed being with him; sitting next to him was like being wrapped in a warm blanket.

"Mr. Speed, me and my daddy went out in the swamp yesterday. That big ol' gator Snaggletooth had a heap of babies around her."

"Good mamas, gators are good mamas. The babies stay with 'em for years."

"I guess that's sort of like a real family and the kids don't want to leave home."

Mr. Speed nodded. "They help each other. The big ones help the little ones, the little ones."

"Yes, sir, I would say that is just like a family would do."

The door to the Last Chance opened, and out sauntered Peckerhead Willy. Right behind him was that Yankee man that had been out to our house. They stood together at the front entry, while the Yankee man ripped open a pack of cigarettes and threw the wrapper on the ground. He turned to Peckerhead. "You haven't found anything yet? You got paid good money, now get out there and do what you're getting paid for." When that Yankee looked over and saw me, he grabbed Peckerhead by the arm real quick-like. "Let's get out of here."

I watched as the two of them walked around the corner and disappeared. I hadn't seen them when I was in the store. They must have been in the back by the three-stool bar, where grown-ups could buy beer.

Mr. Speed held up his index finger. "A finger, it's like a finger."

I studied that finger for a while. "You mean the state of Florida? It does look like a finger. Last year there was a big map of Florida hanging on my classroom wall. And it did look like a finger sticking out in the ocean."

Mr. Speed pointed to his knuckle. "On the knuckle, the knuckle."

"Yes, sir, Mr. Speed, I do believe you are right. We live just about right there."

"Look by the knuckle. When it's dry."

Sometimes I wasn't quite sure what information he was sharing with me, but it didn't make any difference. I knew he had a wisdom I couldn't always understand.

We finished our RCs. I took the bottles back inside and set them on the countertop. "Thank you again, Miss Evelyn."

"You're very welcome, Bones."

I went outside and said, "I best be getting back home, Mr. Speed. I'll stop by again real soon. You have a good day."

"See you later."

On my walk home I kept looking at my finger and the knuckle that Mr. Speed said we lived on.

the champion

Tuesday afternoon, Nolay returned home with one of the biggest surprises of my life. One that made me clear forget about Yankees, legs, knuckles, and knives. Me and Mama were outside working in her garden when the dogs began to bark. Pulling up in our driveway was the most astonishing vehicle I had ever seen. Its heavy body sat low to the ground. The back was squared off, and the front was pointed like a shark's nose. It was the color of ripe limes. Gleaming strips of chrome ran down the sides and sparkled in the sunshine. The convertible top was down. and Nolay sat behind the steering wheel.

Me and Mama, along with the dogs, approached cautiously, as if the car were a rattlesnake coiled to strike. Silver let out a low growl; the hair along her back stood up like porcupine's guills. Nolay laughed out loud and blew the horn. "Y'all come on over here. It ain't gonna bite ya."

Me and the dogs broke into a run to see who would get there first. I began to circle the car, running my hands over the smooth hot metal. The dogs sniffed the huge whitewall tires and wagged their tails. Perched on top of the hood was a shiny chrome angel poised in flight, its wings spread. I came around to the driver's door and asked, "Nolay, what is this?"

"It's a 1949 Studebaker Champion, one of the finest vehicles ever put on a road."

"Is it ours? Can we keep it?"

"It's ours. We don't own it, but we're sure as heck gonna keep it."

Mama stood with her hands on her hips, her eyes drinking in the vision in front of her. She shook her head. "Nolay, where on earth did you get such a thing? And where is our truck?"

"The truck is up at the Fish House. Ironhead's gonna drive it down tomorrow. Don't worry about where this car came from; just get in so we can go for a ride."

Mama continued to stand and stare. "Nolay, we cannot have something like this. What will people say? What will people think?"

"I don't give a hoot what they think or say. They'll probably wish they had one, too. Now y'all jump on in here and let me take ya for a spin."

Mama rubbed her hands over her garden-soiled shirt and said, "Well, I cannot get in that car and go for a ride looking the way I do."

"Then, Honey Girl, go get yourself gussied up so we can go for a ride. How 'bout you, Bones, you ready?"

"Yes, sir!"

"Now, be careful when you open the door, don't let them dang dogs in. They can ride in the truck, but they ain't welcome in here."

I pulled open the heavy door and slid in across the slick green woven seat. I could feel the warmth of the sun-baked material seep through my dungarees. The back of the seat burned my thin T-shirt.

Nolay lifted me onto his lap and let me grab the massive steering wheel; I pulled the headlight switch off and on, blew the thunderous horn, and flicked the spotlight back and forth in different directions. Silver jumped around and howled at the sound of the horn. The Champion was full of power and wonder.

Mama came out dressed in clean slacks, a bright blue scarf wrapped around her head and tied neatly under her chin. She slipped in quietly beside me, looked across at Nolay, and said, "Well, let's go out and give everybody something to talk about."

"Mama, ain't this just the finest thing you ever did see?"

Mama looked over at me. Her face was serious, but her eyes were filled with joy. "It is a thing of beauty."

I turned to Nolay and asked, "Can we go out and visit Little Man? I bet he's never seen anything like this before."

"I reckon that's a good place to start," Nolay said. "What do you think, Honey Girl?"

"Fine by me. I've been meaning to go out and see Miss Melba's new gas stove."

Nolay turned the key, and the Champion's engine sprang to life. He glided the car gently over our deep-rutted driveway, turned left on the county's dull yellow marl road, and headed to Little Man's house.

Soon as we pulled into his yard, we were welcomed by an assortment of hunting dogs. The weathered wooden house sat like a sideways matchbox on stilts about three feet above the ground. At both ends of the house was a single door, so there was no front or back entrance.

Little Man and his daddy, Mr. Cotton, were on the side of the house, starting a fire under a huge black pot. When they saw us, they walked toward the car. Mr. Cotton had the same bird's nest of hair as Little Man, only his was white. He came up to the driver's side, and his tanned face crinkled into a smile as he said, "Whoo-ee, Nolay, you done outdone yourself. That is one fine-lookin' mo chine."

Little Man's eyes sat in his round face like shiny moon pies as he stared in disbelief. That familiar question mark started wiggling up between his eyebrows. Little Man's mama, Miss Melba, walked down the steps, wiping her hands on one of her ever-present flour-sack aprons. Her plump face and arms were covered with brown freckles. Miss Melba was like a second mama to me. I spent nearly as much time out here as I did at home. Sometimes she would run her hands over my hair and say, "Bones, your hair is the perfect color of sweet-corn tassels, it's just lovely." Normally I would not be real happy about someone calling my hair corn tassels, but the way Miss Melba said it, it made me feel good.

Miss Melba came up to Mama's side of the car and said, "Oh, my goodness. Why, Lori, I have never seen anything like this before."

"Melba, I just never know what Nolay will bring home next. And I hear you have a new gas stove. I would love to see it."

"Y'all get out and come inside for a spell. I'm just finishing up some jars of guava jelly." .

Me and Mama followed Miss Melba toward the house while Nolay showed Mr. Cotton and Little Man all the wonders of the Champion.

Inside, the house smelled of old wood and sweet, ripe guavas. A huge wooden table sat in the middle of the room. On one side of the room was Mr. Cotton and Miss Melba's bed; on the other side were three beds where Little Man and his two older brothers, Earl and Ethan, slept. Above the wooden table, hanging from the high ceiling on a long wire, dangled a single lightbulb.

Me and Little Man had spent more nights than I could count curled up on the floor in a thick pile of quilts and feather pillows. In the dim room, we would lie in our beds and listen to the soothing voice of Miss Melba as she read from the Bible, or to Mr. Cotton telling stories of his childhood in the swamps when they were wild and untamed.

At the far end of the house, the kitchen area consisted of a long, rough-hewn countertop, a deep sink with a hand water pump, and an assortment of pots, pans, and cast-iron skillets hanging along the wall. By the open door, where the hulking wood-burning stove once stood, sat a shiny white enamel gas stove.

Mama stood in front of it with her hands on her hips.

"Melba, this is so beautiful, and it must be a treat for you not to have to haul firewood anymore."

A light flush of pink crept up between the brown freckles on Miss Melba's face. She ran her hand gently across the stove's glossy surface. "I sure am proud to have this. It has been a pure luxury not having to chop and tote firewood. The good Lord provides all we need and more." Mama and Miss Melba gazed at the white enamel stove as though it were a pot of gold at the end of a rainbow.

As the two women stood admiring the new stove, I asked, "Mama, can I go out and see if Little Man can come for a ride with us?"

"Of course you can."

Outside, the Champion's hood was open like a giant mouth. Nolay stood on one side; Mr. Cotton, Little Man, Earl, and Ethan were on the other side admiring the powerful engine.

As I walked up, I heard Mr. Cotton telling Nolay, "Yesterday Jakey Toms stopped by. Said Sheriff LeRoy hired him and his hound dogs to go lookin' for that Yankee's body."

Nolay said, "Sure don't make sense why that man would have been out there."

Mr. Cotton shook his head. "Wadn't they the same ones that came out your way and y'all had a little run-in with?"

"If it was the same two, me and Bones saw 'em the next day out on back of my property with the Reems brothers."

"The Reems? What was those scallywags doin' out on your property?"

"No idea, but I can pretty much guarantee they wadn't up to much good."

I looked up at Mr. Cotton and said, "Can Little Man come for a ride with us? We'll bring him back shortly."

"I think that would be all right," Mr. Cotton said. "Ethan and Earl can help me with the chickens." He placed a thick-callused hand on my head. "Bones, I haven't seen you around for a while. How's all them critters of yours? You still got that raccoon?"

"Yes, sir, but just like you said, she's starting to try to run away at night. I tried to get Nolay to build a cage for her, but he said if she wants to go back to the wild it's her choice."

"Well, that's right, she is a wild creature and you don't want to go cagin' something up. I told you when I gave 'er to you that she'd steal your heart and run away with it." He reached into his top shirt pocket, pulled out a packet of loose tobacco, and began spilling it into a sheer rolling paper cradled between his index finger and thumb. "And how's that old pig of yours? That dang thing still sleeping in bed with you?"

"Yes, sir, often as she can."

"I swear, Bones, you got such a way with animals, I think you could take a durn ol' panther and turn it into a house cat."

"I'd sure like to try that. If you ever run across a baby one, you bring it to me."

He placed the perfectly round white cylinder of tobacco in his mouth, lit it, inhaled deeply, and released a thick thread of smoke into the air. "I'll sure keep that in mind."

Nolay looked at me and said, "Bones, you best go get your mama before she talks till dark."

"Yes, sir."

Nolay and Mama settled in the front seat and me and Little Man jumped in the back. Nolay pulled out from Little Man's house, turned right, and headed for the Last Chance and U.S. 1. The Champion's powerful engine purred loudly, its heavy body hunkered low on the hard-topped marl road. A dirty-yellow smoke signal of dust followed along behind us.

At the Last Chance, Nolay idled the engine for a minute. Several men came out front to have a look at what the commotion was. Peckerhead Willy glared in our direction and spat out a long stream of tobacco juice. Me and Little Man waved both our hands at Mr. Speed. He slowly raised one hand in recognition.

Nolay waited so everyone could take in the sight before he maneuvered the Champion out onto the blacktop. He hit the gas pedal, and the huge tires squealed out over the hot pavement. The Champion, with all its power and wonder, roared down the highway.

We drove all the way to Melbourne and back. Along the way, if Nolay saw anyone standing outside, he would blow the horn and me and Little Man would wave our hands high in the air.

Mama shook her head and said, "Nolay, you are making us a spectacle."

Nolay grinned. "We ain't a spectacle, just a sight to behold."

"Well, I'm sure the sight of you riding around in this car will have plenty of tongues wagging."

"Let 'em wag."

By the time we drove back to Little Man's house, the sun and wind had painted our skin a light crimson. Little Man got out of the car and said, "I sure do thank ya, Mr. Nolay. That was a pure pleasure."

As we drove away, I twisted around in the backseat and watched Little Man in his yard, a huge grin across his freckled face, his bird's-nest hair spread out in all directions. We waved to each other until the Champion separated us from sight.

The Champion would take us to places we had never been, and to some places I never wanted to go.

blind spot

That evening during supper, Nolay announced, "What y'all think about us taking the Champion and going for a ride down to the Tamiami Trail and visit Cat Island?"

I started to jump up and down and talk so fast I could hardly understand myself. "Holee, can I bring Nippy with me, can I bring my guns, how long are we gonna stay?"

"Now, slow down, Bones, we're just going for the day. I think we best leave all the critters here. They got enough of 'em down there already."

Immediately, Mama started fretting about what to take out to the island. "I just put up some stewed tomatoes, and there's snap beans and okra in the garden. Bones, you come out and help me get some stuff from the garden."

"Hold on, Lori, it's too dark to be going out to the garden. You don't need to go running around like a chicken with its head cut off. We're just going for the day."

"I will not go see family without showing some appreciation."

The next morning, as the first rays of a new day peeked over the horizon, me and Nolay loaded three croker sacks full of Mama's appreciation into the trunk of the Champion.

Nolay put the top down, I slipped in between him and Mama, and we started the nearly three-hour trip toward the great Everglades. I snuggled close to Mama and asked, "Nolay, tell me the story about when you were a little boy and lived on Cat Island."

"Bones, I told you that story how many times already?"

"I know, but just tell me one more time. Please? Every time I hear it I learn something new."

"Okay, one more time. Let me see, now."

Nolay took a deep breath and glanced at me. "Now, you know it ain't an island at all. It's called that 'cause that's where all the Indian side of my family, the Cat clan lives, pretty much set apart from the rest of the county. My grandmother, Lily Cat, was a beautiful Indian woman, but she was also headstrong, and went and married a white man. Back then, same as now, that was not looked upon kindly, but she did it anyways. The two of them was working down in the Lake Okeechobee area when the hurricane of '28 came blowing through and overflowed them flimsy dikes the Yankees had built. Both of 'em died in that. They had one son, and that was my daddy, your granddaddy. He was raised in the village by my grandmother's people, the Cat clan."

"And then what happened?"

Nolay glanced out over the glassy brown waters of the Indian River as if to find missing pieces of the story. "Well, he married a beautiful Indian woman. My mama was from the Seminole tribe." Nolay quickly looked down at me. "That's how I got my name. We lived in the village until I was about your age. Then they decided to move up here to the old family land in Micco. Money was pretty scarce back in those days, so my daddy went and took on an extra job in Key West. The state of Florida was building a bridge to connect all the Florida Keys. He was down there working on building that dang bridge when the hurricane of '35 hit. He didn't make it out alive.

"The house that me and my mama was living in got blown clear down. What's left of it is sittin' right next to our house now. That's when the two of us moved back down to Cat Island. It wadn't six months after that my mama got sick and died. I still think she died of a broken heart."

Nolay drove along in silence for a few minutes, then continued "I'm a long way from being pure Indian, but my family, the Cat clan, raised me just like I was one of 'em. I wadn't ever treated different. I'm proud of every drop of Miccosukee that I got running through my veins."

Nolay glanced back out at the river. "Couple years after, when I was about eighteen, I come back up here to Micco and, along with some help from my uncles Bob and Tom, built a sturdy little block house on that very piece of property. And that's were we live now. I pretty much lived between the two places till I was about twenty." Nolay looked at me and said, "Hurricanes have been pretty hard on our family, took out a bunch of us."

"Reverend Jenkins says a hurricane is the raft of God," I said. "Or something like that. Anyway, when God gets mad at us, he sends down his raft from heaven."

A little smile tugged at the corner of Nolay's mouth. "So ol' Preacher Jenkins told you God has a raft big enough to put a hurricane on."

"Well, it's something like a raft. What is it, Mama?"

"I think you mean to say the wrath of God," she said, smiling at Nolay.

"Yeah, that's what it is; anyway, God gets mad when we do bad things."

Nolay continued, "Well, Bones, I don't think it has anything to do with God. I think it's nature, the spirit of Earth. When man starts trying to mess with nature and change it around for his own good, then nature comes in and shows 'em who the real boss is. If it hadn't been for men thinking they were more powerful than nature, that they could change it around any way they wanted to, then none of my family or any of those thousands of other people would have been there and none of 'em would have died."

"What happened after you left Cat Island and built our house?"

"Now see, you already know that story, too."

"I know, but you can't stop at the best part."

Nolay winked at me. "Well, one winter I was earning some extra money picking oranges up in the Ocala area when I made friends with one of the other pickers. He was from Georgia and asked me if I wanted to catch a ride with him and go up to Georgia and see his family's farm. And that's when I met the prettiest little green-eyed woman I had ever seen in my life. One look into those eyes and she cast a spell on me. I was a goner."

"Mama, did you really do that?"

"I guess you could say we put a spell on each other," Mama said. "It wasn't long after we met that, against my daddy's wishes, we ran away and got married. Then along came you, and I think you know the rest of the story."

Nolay said, "Well, there was a little spell in there when World War II started and I was gone for a little over a year. I was one of the lucky ones. I got drafted when the war was pretty close to ending. I wanted you and your mama to go up and stay in Georgia with Big Mama and Grandpa." He shook his head and let out a little laugh. "But your mama wouldn't hear of leaving our house and land. The two of you stayed right there."

Mama cut in with, "But you can see that everything turned out fine. I could not bear to leave behind our home that we had worked so hard on. All our neighbors pitched in when Nolay was gone, and we all helped each other out. It wasn't a good time, but we all took care of each other."

Nolay slowed the Champion down as we came up behind a car towing a cumbersome house trailer. He shook his head. "Them things are a nuisance. They remind me of wagon trains. Come down here and park wherever they want. They shouldn't be allowed on the road. Or on the land, either."

Mama said, "Nolay, I don't think the state of Florida is

going to let you put up a gate to keep out people or trailers. People come down here to enjoy the weather."

"Maybe some of 'em do. But you mark my words, Lori, them wagon trains are going to be the ruin of this place. They shouldn't be allowed." Nolay glanced at me. "Bones, I see some mighty sleepy eyes. Why don't you lay your head down in your mama's lap and get some rest? We'll be there soon enough, and you'll be running wild with all the kids."

I curled up between my parents, and the steady hum of the Champion's engine and its big tires singing on the pavement soon lulled me to sleep. The next thing I knew, Mama's hand was gently shaking me. "Wake up, Bones, we're here."

As Nolay pulled into the small village, I sat up and looked out the window. Like oblong birdhouses, several palmetto-thatched dwellings called chickees sat in a horseshoe formation on raised platforms. A thin gray thread of smoke drifted up from the cook chickee that sat in the middle of the village. Before the car stopped rolling, we were surrounded by an array of giggling Indian children and yapping dogs.

I recognized Nolay's uncle Bob Cat as he walked toward us. His face was an older version of Nolay's. His eyes sat in his round face like shiny brown marbles, instead of Nolay's crystal-blue; his wavy black hair hung nearly to his shoulders. Over a pair of dungarees, he wore the traditional multicolored shirt of the Miccosukee and Seminole Indians.

He flashed the same dazzling smile as Nolay and said, "Well, gol-durn, look what the cat done drug in. Now, that is one dang fancy vehicle you are driving. We were just talking about you the other night, and here you show up. Y'all get on out. Tom is up with Blind Spot right now. She'll be mighty happy to see you folks."

Soon as I stepped out of the truck I was surrounded by a group of brown-cookie-faced Indian kids all speaking at the same time.

"Hey, Bones, my dog just had a litter of puppies, you want one?"

"We got a pet skunk, come see it."

"I'm learning how to sew."

Uncle Bob Cat waved a hand in the air and said, "You kids hush up, you gotta talk one at a time. Bones cain't understand a word you're saying."

Nolay got out of the car and opened the trunk. He handed the croker sacks to some of the older boys and said, "Y'all take these up to the cook chickee."

One of the girls grabbed my hand and said, "Bones, come on and meet Two-Stripes, our pet skunk."

Before I could be pulled away, Nolay intervened. "Bones, you come and pay your respects to Blind Spot, then you got the rest of the day to go wild."

We walked with Uncle Bob Cat through the small village. As we passed some of the chickees, women dressed in long rainbow-colored skirts and blouses came to the open doors. They waved shyly and called out, "Hey, Yoo." Nolay and his family were being welcomed back home.

We stopped in front of one of the chickees. Tom Cat, Uncle Bob Cat's brother, came to the open door. He slapped the side of his leg and let out a little hoot. "Y'all come on in." He looked back inside the chickee and said something in the singsong Native language.

Inside the chickee, the rich smell of smoke mingled with the mustiness of dried leaves. Slender fingers of sunlight filtered through the palmetto thatching and danced across the floor. As my eyes adjusted to the dimness, I saw a small woman nestled against the wall on a pile of colorful blankets. In a voice as soft as falling rain, she said, "Hey, Yoo, my family, it is good to feel you again." She lifted her frail arms, like two small, shriveled tree limbs. "Come close so I can touch you."

Her moon-shaped face was as brown and wrinkled as a crumpled-up paper bag. Two small holes the color of clouds sat where her eyes should have been. A halo of thick silver hair twisted around the top of her head. Thick strands of blue and green beads draped around her thin neck. Old and frail, Blind Spot, Nolay's great-grandmother, my great-great-grandmother, sat on her pile of blankets, as elegant as a queen.

Nolay walked over, slowly bent down, and pressed his nose against Blind Spot's wrinkled cheek. Her small, graceful hands ran over his face and hair. "You are still handsome, Grandson. Do you remain as rascally as a raccoon?" A small smile spread across her ancient face. "You still wear the smell of metal toys."

Nolay smiled. "Grandma, it's good to see you again. I never could fool you. You must be smellin' that new car I got."

"It is all over you."

"I'll be happy to take you for a ride."

"Thank you, Grandson, but I am happy just to use my legs."

Mama walked over, squatted down, and hugged Blind Spot's frail body.

She placed a delicate hand on Mama's face and said, "Honey Girl, good for you to be here. And how are you doing with this rascal grandson of mine?"

"It's good to see you again, Grandma," Mama said.

Mama turned in my direction and motioned me forward. "Grandma, Bones is here to see you."

I knelt down in front of her and, as always, was stunned nearly speechless by the great presence of this small woman. "Hello, Grandma Spot."

Blind Spot cupped my face with both hands, her sightless eyes gazing into mine. "Little Bones, I can feel how much you have grown." She ran her hands across my face and down my two long pigtails. "Ah, you've let you hair grow long. Is it still the color of sweet corn?"

"Yes, ma'am, I reckon you could call it that." It made me feel good when Grandma Spot said that, too.

She rubbed her hands over my arms and back up to my face and said, "My precious little Bones, it is good to feel you so healthy."

"Yes, ma'am, and it's good to see you still young and healthy, too."

Blind Spot's face disappeared into a mass of wrinkles as she laughed and said, "You have your father's humor."

Bob Cat walked in and motioned to the floor. "Y'all sit back and get comfortable; we got a lot of catchin' up to do."

As we sat on the floor, family members began trickling into the chickee. The air filled with greetings and questions and laughter. Several of the brown-cookie-faced kids stood by the open doorway and signaled for me to come out. Mama touched my shoulder and said, "You can go out now, Bones, but be back for noon dinner."

bones

I jumped down from the chickee platform and joined up with the kids. Including me, there were a half dozen of us. The three girls—Lily, Rosie, and Daisy—were all about my age or younger. The two boys, Johnny and Jimmy, were a couple of years older and naturally became the leaders of our little gang.

As we explored the paths, trails, and woods of Cat Island, their little pet skunk, Two-Stripes, followed us around, just like Nippy the raccoon did back at home. At the edge of a small tree-rimmed pond, Jimmy turned and pointed. "There's a family of newborn otters over by that side. If we're quiet like, we can sneak up and hide behind that big ol' cypress tree and watch 'em play."

Silent as a family of mice, we slipped up to the side of the gigantic old tree and settled in to watch the otters frolic and chase each other.

At one point Johnny Cat turned to me and said, "Y'all haven't been down here for a while. It's good to see you again."

"I know," I replied. "Maybe now that we have the

Champion, we'll make it down more often. Our old truck used to have a hard time traveling here."

Johnny Cat let out a soft whistle. "That sure is a fancy car. I swear, you never know what Uncle Nolay's going to come up with next. It must be a lot of fun having him for a daddy."

"I guess so. He does keep things interesting."

"My mama and daddy still tell stories about when he lived here in the village. He was always up to something. Like catching snakes to sell to the snake man up in Miami, or the time he came home with a live snapping turtle clamped onto his finger. They wanted to kill the turtle to get it off, but your daddy refused to let 'em. Instead, he had 'em wave a piece of meat in front of the turtle's nose, and sure enough, it let loose and took the bait."

I sighed and shook my head. "I always did wonder how he got that scar on his finger. He told me about having a fight with an alligator!"

Jimmy Cat answered, "All I know is, he's thought of highly here in the village. He's the kind of man that makes you proud to be an Indian."

Johnny Cat said, "What about those stories of him taking people snipe huntin'?"

"Oh yeah. Did he ever tell you about that, Bones?"

"Snipe huntin'? Not that I can recall. What's that?"

Jimmy Cat continued, "Well, sometimes when curious white people would stop by the village to buy stuff like necklaces and such, Uncle Nolay would ask 'em if they wanted to go catch a snipe. He told 'em it was a magnificent little bird that was real hard to catch, but for five dollars he would take 'em out to catch one. After they paid him he would give 'em a croker and walk 'em out in the swamps. He told 'em they had to squat down and stay real still and quiet, and he would circle around and scare the snipe in their direction. When the little bird saw the open croker sack, it would think it was a safe place and jump right inside."

Johnny Cat chimed in. "After he got them folks situated, Uncle Nolay would come back to the village. Everybody got a good laugh out of them people sittin' out there, gettin' ate up by skeeters and waitin' for a imaginary bird to jump in their sack."

I couldn't believe what my ears were hearing. "And people would really do that? They would sit out there getting eaten by mosquitoes and wait for a little bird to run inside their sack?"

"Oh yeah. My daddy said sometimes they would stay out there for hours. And when they made it back to the village they were usually whoppin' mad. But Uncle Nolay would be hiding inside one of the chickees, so nobody ever found him. Daddy said Uncle Nolay had a way with words, he could charm the bark off a tree."

The sound of a shrill whistle drifted out over the swamp and signaled us to come in for noonday dinner. As we walked back to the chickee, I noticed a shiny airboat moored next to several dugout canoes.

"Whose airboat is that?" I asked.

Johnny Cat replied, "That's Uncle Bob Cat's. He's had it

for about a year now. It sure has come in handy. It's a lot faster than our dugouts."

Inside the cook chickee it was a crowded affair as women bustled around, ladling out bowls of sofkee, a traditional Indian dish of boiled corn. In the middle of the chickee, small blue and yellow flames fluttered up from the star-shaped fireplace. Around its edge the women had placed woven mats. On the mats, along with the bowls of sofkee, they sat wooden palmetto-lidded containers piled high with steaming swamp cabbage and wild pork. Stacked beside the customary containers, like leftover Christmas presents, were bright orange, yellow, and red plastic bowls and plates.

The first plate of food was given to Blind Spot; then all us kids filled our plates and found a comfortable place to sit together.

We all sat cross-legged on the floor. The chickee's thatched sides were rolled up to let in a soft cool breeze. The men leaned against poles along the sides of the chickee and laughed over the telling and retelling of stories. They talked of the changes that were rapidly seeping into their way of life.

Bob Cat said, "Nolay, after we eat, maybe you can take a look at my airboat. It ain't been running right. You might be able to help me with it. I need to keep it in good running order. Been making some good side money, taking tourists for rides."

Nolay shook his head. "Bob Cat, I don't know about bringin' strangers here to the village. This is about all we got left of our land and our way of life. Be careful. Outsiders have already done enough harm. They done tried to drain the swamps to build hotels and bridges all over the place. Seems like all they want to do is change and destroy things."

"I understand what you're saying, Nolay, but if we don't change with the times, we're gonna get left sittin' in a hole we can't dig ourselves out of. There ain't many of us left, and there's plenty of them. We're dying, and they keep comin'."

Blind Spot sat, quietly listening. Then she said, "An airboat is like a mindless metal animal. It burns holes in the water and covers the air with its foul smell. It chases life away, instead of bringing it closer." Blind Spot tilted her head as if hearing a silent voice. "Yes, the times have changed and we must change with them. But never lose your respect for Pahay-okee. She is hurt. We need to take better care. If Pa-hay-okee dies, we will all die with her. Man can change what lies on the outside, but he can not touch what lives here." Blind Spot pressed a wrinkled hand over her heart. "Here in the center."

Nolay's voice floated out into the stillness. "Grandma, we will always respect our traditions, and we will do everything we can to to see that our way of life lives forever."

Everyone nodded in silent agreement. The room filled with a quiet admiration for the words Nolay had spoken.

As soon as our food was finished, me and the kids raced each other back to the pond. The day went by all too fast; another shrill whistle signaled us to return to the village. It was time to help load up the Champion and start back home.

As we drove out of the small village, our relatives, dressed in their traditional multicolored clothes, stood waving good-bye. They looked vibrant and solid, like a patchwork quilt of people.

On the drive back home, I sat in the front seat again, between Nolay and Mama.

I asked Nolay, "Who is Pa-hay-okee?"

"It's the old Indian name for the Everglades; it means 'the grassy water.'"

"Is it true, is it really dying?"

"It's hurt, but it ain't so bad yet that we can't fix it."

I looked at Mama and said, "I wish I could live on Cat Island. It's always so much fun there."

Mama put her arm around my shoulders and said, "Bones, it's fun because you're visiting. If you lived there, it would be like home. You would still have chores to do, and you would still go to school, just like all the kids there do."

"I reckon so."

Mama's fingers found the string necklace hanging around my neck, and she asked, "What is this?"

"It's a gator tooth. Jimmy Cat gave it to me; he said it was good luck and would keep away bad spirits."

At that moment, Nolay jerked the Champion into the other lane so hard, it shoved me and Mama into each other.

"Sorry, ladies. I didn't want to run over that possum cros-sin' the road. There's too many danged things trying to get across the road these days."

I dangled the alligator tooth in front of Mama. "See, it must work. That was pretty good luck."

"It was good luck for the possum."

"Mama, did you know that the possum is a mammal and that there are over four hundred different kinds of mammals that live right here in Florida?"

"I did not know that."

"Well, it's true, and the possum is the only one that is kin to the kangaroo. It's a mar-soupel just like a kangaroo. Kangaroos live in Australia."

"You mean a marsupial?"

"Yes, ma'am, 'cause it keeps its babies in a pouch just like a kangaroo. And do you know how it gets its babies into its pouch?"

"Do tell."

"Well, it keeps its babies in its nose and when it's ready it sticks its nose down in the pouch and sneezes them in there."

"Good Lord, Bones, did Mr. Speed tell you that?"

"No, ma'am, he told me the part about the four hundred mammals and the kangaroo. Nolay told me about sneezing the babies into the pouch."

Mama glanced in Nolay's direction. "Well, isn't that interesting. And just where did you come up with that sort of information, Nolay?"

"I just might of seen it happen a time or two," he said.

"Well, the next time you see it happen, please let me know, because I would certainly like to witness such an event."

I looked up at Nolay and said, "You know, today when I was out with the kids, they told me a story about when you used to live in the village. Johnny Cat said you used to take people out snipe hunting."

Nolay let out a little chuckle. "We used to have some good times growing up."

"But what if something happened to someone out there? You know, like if they got snakebite or something?"

"I didn't take 'em anyplace dangerous. Just having a little fun is all." Nolay glanced down at me. "Bones, if you couldn't have fun in life it would be pretty boring, don't you think?"

"Yes, sir. I reckon so." I snuggled in closer to Mama. "Nolay, why is Grandma Spot called Blind Spot?"

"When she was younger, before she lost her sight, she was known as Spotted Cat. I reckon as she aged and her life changed, her name aged right along with her."

"I wish she could still see."

"Grandma probably sees more than most people do with two good eyes. She sees from the inside, from her heart."

I sat and pondered on that. It was sort of the way Mr. Speed saw things, too. I guess him and Grandma Spot had a lot in common.

I looked up at Mama. "Mama, tell me again about how Grandma Spot named me."

"Bones, you do love your stories, don't you?" Mama scrunched down and settled herself on the seat before she began. "When you were born, you weren't much bigger than a puppy with its eyes still closed. For a solid week at the Melbourne hospital, the doctors tried their best to get milk or any kind of nourishment into your tiny body. They finally gave up and told me and your daddy to just take you home and enjoy the short time we would have with you. I cried so much, I felt like an empty bucket."

Mama placed her hand, soft as a feather, on my head as she continued. "We wrapped you up in a blanket and got in the truck, and Nolay drove us straight to Cat Island. The moment I placed your little body in Grandma Spot's arms, she peeled the blanket away and ran her hands all over your body. She started saying, 'Bones, precious little bones.' She had some different herbs and powders brought to her, and for three days and three nights she kept you right there next to her. You never left her side. She would dip her fingertip into the herb-and-powder mixture and put it in your mouth; she whispered words that only the two of you could understand. Then she would rub her hands over you and say, 'Bones, precious little bones.' It wasn't long before your eyes had a sparkle to them and you were sucking from a baby bottle."

"I like that story, Mama. Sometimes at school I get teased about my name, but it don't matter, because I know how special it is."

"It is a special name given to you by a special person. Precious Bones. At first I wanted to call you Precious, but Bones just sort of took over."

Exhausted from the long day, I laid my head in Mama's lap and let the steady hum of the Champion's engine lull me to sleep.

I awoke to the sound of unfamiliar voices. I sat up and rubbed the sleep from my eyes. Darkness had already covered over the day. The only light was the moon's long silver shadows. We were parked in front of the Last Chance gas pumps; Nolay stood outside, filling up the Champion's hungry tank.

I looked into the dimness and made out the massive frame of Sheriff LeRoy Hasket as he leaned against the side of the car, facing Nolay. Hanging from the thick leather belt wrapped around his broad waist were a set of handcuffs, a flashlight, a collection of keys on a metal ring, and an enormous black-handled .357 Magnum pistol.

I recognized the pistol because Sheriff LeRoy let me and Little Man hold it one time. It was almost as heavy as a sawed-off shotgun. The sheriff had told us how valuable it was, and I could tell from his voice how much he treasured it.

Little Man had said Sheriff LeRoy was like a walking jukebox. Every step he took was accompanied by the squeak of leather, clinking of metal, and jingling of keys.

Sheriff LeRoy spoke in his slow, steady voice. "That's a mighty fine vehicle you got there. Fishing must be good."

"Yep, there's a lot of fish jumpin'," Nolay said.

"I heard you had a little disturbance with a couple of Yankee boys out at your place. Last week one of 'em stopped by my office to report his partner missing. Told me they had drove out to your place and you attacked 'em and run 'em off with a gun."

"Durn it, LeRoy, that was nearly two weeks ago them Yankees came out to my place. Never even got out of their car. How come they're only telling you about it now? They're just troublemakers."

"Now, like I said, there was only one of 'em, and he was reportin' his partner missing." LeRoy shifted his body and folded his arms across his chest. "You do know that all that turned up of that Yankee was one of his legs?"

"I heard that."

LeRoy leaned down and looked inside the car. "In fact, little Miss Bones and her friend was the ones that found that leg. Right out in back of your land."

"LeRoy, we know good and well that's what happened. So what?"

"Well, sir, seems like the rest of 'im got found. I hired Jakey Toms and his hound dogs and they found the body—or what was left of it—buried in a muck pit. Out at about the end of your swamp."

"Is that so? Well, it's a big swamp, LeRoy; if you're stupid and you don't know what you're doing, a swamp will eat you right up."

"That may be true, but the interesting thing about that body is the bullet hole in that man's head."

"You don't say. And just what's the point of tellin' me about this, LeRoy?"

"Just doin' my job is all. I'll be doin' a little more po-lease work. Might be stoppin' by your place to ask a few questions."

"You do that, LeRoy, you just do that. Now, if you'll excuse me, it's been a long day. I need to get my family home."

Sheriff LeRoy turned toward me and Mama; he tipped his oversized Stetson and said, "Evenin', Miss Lori." He turned slowly and squeaked, clinked, and jingled off into the gloom of dusk.

As Nolay slid into the driver's seat, Mama asked him, "What was that all about?"

"Lori, Honey Girl, it was just LeRoy being LeRoy. Don't worry your pretty little head about a thing."

We *weren't* worried about it then, but maybe we should have been. It would be all too soon that Sheriff LeRoy would come jingling back into our lives.

white trash

After we returned from our trip, Mama went on one of her cleaning rampages. She cleaned out our closets and dug through the big cedar chest she kept at the end of her bed. That cedar chest was where we stored clothes and anything else of value to keep them from being devoured by bugs.

When I came in for noon dinner, Mama announced, "Bones, I have some boxes of clothes and other stuff you've outgrown, and we need to take them out to the Reems family."

"The Reemses! Mama, do I have to go out there?"

"Well, if you don't come along, it won't look like a friendly visit, and they might take this as charity."

"Mama, I know you been gathering clothes and stuff up from all our neighbors for a week now. Can't you just drop those boxes off by yourself?"

Mama's eyes were soft and mirrored as she quietly said, "Because you are too busy, those poor, innocent little children will have to do without?"

Without thinking, I opened my mouth and blurted out,

"Mama, those Reems boys are meaner than a cornered pole-cat. I nearly hate being around them. I don't want to go out to that white-trash place. Everybody knows—" Before I could finish my act of stupidity, Mama reached over and pulled so hard on my ear I thought my face would be permanently lopsided.

"Bones," she said, "I better never hear that come out of your mouth again. Just because someone doesn't have as much as another person doesn't make them trash. And don't you ever forget that."

"Yes, ma'am. But Mama, it was you yourself told me any-one that didn't have at least one copy of the *Saturday Evening Post* just wasn't civilized and could be considered white trash."

"Bones, I do not recall ever having said such a thing, although it could be true. Now, let's just move on. After you finish your dinner, you help me put those boxes in the truck and we are going to the Reemses'. And you are going to act civil."

"Yes, ma'am."

After we loaded the back of the truck with boxes of clothes and canned vegetables, we started the butt-bruising ride out to the Reems compound.

The Reems family had a hundred-acre track of land that bordered ours. Most of their land consisted of scrub palmetto and pine trees. As we pulled into the bare dirt yard, a couple of half-starved hound dogs and two dirty-faced little boys came out to meet us. Mama looked in my direction and whis-pered, "Bones, you will be kind."

With my ear still red and burning, I answered, "Yes, ma'am."

The main house, where Peckerhead Willy and his young wife, Miss Alvie, lived was a dilapidated two-story clapboard structure. A board was nailed across one broken window and another had a piece of tar paper hanging over it. Off to the side was a barn with both doors missing and an old smoke-house that leaned so far to one side it was propped up with logs. Past the old barn, I could see the smaller house where Whackerstacker Joe lived with his three boys. Their mama, Miss Alice, died when the youngest boy was born. The boys—Fats, Skeeter, and Smokey—ranged in age from seventeen to nine, and each one of them was meaner than a bee-stung bull.

On the sagging front porch, old Ma Reems sat in her rock-ing chair. The screen door squeaked open and Miss Alvie stepped out. Mama got out of the truck, walked up to the porch, and spoke to Ma Reems. "Morning, Miz Reems."

Old Ma Reems didn't even look in Mama's direction, just rocked back and forth, chewing on her wad of tobacco. Mama turned her attention toward the screen door. "Morning, Miss Alvie, how are you doing today?"

Miss Alvie held Baby Teddy in her arms. She came down the steps and walked out into the sunlight. A small bulge in her belly poked at the front of her thin cotton skirt. The two dirty-faced boys, Tim and Tom, rushed over, dug their faces into her skirt, and wrapped their arms around her like little octopuses.

In the bleak front yard, Mama looked as out of place as a peacock in a henhouse. She wore a white blouse and a pair of blue corduroy pants; her honey-blond hair fell to her shoul-ders and sparkled in the bright Florida sun. Miss Alvie stood next to her in a skirt and blouse that had been washed to drabness; she resembled a little gray rag doll.

The screen door opened again and two girls walked down the steps. I recognized Martha and Ruthie from school and from other non-charity visits to this house. Mama turned to me and said, "Bones, you get out of the truck and come say hello to Miss Alvie and the kids."

The girls, like their mama, were frail and small-boned; they reminded me of little whooping cranes wearing dresses. Their skin was the color of fresh milk. Huge brown eyes peered out from their thin faces. Their coal-black bangs were cut straight across their forehead, and their hair hung down to their bony shoulders. Martha was two grades ahead of me; Ruthie was two years behind me. We had an unspoken pact. Sometimes, when Martha wasn't around to protect her, Ruthie was tormented on the playground by Betty Jean Davis and some of her butterfly girls. They made fun of Ruthie's worn clothes, the muck sores on her legs, any flaw they could open and pick at. There were a couple of times when me or Little Man had stepped in and put a stop to it.

"Hey, Martha," I said, "Hey, Ruthie."

"Hey, Bones," Ruthie said. "You want to come see some kittens? My calico had five babies a couple days ago. They still got their eyes closed. They're in the barn, you want to see 'em?"

"Sure, Ruthie, I'd like that. Mama, we're going over to the barn."

"Bones, before you go, just help me carry these boxes inside the house."

Mama went to the back of the truck, handed a box to me, one to Martha, and picked up another one. Ruthie ran up the steps and opened the screen door for us.

Miss Alvie said, "Just put them right there on the floor. I'll tend to them later on. Thank you so much."

"Don't stay too long now," Mama said. "We have to get back and finish up our chores."

Inside the barn, the air was filled with the pungent smell of hay and manure. Thin gray lines of light crept in through cracks in the roof and walls. Ruthie took us over to a corner where a small calico cat lay nestled in a box, nursing her kittens. As the three of us squatted down to see the kittens, the bottom of Ruthie's thin cotton dress got caught on some hay and rose above her skinny thigh. Several purple marks, the perfect shape of a belt buckle, stained her white skin. Martha reached over and quickly pulled the dress down. I had seen those marks before, at school, only then they had been on Martha's legs.

Ruthie stood up and said, "I only see three kittens. Two of 'em are lost; we gotta look for 'em."

"Then you better go out and dig in the pig muck, 'cause I done fed 'em to my hawgs."

Startled, we looked up to see Skeeter, Whackerstacker Joe's twelve-year-old boy, saunter toward us with his younger brother, Smokey, in tow. Their greasy, freckled skin glistened as they walked through the dim rays of light. The boys were the mirror image of their father, both in looks and disposition. They resembled fat, brown-haired possums. Skeeter hooked his chubby thumbs in the tops of his dirty overalls. "My hawgs et 'em up like little gumdrops. We don't need no more mouths to feed round here. I'm a-gonna take the rest of them little rats and drown 'em in the creek. Might take the mama this time, too."

Ruthie's huge brown eyes filled with tears, and she began to sob and plead. "Please don't hurt 'em, Skeeter. I'll take care of 'em. Please don't hurt 'em." Skeeter swaggered toward the little nest. I stood up and stepped in front of him. He stopped and leveled his beady eyes at me.

I stood my ground. I could hear Nolay's voice echo in my ears. "Remember, Bones, it don't matter the size of a man, it only matters the size of the situation. A man's fear can be bigger than he is. Never show your fear, and you'll always be bigger than your situation."

Skeeter squinted down at me. "What you gonna do, swamp monkey, you gonna stop me? You ain't nothin' but a puny little ol' swamp girl. I'll break your scrawny neck and feed you to my hawgs."

Smokey stood behind his big brother and chimed in, "Yeah, you ain't nothin' but a swamp monkey, a girl swamp monkey."

I took a deep breath and puffed myself up like a barnyard rooster. "Skeeter Reems, you possum-faced pig head, you're lower than a dried-up booger. If you want those kittens, you're gonna have to come through me to get 'em. You might win, but you're sure gonna know you tangled with somethin' bad."

I saw movement from the corner of my eye and felt something warm move close to my side. I looked to see Martha standing there with a pitchfork. She looked directly at Skee-

ter and whispered, "Get on outta here, Skeeter. If you touch
Ruthie's kittens, I'm gonna stick you, I'm gonna stick you
good."

Skeeter stepped back so quick he stumbled into Smokey,
and both of them almost fell down. He glared at us and said,
"I ain't scared of you girls. I'll get my knife and gut you like
dead mullets."

"Shut your mouth, Skeeter!" The doorway to the barn
filled with the hulking frame of Fats Reems. Fats was the oldest brother. He also looked like a possum, just a fatter one. As
Fats ambled toward us, the two younger boys began to back
away. "Get on back to the house and keep your stupid yaps
shut." Fats turned toward us. "You girls take them cats up to
the house and keep 'em out a sight." He turned and waddled
back toward the door.

Silently, the three of us gathered up the mama cat and her
kittens and walked back up to the house. Ruthie got a wood
box and we made a nest for the kittens on the far end of the
sagging porch. Ma Reems sat in her rocker like an old sack of
potatoes and slowly squeaked back and forth. Her only other
movement was an occasional twist of her head as she spat
out a black stream of chewing tobacco. Thin brown lines of
tobacco ran down the wrinkles on both sides of her craggy old
face.

Just as Mama and Miss Alvie walked out the screen door,
Peckerhead Willy staggered around the corner and leaned up
against the stair railing. His body reeked of stale sweat and
sour mash. He spoke to Mama in a voice thick and slurred.
"What kind of charity you bringin' to my house this time?"

Mama softly replied, "I haven't brought any charity, Mr. Reems, just sharing an overflow of abundance from the good Lord."

He glared at her. "The Lord ain't never give me nuthin' but trouble. I don't care for nuthin' he got to give out."

Mama turned toward Miss Alvie. "It's been a pleasure, Alvie, and we'll have to get together again soon. Bones, you say goodbye to Miss Alvie and the girls." Then she brushed past Peckerhead Willy as though he were a pile of dried dog poop and curtly said, "Good day, Mr. Reems, and I hope the good Lord continues to rain his blessings on you."

On the drive home Mama gripped the steering wheel so tight her knuckles turned white. I broke the silence and asked, "Mama, do you think there is a *Saturday Evening Post* at the Reemses' house?" She glanced at me sideways but did not reply, so I continued. "I like the girls, it's just those boys. I would rather have a boil on my butt than spend time with them." Mama continued to look straight ahead and drive in silence. "Seems like they get pleasure out of being hurtful to things. I don't know why Soap Sally hasn't turned them into a bucket of soap by now. And Mama, why does Miss Alvie look so much younger than Mr. Peckerhead?"

"Because she *is* younger, Bones. There are some things that you are just too young to understand." Almost absently she muttered under her breath, "I don't understand some things myself." The rest of the ride home was made in silence.

• • •

That night after supper, I lay in my bed, surrounded by several cats and Nippy Raccoon purring contentedly. The muffled voices of Mama and Nolay drifted out over the quiet and into my room. "That poor woman," Mama said. "She's been with that awful man nearly her whole life. In a couple of months, she'll give birth to their fourth child. Although she had powder on it, I could still see the bruise around her eye. No one should have to live like that. That hateful old man!"

Nolay said to Mama, "Lori, Honey Girl, I've known that family my whole life. Seems like every one of those Reems boys grows meaner than the one before. You be careful, Lori. They ain't stupid. Every one of them is slicker than a slug and twice as nasty. They ain't never been up to no good and they never will be. I know how you feel about Alvie and them kids, but you stay clear of them Reems brothers."

It was too bad Nolay was better at giving out advice than he was at taking it

ol' blue and
chicken charlie

Little Man was over visiting the next day, when Mama asked if we would walk to the Last Chance to buy her some Lucky Strikes. We had just started down our dirt road when Nolay drove up in the Champion. He had left early in the morning to go fishing with Ironhead.

He stopped and called out to us, "Where y'all goin'?"

"Down to the Last Chance," Little Man replied "We had a dang good fishin' trip. I brought home some extra fish, and I'm gonna go drop some off for ol' Blue and Chicken Charlie. If y'all want to wait a few minutes, I'll give ya a ride."

Me and Little Man answered at the same time. "Yes, sir!"

"Y'all get in, I just want to go to the house and give this fish to Honey Girl."

When Nolay returned, he was carrying a small sack with him. "You kids jump in the front seat of the truck. I don't want to take the Champion out to Charlie's. It'll get scratched to pieces." I slid in the front seat between Nolay and Little Man.

Nolay placed the sack in back of the truck and smiled as he told us, "Some of your mama's abundance that she wants to share with ol' Charlie."

Nolay turned right on the county road and took another right when he got to the railroad tracks. A small, sandy road ran along the side of the tracks. On the left-hand side, between the tracks and the road, sat a one-room church painted bright blue; a white wooden cross stood sentinel on its pointed roof. Past the church was a row of neat whitewashed shanties. The yards didn't have a sprig of grass; the iron-gray sand was raked smooth and flat in the form of a giant sandbox.

The door and window frames of each shanty were painted a different vibrant color: blue, green, orange, and yellow. Curtains the same color as the frames fluttered in the open windows.

At one end of the sandbox-yard stood an enormous oak tree. Its huge limbs stretched out and reached up into the clear blue sky. A swing hung from one of its gnarled branches; under its protective shade sat a wooden table and an assortment of chairs.

As we pulled into the immaculate little yard, Nolay lightly tooted the truck horn to announce our presence. Like little jack-in-the-boxes, an assortment of faces popped up in windows and open doorways.

From one of the doorways emerged a tall, thin black man. He wore the blue-striped overalls of a railroad worker. His shiny skin stretched so taut over his sharp cheekbones it gave a blue tint to his face. His head was covered in a mass of white cotton-candy hair.

As he approached the truck, he kept his eyes cast downward. "How do, Mista Nolay?" he said in a soft voice.

"Howdy, Blue. I been out fishing and come back with more fish than we can handle. Thought you and the family might like some fresh mullet."

"Yessah, shore 'preciate it." He turned toward one of the shanties and called out, "Jackson, come on over here."

A younger version of the man walked across the yard. Where his left arm should have been, the sleeve of his blue shirt was tucked neatly inside his overalls. Unlike his father, Jackson held his head up and looked straight into Nolay's face. "How do, Nolay."

"Howdy, Jackson. Grab that sack of fish in the back of the truck."

A smile creased Jackson's face and exposed white teeth. "Shore do thank ya. You can count on us having a fish fry with hush puppies tonight."

As Nolay turned the truck around and we pulled away, an array of people spilled out of the little shanties and into the yard. As we drove toward Chicken Charlie's, I asked Nolay, "Why does ol' Blue call you mister, but Jackson doesn't?"

"'Cause Blue is older and he's experienced things that Jackson has never had to. An older colored person would never call a white man—or an Indian for that matter—anything other than mister." Nolay glanced over at me. "Bones, I know you been taught to mind your manners with adults, but if you were to ever call Blue or even Jackson mister or sir, they would be mortified. And I ain't got an answer for that, either. It's just the way it is. For now."

"Nolay, what happened to Jackson's arm?

"He lost it in the war."

"He fought in the same war with you and Mr. Speed?"

"He fought in the same war, but not with us. Colored folks didn't fight alongside white people. They were sent some-place else."

"Nolay, did you fight alongside white people?"

Nolay let out a little laugh. "Now, that did become a funny situation. Same as when I went to school. Seeing that I'm a pretty watered-down Indian and really wasn't living on the reservation, they didn't know what to do with me. I wasn't dark-colored enough to go with the blacks, so they just put me in with the whites."

Little Man asked, "You mean there was colored people in the United States Army? I sure never knew that before."

"Oh yeah, there were lots of colored people, but they were separated from the whites."

I squirmed in my seat and said, "Well, that just don't seem right. If they could fight in the same war, and I reckon for the same reasons, why were they separated?"

Nolay shook his head and said, "You do ask some interest-ing questions, Bones."

"And Nolay, I have another question—why are they called colored people? They're not colored, they're just differ-ent shades of black and brown."

Nolay looked at me and winked. "You got me on that one too, Bones. I ain't got a clue. I just know that's how it is."

Little Man said, "You just said they're different shades of black and brown. That's colored, ain't it?"

"No, it's not," I said. "Colors would be blue or green or something. And I have never seen a blue or green person, and I know you never have either."

Little Man rolled his eyes. "Bones, where do you come up with some of this stuff? You don't think it's right to keep a hog in a pen and kill it for food."

"If you go out and hunt something that's been wild all its life and use it for food, that's something else. But I sure wouldn't put Pearl in a pen and then eat her."

"That's because she's a pet," said Little Man. "Nearly every animal you set eyes on becomes a pet. I reckon if it was up to you, all the animals in the world would be pets and us people would eat vegetables and dirt or something like that."

Nolay laughed and said, "Bones, there's a lot of things in the world that ain't quite right. Maybe it will take you young'uns to change things. All I know is the way things are now."

Out past the Reems place, Nolay began to slow down so he could find the nearly hidden entrance to Chicken Charlie's. He turned off the county road and said, "Y'all roll up the windows. You know Charlie grows some mighty big skeeters. They can eat us when we're outside, but we'll try and keep 'em out of the truck."

The road wasn't much more than a tunnel that led through a massive tangle of guava trees. The truck bumped and scratched its way along until we pulled out into a clearing. Rays of sunshine leaked in through the thick guava trees, sending down long gray ropes of light into the little yard.

In the middle of the clearing rested a small ramshackle

house. The front yard was a living carpet of chickens. On the sagging front porch, fat hens nested in boxes, crates, and broken-down chairs. White icicles of chicken manure dripped from the lower branches of the surrounding guava trees.

Parked in front of the house was a rusty pickup truck. Nolay said, "Looks like Charlie has company."

Little Man leaned in for a closer look. "That looks like Peckerhead Willy's truck."

"I think you're right, Little Man. What's that ol' cock roach doing out here?"

The screen door opened and Peckerhead Willy sauntered out. He glared in our direction, walked to his truck, got in, and drove off into the guava-tree tunnel.

Nolay mumbled to himself, "Wonder what that was all about." He looked in our direction. "Y'all ready to give some blood to Charlie's skeeters? Little Man, grab that sack in the back from Lori. Let's go say howdy."

We stepped out of the truck and were immediately assaulted by the sharp smell of chicken manure and rotten guavas. A black cloud of hungry mosquitoes swarmed toward our face and hands.

The screen door opened and out walked a man so large his body wobbled from side to side. When he saw us, a broad grin split his chubby face. A wave of fat rippled under his chin and down his neck, disappearing inside his faded overalls.

"Howdy, Nolay," he said. "Whut y'all doin' over these parts?"

"Just got in from a few days fishin'. Brought in a big catch, too much for us to eat. Thought you might like some fresh mullet." Nolay placed some fish wrapped in newspaper in one of the old chairs alongside a clucking hen. "And of course Lori canned up too much stuff again, so she sent a few things. Just put that sack over there, Little Man."

Charlie rubbed a puffy hand over the top of his balding head. His pale blue eyes wandered in our direction. Inside that huge body lived the mind of a child. "Well, I sure do thank ya, Nolay. Miz Bones, Little Man, how y'all doin? I ain't seen y'all in a heap a Sundays."

"Just fine, Mr. Charlie," I said. "It's been a busy summer. I can't believe it's almost over."

"Now, if y'all want some guavas, you just go pick as many as you want. Nolay, you wait right here, I'm goin' in the back and get you a sack a dried chicken ma-newer; I know how Miz Lori loves her garden. You wait right here."

Charlie wobbled around the back of the house; his huge, flat bare feet padded softly in the dirt. When he returned, he had a croker sack in one hand and a little basket woven out of dried guava branches in the other. He handed Nolay the croker sack. "This here ma-newer is already dried, so Miz Lori can put it right in the ground." He handed the little basket to me. "Now, I know you got your own aigs, but these here are special. Every one of 'em has a double yolk. I got a special hen only lays double-yolk aigs."

I said, "Thank you, Mr. Charlie. I know we'll enjoy them."

"Miz Bones, you still got that big ol' rooster of yourns? It's been a while since I was last out to your house, but I won't never forget what a beautiful fella he was. I shore would like to have one of his babies, if ever you could let go of one."

"Don't you worry, Mr. Charlie," I said. "There's a hen sittin' on a nest right now, and if one of the biddies is a rooster, I'll make sure you get it."

Nolay picked up the croker sack and said, "Sorry we cain't stay longer, Charlie. I gotta get down to the Last Chance and get in a few supplies. Just wanted to stop by and say howdy."

A huge grin filled Charlie's face. "Well, I sure am proud you did. Y'all come back again."

As Nolay walked away, he turned and said, "Charlie, ol' Peckerhead come out and visit you very often?"

The smile disappeared. Charlie lowered his head and said, "Naw, just sometimes."

"Everything all right, Charlie?"

"Oh yeah, everything is fine."

"Okay then, we'll be seein' ya. You need anything, you let me know, okay?"

"I'll do that, Nolay."

Little Man and I sat in the truck and scratched the welts on our arms and face. "Do you think Mr. Charlie is happy living like he does?" I asked Nolay.

"Well, I cain't say if Charlie is happy or not, but I would think that he is content. He has everything he needs: his chickens, his house, and half the dang skeeters in the state of Florida. I reckon happiness is what you make it. I've known Charlie pert near my entire live, and I ain't never heard him complain." Nolay pulled up to the Last Chance and handed me a dime. "You two get a moon pie or something."

As we dashed inside the store, I waved to Mr. Speed sitting on his bench. "We'll be right back," I called out to him.

I heard Nolay say howdy to Mr. Speed before he walked inside the store.

We bought our moon pies, came back outside, and sat down on the steps next to Mr. Speed's bench. Little Man took a bite and said, "Howdy, Mr. Speed. I can't believe it's almost the end of summer. We'll be starting back to school soon."

I said, "Me and Little Man are going to the movies this Saturday. It's a double feature; one is a war movie, but I'm sure it will be good, because it has John Wayne in it."

Mr. Speed tilted his head to one side and said, "During the war, America made a bomb, called the a-to-mic. Dropped it on Japan. Two times, two times. It melted people, like Popsicles in the sun. Yes, sir, like Popsicles in the sun."

"Mr. Speed," I said, "we did that? We dropped a bomb that melted people?"

"Yes, sir, like Popsicles in the sun."

"That don't sound like a nice thing to do."

Little Man shook his head and said, "Good Lord, Bones, it was during the war. What you think people do during a war, come out shakin' hands?"

"Well, of course I know it was a war, but it still don't seem like a nice thing to do. I mean, melt people with a bomb?"

A car with a New York license plate pulled up to the gas pumps. The car door opened and a thin man got out. He wore a white shirt and blue plaid shorts that reached down to his skinny knees. His white legs and arms were blotched with patches of pink and crimson where the sun had burned away the top layers of skin. He walked past us and into the store.

Little Man made a clucking sound. "I swear, some of these

Yankees wear the dangest things. Did you see them shorts he had on?"

"Of course I saw 'em, and I know what they're called: Bermuda shorts. Ain't that right, Mr. Speed?"

"Yes, sir, Bermuda shorts, they are called Bermuda shorts."

Little Man scrunched up his face and said, "Why are they called that?"

"I don't know why," I said. "I just know that's what they're called. Maybe they were made in Bermuda or something."

"Well, I swear you never will see me in a pair of them things."

The Yankee man walked out of the store, got back in his car, and drove away.

Little Man nibbled on his moon pie and said, "Now, that man's sunburn looked like it would be mighty painful. I can't believe people come down here and just sit in the sun like that. I like going to the beach, turtle huntin' and fishin', but I sure ain't gonna lay down and fry like a piece of sausage."

Mr. Speed bobbed his head up and down and said, "Florida got thirteen hundred miles of beach, thirteen hundred miles. Most of it fish poop. Just plain ol' fish poop."

Little Man and I exchanged looks before he replied, "Lordy, Mr. Speed, you mean to say all that sand is no more than a fish outhouse?"

"Most of it. Just parrot fish poop. They eat the coral and turn it into sand. Gets washed up and makes a beach, thirteen hundred miles of beach."

Little Man slapped the side of his leg and let out a little hoot. "Now, if that ain't a sight, all those Yankees come down here and pay money to get sunburned while lying on top of fish poop."

Nolay walked down the steps carrying a cardboard box of supplies. "Be seein' you later, Speed. You kids ready to go?"

"Yes, sir," I replied. Turning back to Mr. Speed, I said, "I'll try to stop by this Monday and tell you all about the movie picture. Okay, Mr. Speed?"

Mr. Speed was having a good day, the pages in his mind dry and turning nicely.

He tilted his lopsided head in my direction. From under his green baseball cap he looked at me, his bright brown eyes shimmering with little flecks of gold. His head slowly bobbed up and down. A crooked smile crossed his face. "The movie picture, the movie picture."

I didn't know it then, but Mr. Speed and John Wayne had a lot in common.

invisible walls

All Saturday morning, me and Little Man patiently waited for Mama to drive us up to the railroad tracks so we could catch the train and go to the movies. We finally got her out to the truck, only to look up and see Ironhead's pickup bouncing its way along our driveway.

He got out of his pickup and walked, stiff legged, over to our truck. We could tell by the way his breath came in little spurts that he had some important news to share. He leaned one hand against the car and scratched his fiery red hair. "Morning, Miss Lori. Is Nolay around?"

"No, Ironhead. Actually, I thought he was off fishing with you."

"No, ma'am, Miss Lori. I ain't seen Nolay for a week or so."

Mama cocked her head to one side. "Well, he must have changed his plans."

Ironhead huffed and puffed and shuffled his feet in the

dirt. Finally he said, "I tell you what, I just tell you what, I don't know what's goin' on in these parts anymore. Early this morning, Jackson, Blue's boy, found ol' Peckerhead Willy lying across the railroad tracks, cut plumb in two. Deader than a doornail."

"Good Lord, Ironhead," Mama said, leaning against the truck. "Where about did they find him? What happened?"

"Ain't sure, Miss Lori. They found him up near where the shortcut goes back of Charlie's place and into the Reemses'. They figure he musta passed out, and the early-mornin' freight train run 'im over."

Mama shook her head. "Alvie, that poor woman. What will she do now? Good Lord, I have to go see Melba. We have to start getting stuff together for Alvie and the kids."

Me and Little Man looked at each other. It was plain to see that Mama's mission was no longer to get us to the railroad tracks. Her sole intent now was to gather up an abundance of comfort food to share with that poor woman and those poor kids. I cleared my throat and said, "Mama, maybe Ironhead could give us a ride to the railroad tracks. That way you could get started on what you need to do."

"Well, that would be fine, if it's no bother for Ironhead."

"No, ma'am, I'm headin' back that way right now."

As we got out of the truck, Mama said, "Now, you remember to catch the six o'clock Greyhound bus back home. I'll meet you two at the Last Chance."

On our ride to the tracks, Little Man asked Ironhead, "What do you think happened?"

"Don't rightly know. He musta got liquored up and stumbled onto the tracks. I don't know. There's just too much strange stuff happenin' around here, I can't keep track of it anymore."

When we arrived, Blue and a group of colored kids were already standing at the railroad crossing. When we were going to catch a ride on the train, Blue was always there to make sure everyone got on board safely.

As we got out of the truck and walked toward the group, the air was thick with excitement. We chattered about Peckerhead Willy's body and our big adventure going to the movies. The movie was a double feature: Roy Rogers in *The Golden Stallion* and John Wayne in *Sands of Iwo Jima*.

One of the older colored boys told us, "It was my pa that found 'im this morning. He went out to check on rail spikes and come across the body. He went down to the Last Chance and asked Mr. Ball to call the sheriff to come out."

Little Man let out a whistle. "That musta been something, coming across a sight like that in the morning."

Even though it was Saturday, everyone wore their Sunday best—we were going to town to see a movie! The colored girls had on bright starched dresses; their hair was braided in multiple pigtails and adorned in a rainbow of colored ribbons. The boys' overalls were clean and crisp, a knife-sharp crease ironed down the front of each leg. Me and Little Man had on our best dungarees and polished cowboy boots.

At the sound of the train whistle, Blue took out a white handkerchief, stepped up to the tracks, and began to flag down the approaching train. The huge locomotive slowed, its steel wheels screeching and whining against the tracks.

As the train came to a stop, an invisible wall of separation silently slid between us and the colored kids. Me and Little Man handed the conductor a quarter and boarded the first car. The colored kids walked down to the last car.

We picked a window seat in the middle of the car and sat down. As the train jerked and squeaked to a start, I looked around the nearly empty car and said, "It don't seem right that they can't just sit up here with us."

"You know whites don't sit with coloreds."

"Well, it still don't seem right."

"I swear, Bones, I don't know where you get some of your ideas from. It's just natural. You don't see blue birds mixing up with red birds. And whites don't mix with coloreds. Next thing, you'd have us marryin' up with 'em."

"I didn't say I wanted to marry one of 'em, but I don't see no harm in sitting together or even going to school together. Blue birds and red birds sit in the same birdbath, don't they?"

Little Man's big brown eyes rolled around in his freckled face as he groaned, "Good Lord, Bones."

Suddenly, he pointed out the window. "Looky yonder, there's the sheriff's car and the funeral car. We must be going over the very place where ol' Peckerhead got run over. I bet his body is in that funeral car."

I looked out the window and saw Sheriff LeRoy and several other men as they stood by a big black hearse. The sheriff was looking down into his right hand at something bright red. Something that looked very familiar.

"Little Man, that is a terrible thought. I don't want to

have that picture in my mind. I don't want to think about a train running over ol' Peckerhead's fat body. Let's talk about something else."

"Well, it did happen."

"I know it happened, but I don't want to think about it."

"What do you want to talk about?"

"I don't care, anything but that."

"Okay, suit yourself, I don't have to talk about nothing. I can just sit here and be quiet."

It wasn't that I didn't want to talk to Little Man. I just couldn't get my mind off what Sheriff LeRoy was holding in his hand.

Me and Little Man leaned back in our seats, and the rest of the ride was spent listening to the steady click-clack of the train wheels speeding along the steel tracks.

When the train finally pulled into the Melbourne train depot, Little Man and I started the short walk to the theater. The colored kids followed at a respectful distance. We paid our dime, got a box of popcorn, and entered into the dark, damp, magical world of the Van Croix Theater. At the front entry was a sign with black letters that said *Colored Section*, with an arrow pointing toward the balcony.

For the next few hours, we sat spellbound as John Wayne and his loyal band of Marines smoked hundreds of cigarettes and killed thousands of Japanese. The auditorium filled with sniffles and tears when John Wayne died. At the end, when the American flag was raised in all its glory, we clapped and cheered.

We watched as Roy Rogers went to jail before he would let his best friend, the beautiful palomino Trigger, be killed. All too soon, Roy and Trigger rode off into the sunset while "Happy Trails" played. The lights inside the theater came on, and reluctantly, we got up and slowly moved with the throng of kids toward the doors.

Once outside, like ducks in a row, with the colored kids a respectable distance behind us, we headed toward the Greyhound bus station. Being that there was only one passenger train a day, we had no choice but to catch the bus back home.

At the bus station, we purchased our tickets and sat on a bench out front and waited for the bus to come. There were two water fountains along the outside wall. A sign above one said *Whites Only*, and above the other one it said *Coloreds Only*. I had no idea what would happen if someone white drank out of the Coloreds Only fountain, but I always wanted to sneak a try. The picture of all those different-colored birds splashing around in the same birdbath popped up in my mind.

Finally, the bus arrived, belching gray smoke and gasoline fumes. Me and Little Man got on and sat in the front seats and watched the colored kids silently walk by, heading for the back of the bus.

"Little Man," I said, "do you know when I was little, I thought I was going to grow up to be Roy Rogers?"

"You cain't grow up to be somebody else."

"Well, I know that now, but when I was little I didn't.

Anyway, when I grow up I'm gonna be a veterinarian. I'm gonna open up an animal hospital and live right here for my whole life. Do you know what you want to be?"

"I sure do, I'm gonna join the army and be a soldier. I'm gonna go out and see as much of the world as I can."

"A soldier! But what if you get hurt, like Mr. Speed or Jackson?"

"I ain't gonna get hurt 'cause there ain't gonna be no more wars. You heard Mr. Speed; we got a bomb that melts people. Do you think anybody is gonna be crazy enough to go to war with someone that can melt 'em? Anyway, my daddy and your daddy were both in the war, and neither one of 'em got hurt."

"Well, I reckon not, but I still wish you would think about being something else."

For the next hour, the bus swayed and lurched down the highway. Finally, it jerked to a stop in front of the Last Chance. Our pickup was parked alongside the store. I could see Blue leaning against the side of the building. Mama was sitting on one of the benches with a small group of women listening to the radio, the sounds floating out through one of the store's front windows. Mr. Speed was nowhere to be seen. He had already gone home for the night.

We got in the truck with Mama and started to head home. The colored kids, along with Blue, were walking up the road. Mama stopped and told them, "Y'all jump in the back and I'll give you a ride home." After she dropped them off at the neat row of shanties, we headed to Little Man's house.

More to myself than anyone in particular, I said, "Do you

think one day we'll go to the same school and sit together on the same bus as colored people? I mean, it just don't seem right that we can be friends and talk with each other here, but we can't do anything in public together. We can't even drink out of the same water fountain."

Little Man was first to answer. "There you go again, Bones, with your strange ideas. What difference would it make? They got their place and we got ours."

Mama let out a little laugh. "Little Man, you might be surprised, it just might happen someday. We don't know what the future will be."

"Well, if it happens, I sure will be surprised."

Mama looked over at Little Man with that smile in her eyes. "Little Man, you do know that Nolay isn't exactly considered white, but he's married to me, a white woman?"

"Well, yes, ma'am, course I know that, but it ain't the same. Mr. Nolay is a Native American, and that's something to be mighty proud of."

"That's one way to look at it. But I can assure you, that's not the way everyone sees it. And we might all be surprised what could come about in the future."

I looked over at Little Man, and sure enough that question mark was crawling up between his eyes. I had to turn away to hide my smile.

Soon as we pulled into Little Man's yard, Miss Melba came out to the truck and told Mama about the final plans for Peckerhead's funeral. "Since Willy was not a churchgoin' man, his brother, Joe, wants to have the funeral this Tuesday at their house."

Mama shook her head. "Thanks, Melba. We'll be sure to be there."

On the ride home I asked, "Mama, are you sad that Peckerhead Willy died?"

"No, Bones. The death of that mean old man doesn't make me sad. It's Alvie and the kids I'm concerned about."

"Mama, you know this morning, when Ironhead came out to the house and told us about Peckerhead, he said Nolay wasn't out fishing with him. I thought that was where he was supposed to be."

"I thought that was where he was, too."

"Well, if he wasn't fishing, where was he?"

"You know your daddy. He can change his mind like the wind changes directions."

I sure agreed with how fast Nolay could change, but it wasn't the wind that bothered me. It was what I had seen the sheriff holding.

the funeral

Sunday morning, Mama had one of her callings, and we ended up at the Bethany Baptist Church. Everyone was buzzing around like bees, talking about Peckerhead's death. Preacher Jenkins had us all bow our heads as he said a special prayer. "Lord, look down on the Reems family, and bring them your comfort, as only you can comfort, for their tragic loss. And Lord, reach out your loving arms and embrace this lost sheep back into your fold. Forever and ever. Amen."

During the prayer I had my eyes squeezed shut, but when he asked the Lord to reach out and embrace Peckerhead, I had to open them. I looked around to make sure Preacher Jenkins wasn't playing a joke on us. But he was standing in front of the pulpit, eyes closed and arms raised toward heaven.

When we got back from church, Nolay was home. Soon as Mama parked the Champion I jumped out and ran inside the house. Nolay was sitting at the kitchen table finishing up a bowl of grits. "Nolay, did you hear what happened to ol' Peckerhead Willy?"

"Nope. I just got in. What happened to that ol' scally-wag?"

"He's dead. He got run over by a train."

Nolay turned his full attention on me. "What are you saying? When did that happen?"

"I think it happened Friday night, the same day you, me, and Little Man went out to visit Mr. Charlie. Yesterday morning Ironhead came out and told us. And when me and Little Man went to the movies we saw right where it happened."

"You don't say. Now, that sure is curious."

Mama walked in the kitchen and continued, "It is such a tragic thing. The funeral will be this Tuesday." She turned and stood in front of Nolay. "And I do hope you will be here to attend and pay your respects."

"Of course I'll attend. But I ain't gonna pay no respects."

Mama shook her head and rolled her eyes. "And Nolay, when Ironhead came over, he said you weren't out fishing with him."

"Yeah, I changed my mind and went up Jacksonville way." Nolay stood up and took his bowl over to the sink. "I gotta go change out of these clothes." He turned and walked out of the kitchen, leaving me and Mama standing there looking at each other.

Monday afternoon I strolled down to the Last Chance to sit a spell with Mr. Speed. On the walk there, I decided it would not be a good idea to tell him about John Wayne and the war movie. I would stick with Roy Rogers and Trigger.

After I got settled in on the bench next to Mr. Speed, I told him the story from start to finish. The whole time, he bobbed his head up and down. At the end I said, "Mr. Speed, that Trigger sure is something. I think horses must be the smartest animal there is."

"Pigs are smarter. The smartest animal is a pig. A pig."

"Pigs? You mean like my Pearl?"

"Yep, smarter. Pearl is smarter."

Mr. Speed had met Pearl on several occasions when me and Nolay had taken her for a ride in the back of the truck. She sat back there with her snout sticking out over the edge, just like a dog.

"Golly, that sure does make me proud to have Pearl as a friend."

"Friends, good friends."

I looked over at Mr. Speed and thought about what a good friend he was to me. Nobody else would let me carry on without laughing or saying what strange ideas I had. I couldn't always tell for sure, but I was pretty certain Mr. Speed felt the same as I did about things—the important things, anyway.

Mr. Speed was holding up his finger. "Shines by the knuckle. Heard 'em talk, talk, it's by the knuckle."

I pointed to the side of my finger and said, "You mean here, this is where we live?"

"The swamp will dry up. Soon. Dry up."

"Yes, sir. It's starting to do that right now. It's nearly autumn already."

"Heard talk. Look for it here, shines gold, gold."

"Yes, sir, I will do that."

Right now, I had no idea what Mr. Speed was trying to share with me. We sat in each other's silence for a while longer as Mr. Speed bobbed his head up and down. The pages in his mind seemed pretty soggy today.

I looked over and said, "Mr. Speed, I best be getting back home. I still got some chores to do. I'll be seeing you again soon."

"Again, soon."

On my walk back home, Mr. Speed's words hung on to me like leaves on a tree. I couldn't stop a smile spreading across my face at the thought of my Pearl being smarter than Roy Rogers's Trigger.

Tuesday morning, the day of the funeral, Mama took charge. She insisted I wear a dress. "It would not be proper for you to go dressed as a cowboy." Armed with a huge bowl of potato salad, Mama herded me and Nolay into the truck. "This is not an occasion for the Champion; we are to be humble and civil."

At the end of our driveway, before we turned onto the county road, a group of colored people stood on the side of the road. I recognized Blue and several of the colored women from the shanties. Nolay stopped the truck. Blue shuffled over to Nolay's side, holding his worn straw hat in his hands, his eyes cast respectfully downward.

"Mr. Nolay, Miz Lori, the ladies here have some offerin's for Miz Alvie and the chilluns. We was wonderin' if we could trouble you to take 'em out to her place when y'all go. We know Mr. Joe don' take kindly to colored folks, but the ladies here would like to do the Christian thing and give somethin' to Mr. Willy's famlee. Don't intend to be no bother, Mr. Nolay, but shore would 'preciate it."

"No bother at all, Blue, just put the stuff in the back of the truck. We'll see that it gets there."

The ladies began to load brightly printed flour sacks filled with fresh garden vegetables in the back. Mama looked at the precious sacks being used. She leaned out the window and said to one of the women, "Bertha, do you want the sacks returned? I can bring them back if you like. It won't be a bother."

"No, Miz Lori, it's all a offerin'. We sure do 'preciate you doing this. If you could, you let Miz Alvie know in private that our prayers are with her and the chillun."

"I will do that, Bertha, I will surely do that. And thank you and the rest of the ladies."

On our ride out to the Reems place, the cab of the truck was filled with a deafening silence.

As we drove up, we saw an assortment of cars and trucks parked haphazardly in the Reemses' desolate yard. I recognized Mr. Cotton's blue pickup and swallowed a sigh of relief that Little Man was somewhere close by. There was a gathering of men milling around the old broken barn door. Whackerstacker Joe leaned against the wall and passed a jar of moonshine around the group of men.

Mama leveled her eyes on me and Nolay. "Nolay, you keep away from that moonshine. And Bones, you conduct yourself like a young lady. This is a funeral; you are here to pay your respects."

"Yes, ma'am," Nolay replied in a squeaky little-kid voice, then looked down at me and winked.

Women clad in their best dark-colored dresses filled the front porch and spilled out into the yard. Old Ma Reems sat in her decrepit rocking chair, tobacco stains dripping down both sides of her chin. The usual blank stare covered her craggy old face.

I found Little Man around the side of the house with a group of kids. We were just getting ready to start a game of tag, when Miss Melba came around the corner and said, "Little Man, you and Bones come inside and pay your respects."

As we climbed up the dilapidated steps, I whispered to Little Man, "I ain't ever been inside the Reemses' house, have you?"

"Naw, this is the first time."

On one side of the rickety front porch, several boards had been set on top of a couple of sawhorses to make a table. It was covered in worn bedsheets and laden with bowls and platters of comfort food brought by well-meaning neighbors.

Little Man stepped up and pulled open the squeaky screen door. I slid in behind him and stuck my hand in his back pocket. The only light inside the room was from flickering kerosene lanterns and some candles. The sour smell of misery rushed over us. I blinked to adjust to the dimness. People stood in small groups; some sat in chairs and on an old couch that was set along the wall. Muffled voices and the cries of babies hung in the thick, stale air.

I was just ready to tell Little Man I wanted to leave when

he let out a sigh and whispered, "Lordy, Bones, looky there." I tightened my grip on his pants pocket and peeked around his shoulder. A long pine box sat in the middle of the floor. An assortment of candles and wilted flowers was on the top.

Seated beside the pine box was Miss Alvie. She cradled a baby in one arm, her other hand limp as a dishrag on top of her protruding stomach. Next to her sat Martha, Ruthie, and the dirty-faced little boys. Today the boys' faces had been scrubbed pink-clean.

I turned to bolt out the door, but the soft hand of Miss Melba wrapped gently around my arm. She whispered, "Bones, you and Little Man go up and give your respects to Miss Alvie."

Even in the dark, Miss Melba must have seen the terror in my eyes, because she kept her hold on my arm and began to nudge me and Little Man. Sandwiched between the two of them, I felt my wooden legs jerk forward.

Little Man shuffled up and stood in front of Miss Alvie. "My condolences, Miss Alvie." I peeked around his side and whispered, "Me too." Martha and Ruthie sat still as little sticks, their eyes glued to the floor. Shadows shimmered across their pale white skin. Miss Alvie looked at us; her eyes mirrored the hopelessness of a trapped animal's. I watched her thin lips form the words "Thank you" but no sound came out.

I was still clutching Little Man's back pocket as we turned in unison and walked toward the light of the screen door. When we stepped out on the porch we saw, parked directly in front of the steps, a shiny black hearse. The two back doors were open, and a small crowd of boys was hanging around, looking inside. Little Man let out a whistle and headed straight down the steps to join the other boys.

Sheriff LeRoy's car was parked in front of the hearse. I watched as he walked down the steps and headed for his car.

A group of men began to make their way up from the barn to the house. Whackerstacker Joe swaggered in front, followed by his three boys. He walked past the back of the hearse and said, "Y'all get on outta here. We got bizzness to do."

The men went inside the house. In a few minutes, the screen door squeaked open, and they carried out the pine box. Miss Alvie and her brood walked down the steps and stood behind the hearse as the pine box was slid inside. Martha's and Ruthie's milk-white skin glistened in the hot sun. Standing next to the pink-skinned Reems boys, they looked like two white cranes that had landed in a pigpen.

The Reems clan loaded up in cars provided by neighbors and proceeded follow the long black hearse, with Sheriff LeRoy's car leading the way down the road.

Mama came out of the house and signaled it was time for us to go. On the way home she kept saying, more to herself than to us, "That poor woman and those poor kids. What will she do now?"

Nolay cleared his throat. "I was talking with some of the boys and Sheriff LeRoy about what happened to Peckerhead. LeRoy seems to think it wasn't an accident. Says he's investigatin', but it looks like ol' Peckerhead was laid across the tracks on purpose."

Mama turned her head. "On purpose? You mean LeRoy thinks it was murder?"

"He didn't say those exact words, but I do believe that's what he's thinkin'. Says there appears to have been a scuffle of some sorts and he's collecting evidence."

Evidence. That word bounced around inside my head. Was that what I saw Sheriff LeRoy holding when we passed him on the train? And where was Nolay that night, the very night he was supposed to have been fishing with Ironhead? He said he was up in Jacksonville, but doing what?

I turned to ask Nolay a million questions, but I could tell by the way he held his chin to one side that I wasn't going to get the answer to even one.

the sheriff

Wednesday morning arrived and plopped down on us hot and damp as a soggy cotton ball. I was sitting at the kitchen table trying to enjoy a bowl of warm grits with Nolay and Mama. It was early; Ikibob had just let out his first crow of the day. I slowly stirred my bowl of grits and mumbled, "I can't believe school starts in little over a week. The summer went by too fast. I wish I never had to go back to school again."

The dogs started to bark; Nolay and I went to the picture window to see who would visit this early in the morning. Sheriff LeRoy's car pulled up in our driveway; right behind him was a black Ford with the inscription *Dade County Sheriff Dept.* on the side.

I followed Nolay outside. Halfway to the car he turned and told me, "Bones, call the dogs and keep 'em over there by the tree."

Me and the dogs stayed at a respectable distance, but within hearing range. From where I sat, I could see two strange men in the front of the black Ford and another hidden in the dimness of the backseat.

Sheriff LeRoy unfolded his massive body from the patrol car and ambled over to Nolay. "How do, Nolay. I know it's early, but these two detectives from Dade County want to ask you a few questions. Sure would appreciate you takin' a ride up to the station with me."

"LeRoy, I don't know what this is all about, but I got a busy morning ahead of me. If they want to ask me anything, I'm right here right now." Without waiting for LeRoy to reply, Nolay walked over to the black Ford, leaned inside the open window, and said, "Y'all get on out if you got something to say. My little girl there has ahold of the dogs, they won't bother you." When Nolay turned away from the car he looked over at me and made a face like he had just taken a bite out of a lemon.

Reluctantly, the two men in the front seat got out and came around to the side of the car. The man in the backseat didn't move. They were dressed in dark heavy suits; one of them had a little bow tie perched at the base of his neck. I could see beads of sweat glisten on their foreheads and trickle down the sides of their faces.

One of the men leaned against the car and said, "Well, sir, we would rather do this at the station, but seeing that you are willing to answer some questions now, we can accommodate you. There have been two murders in these parts, and there appears to be evidence that you had a run-in with both of the victims."

"If you're talking about that Yankee man and old Pecker-head, I didn't have a run-in with either one of 'em."

The man with the bow tie pointed toward the backseat and continued. "Well, sir, it seems Mr. Decker here is of a different opinion. He states that he and his partner, Mr. Robert Fowler, came out to this house inquiring about real estate and that you not only did physical damage to their car but threatened their lives with a gun. He also states that not long after that incident, you threatened them again, as well as one of your neighbors, a Mr. Willy Reems. It is also rumored, sir, that you are the owner of numerous guns."

Now I recognized the man in the backseat; he was one of the Yankee men Nolay had chased down the road. He had also been with the Reems brothers when Nolay and I saw them at the back of our land.

Nolay shook his head and laughed. "You quacking at the wrong duck, mister. You are right about one thing; I do have plenty of guns. Everyone in these parts does. But I don't use 'em to shoot people. If I had wanted to kill someone, you surely would not have found a body. I wouldn't have been stupid enough to drag a body up to the railroad tracks, especially someone as useless as old Peckerhead."

This conversation made Sheriff LeRoy look even more uncomfortable; he leaned against the car, pulled his huge Stetson further over his eyes, and began to dig the heel of one of his colossal boots into the soft sand.

Nolay pointed to the man in the backseat. "As far as those two Yankees are concerned, they came on my property uninvited, and they insulted me and my family. If I had wanted to do 'em harm, both of 'em would be dead, not just one. Now, if you don't have any more questions, I would appreciate it if you folks moved on, 'cause I got more important things to do."

"Well, sir, you are a prime suspect for these two murders, and we will need you to come down to the station so we can further investigate this situation." The bow-tie man turned to Sheriff LeRoy. "Sheriff LeRoy Hasket, it's about time for you to do your duty and bring this man in."

The two men turned around and walked back to their car. One of them mumbled, just loud enough for us to hear, "Dumb Florida crackers."

Again, just hearing the way that man said *cracker*, it made me feel uncomfortable. Then I remembered Nolay's words, took a deep breath, and made myself feel proud.

Sheriff LeRoy ambled away from his car and over to me and Nolay. He leaned his head down and very softly said, "Now, Nolay, you and me goes back a long ways. I gotta ask you to do me this one favor and just accompany me down to the station. If you don't, I'm gonna look mighty bad in front of these here city fellas. Now, I need you to hep me out here. I'm just doing my job."

Nolay looked up at the massive man in front of him and replied, "Blast it, LeRoy, if it was anyone else but you, I would tell 'em where to go."

"Sorry 'bout all this, Nolay, I'm just doing my job."

Mama walked out of the house, frowning. "What's going on? What's all this about?"

Nolay went over to her. "It's just a misunderstandin', ain't nothing to worry about, Honey Girl. I'm going for a ride down to the station with LeRoy. He'll bring me back home in a little while."

Sheriff LeRoy tipped his huge Stetson in Mama's direction. "Miss Lori, I'll have 'im back as soon as possible."

Nolay walked over to the car and opened the front door. He turned to the sheriff and said, "I ain't getting in the back, I'm riding up front with you."

After the other men got back in their car, I let the dogs go. They circled the car a couple of times, yapping and snapping their teeth.

Mama and I stood in the yard and watched as the two cars disappeared down our driveway. She still had a frown on her face. I said, "Mama, do you think Nolay is in trouble?"

"I hope not." She turned and began walking back to the house. "Don't worry, Bones. LeRoy won't let anything happen to him."

I followed behind Mama and said, "What's a prime suspect?"

"It means they don't have anyone else to be suspicious of."

"Well, that don't sound very good, does it?"

"Don't worry, Bones. Sheriff LeRoy will get it all straightened out."

For the rest of the day, me and Mama both tried to keep busy and not think about Nolay being up at Titusville. But I couldn't stop from thinking about Nolay's missing red handkerchief and that knife I'd found out in the swamps.

The sun had already dipped behind the flat horizon when

the dogs started to bark. The smoky beams of two headlights cut into the darkness as a car made its way up our dirt road. We heard the beep of a horn. Me and Mama went outside to see Sheriff LeRoy alone in his car.

"Where's Nolay, LeRoy?" Mama said.

Sheriff LeRoy's massive head rolled to one side as he said, "Miss Lori, them two fellas done had Nolay arrested."

"Arrested for what?"

"On suspicion of the murder of that Fowler man and old Peckerhead Willie. I shore am sorry, Miss Lori. I shore am sorry."

"Sorry? My God, LeRoy, you were just going to take him in for questioning. You were supposed to bring him back home. Where is Nolay now?"

"They done booked him into the Titusville County jail. You can go up tomorrow and see if you can bail 'im out. I tried to tell them fellas Nolay could just come back home, wadn't no way he was gonna run away, but they wouldn't have it. Them city slickers wanted to take him down to Dade County, but I refused to let 'em. Them crimes were committed in my jurisdiction, so he's gonna stay right here in Brevard County. Long as I can keep 'im."

"LeRoy, how did you let him get arrested for murder?"

"Miss Lori, them city po-lease have evidence. I cain't discuss it with you, but they have evidence."

Mama pressed her lips together and let out a deep sigh. She looked at the huge man in the car and said, "It's not your fault, LeRoy. Thanks for coming by. I'll go up and see him tomorrow and we'll get this straightened out."

Sheriff LeRoy hung his massive head and said, "I shore am sorry. I'm just doin' my job, but I promise you I'll do everything I can to hep. I don't want to see Nolay being sent down to Dade County, not with him being . . . you know . . . not with him being part . . ."

"Indian, LeRoy, is that what you're trying to say? Not with him being part Indian."

Sheriff LeRoy managed to mumble, "I shore am sorry."

Next morning, right after Ikibob crowed, I padded into the kitchen to find Mama at the kitchen table, her coffee cup and a pack of Lucky Strikes in front of her. "Bones, hurry up and get ready, we're going to visit your daddy."

"Do I have to wear a dress?"

"No, you can wear your dungarees."

Mama had the top up on the Champion. I opened the door and slid inside, onto the cold seat. Nothing about the Champion felt like it had on the days we'd gone for rides with Nolay. On the ride up, Mama told me over and over, "Now, don't you worry, everything will be just fine. We'll get this straightened out."

I had always looked forward to a ride up to the Titusville Courthouse; we had retrieved Nolay from there on numerous occasions. But those times, it wasn't anything as serious as this. Nolay had a knack for breaking what he called "stupid white law." He had been known to pick up other people's possessions when they were just laying around idle. He had also been known to drive off at a gas station without paying for gas. Of course that never happened at the Last Chance, because we had a running tab there and Mr. Ball knew Nolay would come in and pay when he got the money.

The Titusville Courthouse was the only building in the county that had an elevator; it was like a free carnival ride. Usually Nolay's fines weren't more that twenty dollars. We would pay at the front desk, get on that marvelous elevator, ride up to the second floor, retrieve Nolay, and ride back down.

Mama parked the Champion in front of a two-story gray building with bars across the top windows. "Bones, I don't think it's a good idea for you to wear your cap pistols into the courthouse. Just leave them here in the car until we come back."

She signed in at the front desk and told the officer who she was there to see. He looked over at me and said, "Sorry, but children aren't allowed on the top floor."

Now, that was news to me, because I had ridden that elevator up to the top floor on numerous other occasions. Must have been news to Mama, too, because she stepped back, looked directly at the officer, and said, in a voice with a little more Southern charm than usual, "Sir, we have just endured a long ride, and my little girl needs to go up and see her daddy. Now, if you will be so kind as to show us the way . . ."

The police officer blinked his eyes like a stunned rooster, then nodded and replied, "Being that you drove all the way up here, I reckon it will be all right for her to go see her daddy." He escorted us to the elevator and pushed a button, and two doors slid open. We stepped inside the small room, he pushed another button, and the doors slid shut. We magically floated up to the second floor.

The visiting room wasn't much bigger than a closet with a table in the middle. We sat down, and after a few minutes Nolay strolled in. He walked around the table and hugged me and Mama.

He sat down and flashed one of his smiles, but his eyes were dull and haunted. "Lori, did you bring me some fresh clothes? I been sleeping in these, and they're pretty durn ripe."

"No, I didn't. I was in such a hurry to get up here. Anyway, you'll be coming back home tomorrow, won't you?"

"I don't know, Honey Girl. The judge set my bail at three hundred dollars."

"Three hundred dollars! My goodness, you live here, you're not going to run away. Besides, you don't have anything to run away from."

"If I don't come up with three hundred dollars, those big-city police are gonna take me down to Dade County. I don't stand a chance for a fair trial there."

"Trial? There's going to be a trial?"

"Lori, I don't know what all is gonna happen. Everything is just crazy mixed-up right now. All I know is I gotta get out of here, but I need three hundred dollars to do it."

"Nolay, where are we going to get three hundred dollars? Maybe I could mortgage the land."

"No, you don't even think about that. We'll get the money, but you don't think about doing nothing with the land. That's my family's land. It ain't for sale or mortgage."

Before we left, Nolay reached across the table and held one of my hands and one of Mama's. "Now, I don't want y'all to worry about this. You hear me, we'll work this out."

Mama looked at Nolay. "I *am* worried. How am I going to get three hundred dollars? I don't do what you do. I don't go fishing. I don't . . . I don't do a lot of things that you do. How am I going to get this money?"

Nolay looked down at the table. "Honey Girl, I ain't got no ideas at the moment, but something will come up. I just know I gotta get outta this place."

I squeezed Nolay's hand. "Don't you worry, Nolay, I'll take good care of all the animals and the land till you come home."

I didn't enjoy the elevator ride back down.

It was a long, quiet ride home. Mama's eyes were riveted on the road; both her hands gripped the steering wheel. The Champion felt like an old empty refrigerator on wheels. It was like all the joy we had shared in it had been sucked out.

That night, as we sat at the kitchen table, I said, "Mama, can we just go to the bank and get some money?"

"No, Bones, the bank won't just give us money."

"Can we sell the Champion?"

"We don't own the Champion. I have no idea what kind of wheeling and dealing your daddy did to get it. All I know is, it doesn't have a title, so we can't sell it."

"Mama, you know what we need? We need a miracle."

Mama looked at me and shook her head. "What is a miracle, Bones? You just tell me what a miracle is. We need money. Don't you understand? We need three hundred dollars, and we don't have it." She cupped her face in both hands and leaned her elbows on the table.

"I was just trying to help, Mama."

She lifted her head. "I'm sorry, Bones, I didn't mean to take it out on you. It's just . . ."

I watched as her eyes turned into green pools of sadness. Tears brimmed up and slid slowly down her face. "Three hundred dollars. How am I going to find that kind of money?"

I had no idea where she could find three hundred dollars. All I knew was, right about now, we needed three hundred miracles.

miracles

The next morning, breakfast was a silent event. I watched as Mama absentmindedly used her spoon to stir a figure eight in her bowl of grits. She let out a little sigh and said, "I'm going up to see your daddy this morning. I'm taking some clean clothes. Maybe the two of us together can come up with an idea to raise the bail money. I'll drop you off at Little Man's for the day."

I looked over at her and said, "Mama, when you see Nolay, tell him hey for me and let him know everything is fine here with the animals and the land."

"I will, Bones. I sure will."

Me and Little Man spent most of the day doing chores around his house. We collected eggs and cleaned up inside the henhouse and went over to see the new batch of baby pigs. I wanted to hold one of the babies, but Little Man said, "I don't think that's a good idea, Bones. Them babies is pigs, not pets, so best you keep it that way."

Mr. Cotton, Earl, and Ethan spent most of the day out in

the sugarcane patch. When we went in for noon dinner, Miss Melba had made a special batch of biscuits, and there was a pitcher of fresh sorghum syrup sitting in the middle of the table. I knew she was trying pick up my spirits because I felt lower than a doodlebug in the dirt.

When we sat down at the table, Mr. Cotton said a special grace asking the Lord to bring Nolay back home to us soon as he could. After he finished, Miss Melba looked over at me and said, "Now, Bones, don't you worry yourself, your daddy will be back here with us real soon. The good Lord will see to it."

Saturday, me and Mama went to visit Nolay. Mama kept the top up on the Champion. On the ride to Titusville, a thought kept popping up in my mind like a jack-in-the-box. I wanted Mama to slam on the brakes and turn that big car around and head back home. But it just kept rolling down the highway, heading to the Titusville Courthouse. I sure did want to see my daddy; I just didn't want to see him where he was.

When we walked inside, the officer behind the counter leaned his head down and studied real hard on some papers. Me and Mama walked over, got in the elevator, and were swished away to the top floor.

When Nolay came out, he gave us both big, tight hugs. We sat down across from him at the wooden table and Nolay reached across and held one of Mama's hands. Nolay's blue eyes looked like gray storm clouds were passing over them, but he still flashed a bright smile. "How you two doing? Everything going all right?"

Mama let out a deep sigh, but I answered, "Well, it would be a lot better if you were back home with us."

"I wish I was back home, too, Bones."

"And we are having a hard time trying to figure out how to get that three hundred dollars. You got any ideas, Nolay?"

Nolay wagged his head back and forth. "Not right at the moment."

Mama let out another deep sigh and I figured I better change the subject.

"Nolay, when I was out at Little Man's yesterday their mama pig had six babies. They were the cutest things, but Little Man wouldn't let me hold one because he thought I might want to take it home for a pet."

Nolay looked at me and smiled. "I think Little Man is a bright boy. You don't need any more pets right now, especially another pig."

For the next hour we sat and acted like we were still back home. All too soon the guard came and told us our time was up. We hugged each other again. Mama said to Nolay, "I'll be back tomorrow after church."

"Honey Girl, you don't have to come up here every day. That's a long ride. And hopefully next time you come up I'll be riding back home with you."

When me and Mama walked out the door, I said to her, "Mama, why don't we just take the stairs back down?"

"You don't want to ride the elevator?"

"No, ma'am, I can do without riding in it for the rest of my life."

"Maybe the stairs will be better. It is a long sit in that

car going back home. Walking down the stairs might do us good."

Nolay had been in jail for three long days. Sadness grew around Mama like the roots of a strangler fig. All I could do was watch as it slowly wrapped around her and choked out her happiness. The green of her eyes dimmed to a dull olive. Dark half-moons rose under them. Sometimes at night, I would wake up and see the flickering of a kerosene lantern spilling out from her bedroom. No matter how early I got up, she was already at the kitchen table with a cup of coffee and an ashtray with crumpled Lucky Strikes spilling out over its edge.

Like particles of dust, the news about Nolay and the need for three hundred dollars drifted out and spread over our community. Of course no one spoke of it, that would have been uncivil; it was just a known fact.

Sunday morning me and Mama went to church where I prayed extra hard for Nolay and the Lord to be on good terms. There was nobody there to teach Sunday school, so I had to sit on that hard pew and listen to Preacher Jenkins give an extra-long-winded sermon about the lost son coming back home. Of course he didn't mention any names, but I had a pretty good idea who he was talking about.

On our way home, Mama stared straight ahead and spoke to her reflection in the windshield. "I just don't know what I'm going to do. I can't find a job and I can't borrow money from the bank. And no one in our family has that kind of money. I need to get it soon, or they're going to send him down to Dade County. Thank goodness Mr. Ball lets us keep a running tab at the Last Chance, or I wouldn't even have gas for the car."

I reached over and touched her arm. "Mama, do you remember the time Nolay took us up to St. Augustine to see the fort? And we went by that roadside zoo, and I thought it was a real zoo and I wanted to go see the live Florida panther. And you told me not to go in there, but I wanted to anyway?"

"Yes, I remember."

"You remember what those animals looked like. Some of 'em were crippled or had their paws cut off from being caught in those steel traps. And that poor old panther, sitting in that dirty, smelly cage with its hair all matted and flies eating on its ears. It was just about the saddest thing I ever did see."

"Yes, I remember. I tried to tell you it wasn't going to be a good place to go. But you insisted."

"Do you remember what me and Nolay did?"

She turned to me, a flicker of happiness crossing her face. "I remember what you two did. How could I forget? You opened all those cages and set those animals free."

"That was so much fun, Mama. And that big ol' panther, at first it wouldn't even come out the door. Nolay had to shake the cage to get it to move. It slinked down to the edge of the woods, then turned and looked back at us. It just stood there and then it shook its body all over, like a dog does when it gets out of the water. When it looked back at us, it was a panther again. Its eyes were big and wild. It was a beautiful sight to see. Then it ran off into the woods."

We rode in silence for a while. "Mama, I wish I could do that for Nolay. I wish I could just open up that jail door and set him free."

"I wish it was that easy, Bones. But wishing won't help."

We pulled into the yard and were welcomed by the dogs, Pearl, and Harry. As I got out of the car, the animals surrounded me and almost knocked me to the ground in their need to give and receive attention.

At the front door Mama stooped down and picked up a small tobacco tin leaning on its side. She pulled off the top. Inside were ten neatly folded one-dollar bills. She looked around the yard as if whoever put it there might still be standing in the shadows. She held the folded bills in her hand. "What on earth. Bones, what do you think this is?"

It was plain to see what it was, and I told her. "Mama, that is a miracle."

And that was when the miracles started to rain down on our lives. Mama found an envelope with five dollars on the front seat of the Champion, a box of sweet potatoes at our front door with six dollars, a paper bag with three dollars' worth of nickels and pennies. They arrived in mason jars, snuff bottles, tins, bags, boxes, and envelopes. Each one filled with its own special miracles.

Mama got out one of her big pickling jars and began to drop the miracles inside, one by one. Her face began to brighten; the dark half-moons drifted away from under her eyes. The tree roots of sadness lost their grip. I watched as she, along with that pickling jar, began to fill up with hope.

• • •

Monday morning, me and Mama had just finished washing the breakfast dishes when the dogs started barking. I looked out the picture window and there were Uncle Bob Cat and Uncle Tom Cat sitting in their truck. We went to meet them. Mama said, "Y'all come inside. The dogs won't bother you."

They came in and sat down on the couch.

Mama asked, "Can I get you some coffee or something?"

Uncle Bob answered, "No, thank you, Lori. We just wanted to come up and see how you were doing. Thanks for getting the message down to us about Nolay. Everyone at home sends their regards."

"Thank you, Bob Cat."

"Grandma Spot is saying some special prayers. Nolay can sure get himself into some mischief, but this one is a real mess."

"I know. But with the help of our friends and family we'll get through it."

Uncle Tom Cat pulled an envelope from his front pocket. "We took up a little collection in the village and wanted to give this to you."

Mama reached out and took the envelope. It would have been uncivil to open it in front of them. She looked at it and placed it in her lap, where it sat like a little curled-up kitten. "Thank you. Please give our thanks to everyone."

"We'll sure do that. We can't stay for long, we just wanted to stop by and let you know we're thinking about you folks."

"That was such a long ride for you. I can't tell you how much we appreciate it."

"Nolay would do it for us, that's for sure."

After they left, Mama opened the envelope. Inside were five ten-dollar bills. I watched as Mama's eyes glistened with hope.

Ironhead stopped by that afternoon. "Miss Lori, you take a break and stay home. I'll be going up to see Nolay tomorrow. I'll stop by and let you know how he is."

"Thank you, Ironhead. I appreciate that. And while you're there, tell Nolay things are beginning to look up."

"I'll sure do that, Miss Lori."

Late Tuesday morning Little Man came strolling up our road. In one hand he carried a small basket woven from guava twigs. It was filled with eggs. In the other hand, he held a flour sack. I went out to meet him.

"Howdy, Bones. I got a few things here for your mama."

"Come on in, she's in the kitchen "

Little Man walked into the kitchen and set the basket and sack on the table.

"Morning, Miss Lori. This here is from Mr. Charlie, and this here is some lima beans from my mama."

"Why, thank you, Little Man."

"And Mama and Daddy want to invite you and Bones over for supper tomorrow. Daddy shot a big ol' turkey this morning and Mama wants to roast it up in her new oven."

"That sounds wonderful, Little Man. I'm going up in the morning to see Nolay. Bones can come over and stay with you if that's all right."

"Yes, ma'am. You know Bones is pretty much family at our house."

Before he left, Little Man placed some wrinkled dollar bills in my hand. "Bones, I been thinking. This here is the Christmas money you and me got saved up. I want you to give it to your mama, for Mr. Nolay."

"But we worked all summer long gettin' that money. Specially you—you worked so hard, helping your daddy and all. Are you sure?"

"Well, it is our Christmas money, and it ain't gonna be much of a Christmas without Mr. Nolay back home."

"Christmas! Do you think Nolay will be gone that long?"

"I sure hope not. I want 'im to be home tomorrow. But anyways, you take this and give it to your mama."

I swallowed down a small lump rising in my throat. "Thanks, Little Man."

Under Chicken Charlie's basket of double-yolked eggs were six shiny quarters. Five ten-dollar bills held together with a paper clip tumbled out with the lima beans.

That afternoon Ironhead came driving up. Mama went out and motioned for him to come inside. He came in the kitchen and placed a newspaper-covered package on the table. "Caught it early this morning. It's a big fat mullet. Thought you might enjoy some fresh fish."

"We sure will, thank you."

Ironhead sat down at the table and ran his hands through his fiery red hair.

"I tell you what; it felt like someone done stomped on my heart to see Nolay in there. But don't you worry none, Miss Lori; he'll be home soon enough. I'm sure of it."

After he left, Mama unwrapped the package. Laying

beside the fish, all neat and tidy in a piece of waxed paper, was thirty dollars.

Wednesday morning Mama dropped me off at Little Man's. Nearly the whole day was spent preparing the turkey and all the fixings that went with it. By the time Mama came back, the table was fixed and Miss Melba had that turkey on the countertop to cool off.

Mr. Cotton placed it in the middle of table, right under the single hanging lightbulb. He stood back and said, "This here is like having Thanksgiving in September. Let's gather around and give thanks."

We stood around the table and bowed our heads as Mr. Cotton said grace. "Dear Lord, bless this here food, bless our family and friends. Thank you, Lord, for all the many blessings you give to us and continue to give to us. And we thank you, Lord, for what you don't see fit to give to us, 'cause we don't need it. Hep us to know right from wrong. We ask all this in Jesus's name. Amen."

After that Amen, a moment of silence fell over us.

Everyone sat down except Mr. Cotton. He leaned over and started carving the turkey and dishing it out to us. We filled our plates with turkey, mashed potatoes, gravy, and butter-topped biscuits. It truly was like having Thanksgiving in September, except for one big emptiness: Nolay wasn't there with us. We all ate until our mouths were tired and then tried to eat some more.

At the end of the meal, I asked Miss Melba if I could have

the wishbone. I told her, "I want to give it to Mr. Speed. He says that wishes can come true, so maybe if the two of us wish on something together, it will be that much stronger."

Miss Melba replied, "That is a very sweet idea. Of course you can have it."

Mama looked over and gave me one of her smiles that had lots of words in it.

Miss Melba's September Thanksgiving dinner had been just the thing to lift me and Mama's low spirits. It was the first time I had seen Mama smile and laugh since Nolay was arrested nearly a week ago.

Mama said, "Melba, that was just wonderful. Let me help you clean up."

"Lori, you and Bones don't need to stay and help. Y'all should get on home before it gets too dark, so you can take care of all the animals."

"Thank you, I can't tell you how much I have enjoyed this."

On the drive home me and Mama actually talked about things other than jail, money, and lawyers. It felt good to have her back.

Thursday me and Mama both stayed home. "Bones, I have gotten so behind in some of my gardening I need to stay home today," she said.

All morning the two of us worked in the garden weeding and getting everything back into shape. After noon dinner, I asked, "Mama, can I go down and see how Mr. Speed's doing?"

"Of course, you've been so much help to me this morning."

When I arrived at the Last Chance, I went over and sat down beside Mr. Speed on the bench. "Howdy, Mr. Speed. I sure do miss my daddy. I hope we can get him back home soon."

He bobbed his head up and down. "Shine in the dirt. At the knuckle. In the dirt."

I guess the pages in his mind were stuck on knuckles again today.

"Mr. Speed, remember when you told me that if you wish hard enough for something that a miracle might happen?"

"Miracles, miracles happen."

"Well, I want to tell you, I think they are starting to happen. I think they surely are. And Mr. Speed, I have a surprise for you. I'm still working on it, but when it's finished I'll bring it down to you."

Half of Mr. Speed's face moved into a lopsided smile. "Surprise."

"Mr. Speed, you want an RC?"

Mr. Speed nodded.

When I went inside to get our RCs, Mr. Ball handed me a carton of Lucky Strikes. "Bones, let your Mama know I did something so foolish, I overordered on cigarettes. Not many people smoke Luckies, so if I don't sell them, they'll just go stale on the shelf. You give her these, all right?"

"Yes, sir, I will. And thank you very much, Mr. Ball."

I went out and sat down next to Mr. Speed. As we looked out at the Indian River, a long line of brown pelicans flew gracefully over the top of the water.

"Look at that, Mr. Speed. I think they are mighty beautiful birds. I know some fishermen don't like them because they think they're fish thieves. But I don't think that. Do you?"

"Not thieves, just smart. Smart birds. The brown ones live here, but the white ones don't. Just come to visit when it's warm. They can herd fish onto shore, just like cows. Like cows."

"The white pelican can herd fish like a cowboy herds cattle?"

"Circle around the fish school and herd them in. Smart birds. Smart."

"My goodness, I have never seen that, but I hope I will get to someday."

The two of us sat together for a while longer, just enjoying each other's silence. After we finished our colas, I said, "I best be getting home. I'll be stopping by again real soon."

"Real soon."

On my walk back home, I saw Blue and Jackson standing by the railroad tracks. Jackson stepped forward and handed me a paper bag. "Tell your mama we done grown too many mustard greens."

Blue kept his eyes averted. Jackson touched his frayed straw hat and looked directly at me. His black eyes were clear and kind.

"You give our regards to Mista Nolay." He spoke as if Nolay were still at home or just out on a fishing trip.

When I got home, Mama was up and looked a little refreshed. I placed the carton of cigarettes and the bag on the table. When she opened the carton, a fifty-dollar bill slid from between the packs. And at the bottom of that bag of mustard greens, rolled into a little tube and wrapped with a rubber band, was thirty dollars.

It took just five days for Mama's pickle jar to fill up with three hundred dollars' worth of miracles, and Nolay's freedom. Friday morning Mama woke me and said, "Hurry up. Never mind any chores today, just get all the animals fed and eat some breakfast. We're going to get your daddy."

To me that sounded like a grand thing to do for the day.

Mama put the top down on the Champion, tied a bright green scarf around her hair, placed her pickle jar full of miracles on the front seat, and started driving us to the Titusville Courthouse. When we reached town, she drove straight past the Melbourne City Bank. I turned to her and said, "Mama, aren't you going to go to the bank and cash all that money in?"

Mama looked over at me with the same little twinkle in her eyes that I had seen in Nolay's and said, "No, I don't think so."

At the courthouse, Mama walked into that cold gray building with her head held high. When the officer at the front desk saw us, he put his head down real quick. Mama walked over and set her pickle jar full of dollars, quarters, dimes, nickels, and pennies right in front of that officer. He looked back and forth from the jar to Mama. In her sweetest Southern drawl, Mama said, "If you would be so kind, sir, as to count out the three hundred dollars for my husband's bail. I will just take a seat over there and wait for you."

Me and Mama went and sat on a small wooden bench

across from the desk. We watched as the officer slowly wrapped both his hands around the jar as though it were going to jump up and run away. He spilled out the miracles and began stacking them in assorted piles. He finally looked in our direction and said, "Yes, ma'am, there is the correct amount of money here. I will go get your husband."

"Thank you, sir."

I said to Mama, "Don't you think that was sort of mean, to make him count out all that money?"

Mama smiled. "Absolutely not. He has never been very polite or cordial to me. What goes around comes around. You remember that, Bones."

Thinkin' about watching that man sort through all those coins and crumpled-up dollars, I replied, "Yes, ma'am, I sure will remember that."

About a half hour later, the elevator doors magically slid open and Nolay stepped out.

We walked out of that building as quickly as we could. Nolay slid into the driver's side of the Champion. I curled up on the seat between my parents. The Champion purred along the hot pavement, Florida's warm air playfully licking at our faces. Nolay took in a deep breath, shook his headful of shaggy black curls, and said, "Smell that sweet air. That was about the longest eight days I have ever spent in my life."

His blue eyes twinkled as he looked back and forth from me to Mama. "Honey Girl, how did you come up with all that money? Y'all didn't rob a bank or anything, did ya?"

Mama laid her arm across my shoulder and gently twirled a strand of my hair between her fingers. I could feel the softness of her eyes resting on me. "No, Nolay, we didn't rob a bank. It was just a miracle, just a plain old miracle."

Over the weekend Nolay was busy going on some of his business trips. I began to notice how things appeared around the house and just as quickly disappeared. Although we still didn't have electricity, he carted home radios, toasters, and cases of lightbulbs. There were sets of tires, fishing rods, guns, and car batteries. Boxes, crates, and barrels, they all came and they went.

He also visited the swamps to check on a little something out there.

On Sunday he showed up with a washing machine sitting in the back of his truck and covered by an old blanket. I walked over to have a closer look and heard Mama question him. "Where did you get something like that and what are you going to do with it? Did you steal this?"

"Honey Girl, I keep tellin' you that some people got more stuff than they know what to do with. I'm just moving some things around. It just ain't right for things like this to set around idle. Ain't doin' any harm."

"That's what you said about running those Yankee men off with a gun, and look where that got us."

"Ain't the same. Don't you fret about it, Honey Girl. If I end up going to trial over all this, we got to have money for a lawyer. I'm taking care of it, that's all."

"Nolay, have you ever thought about getting a steady job?"

"You don't think net fishin' is a steady job? What other sort of job? Working for seventy-five cents an hour? That's a waste of time. I'm doing just fine."

• • •

The three of us were standing out in the yard by Nolay's truck, when none other than Sheriff LeRoy pulled into our yard. Nolay walked over to the car and said, "LeRoy, what brings you out here on a Sunday?"

The sheriff sat in his car and glanced at the blanket-covered object in the back of Nolay's truck but didn't say a word about it. "Sorry about the intrusion on a Sunday. Just wanted to stop by and remind you not to be wandering off. You stick close to home. And stay clear of them Reemses. I got some po-lease work to do. I got me some ideas. I'll be back in touch with you soon as I learn something more. And Nolay, don't go doing anything foolish or you'll end up back in jail."

"I ain't gonna do nothing foolish."

Sheriff LeRoy looked in my and Mama's direction, politely nodded his huge head, started up his car, and drove off.

I wasn't worried so much about Nolay doing something foolish. It was Sheriff LeRoy's ideas and his po-lease work that concerned me.

memories

Monday morning I woke up to Mama's soft voice. "Rise and shine, Bones, it's the first day of school."

Mama dropped me off along the county road to wait for the bus. By the time I got on board, it was half full of freshly scrubbed kids smelling like Ivory soap. Little Man had our usual seat saved. Skeeter Reems looked like an upside-down toad sprawled out in the backseat, and next to him, looking like a frog, was his younger brother, Smokey. I looked around and noticed that the seat where Martha and Ruthie usually sat was empty. "I wonder where Martha and Ruthie are?" I said.

"Miss Alvie must need 'em more than they need school."

"I wish my mama felt the same way."

"Now, looky, Bones, don't you go scrappin' for trouble. Especially with them Barracuda Boys."

"I ain't gonna look for trouble."

"Well, you know things are gonna get said, you just walk away from it. You hear? Now, everything is gonna be all right with Mr. Nolay. Just like my mama says, it's in the hands of the Lord."

"I understand that. I'm just not so sure how Nolay and the Lord are getting along these days."

"Don't worry. Just have faith, Bones. And you're gonna like your new teacher. I had her last year in fifth grade, too, and she's right likable."

"Little Man," I whispered, "do you still have Nolay's knife that I found in the swamps?"

"Course I do. But we don't know that it's Mr. Nolay's," Little Man whispered back.

"Well, you were the one that said we should keep it a secret and not show it to anybody. You must have been having some kind of thoughts on who it belonged to."

"I will admit some strange thoughts came in my mind, but I got rid of 'em. That's not the way I want to be thinking. I got no idea whose knife it is."

I had no answer to that. Sometimes Little Man could be confusing. And I wished I could do the same thing, just get rid of some of the thoughts swimming around in my head.

Being that Micco was located over twenty-five miles from school, it was a long ride in. The old bus jarred us along the highway for over an hour until we finally arrived. The schoolyard was a bustle of old and new faces. The Barracuda Boys were already trolling the new arrivals, looking for the weak and defenseless.

As we stepped off the bus, I watched Skeeter and Smokey Reems saunter over and join up with a group of boys. Little

Man glanced at me and said, "You stay clear of them boys, you hear?"

"I will. I'm not looking for any trouble."

Little Man shook his head and started to walk away. "I'll see you back here after school."

I walked over to a small group of girls and joined in on their conversation. They all lived in town, so we didn't get to see each other all summer. Everyone was talking at the same time about what they had done over the summer, and I realized that I was glad to see some of my classmates again. Maybe school wouldn't be so awful after all.

Then I looked over by the swing set and saw Betty Jean Davis and her select group of friends. I sure did hope that she wasn't in my class again this year. That girl thought she was the best thing since sliced bread. But as far as I was concerned, she was just a spoiled brat and meaner than a stepped-on rattlesnake.

The morning bell rang, and we all went to our new classrooms. There were only two classes for each grade, so most of my classmates and me had shared at least one or more grades.

As I walked down the hall, I saw that one of the first-grade classroom doors was open. Sitting behind her huge desk was the Lizard Lady herself. Quick as lightning her eyes fastened on me like the fangs of a snake. Just the sight of her sent a cold chill down my spine. Not only because she was the meanest teacher I ever had, but because seeing her reminded me of one of the worst days of my life. My first day at school. It was four years ago, but it felt like just last week.

The summer of 1945, Nolay had just returned home from the war, and we were once again a family. I watched as Mama worked feverishly on her old treadle sewing machine. Her little legs pumped up and down and her delicate fingers deftly slipped pieces of cloth under the needle. Mama made nearly all my cowboy shirts and nightclothes. All I had to do was show her a picture of it in the Sears Roebuck catalog. But now she was busy making me cute little dresses.

That first day of school Mama dressed me up like I was a little plastic baby doll. I had on a light blue cotton dress with white flowers spilling down the front and the sorriest-looking shoes I had ever seen, some shiny white plastic things with bows on the front.

She loaded me up in the truck and chattered the entire hour's drive to school. "Bones, you look so nice, and you are going to have so much fun. You'll meet lots of new friends, and you'll learn to read and write. Now, remember, you wait outside your classroom door and Little Man will come and get you so you can ride the school bus home."

Melbourne School stood in the middle of town like three giant pink tombstones. It was home to kids from first grade right up to twelfth. I got out of the truck and Mama latched on to my hand and gently pulled me toward the first building. We entered a bright yellow hallway that smelled of fresh paint and bleach. The muddled sounds of laughter and children's voices drifted out of several classrooms as we passed by. Mama stopped at a door with colored paper numbers plastered all over it and whispered, "This is Miss Harms's room, and she's going to be your teacher."

She opened the door and pulled me inside. The classroom was filled with the most kids I had ever seen in my life; there must have been twenty of them. All eyes turned in our direction. Seated behind a large desk at the front of the room was a woman so wrinkled and gray she resembled one of my pet lizards. She wore a black polka-dot dress. Her blue-gray hair was pulled back in a bun so tight it made her eyes slant and pop out from her head. She stuck a bony finger in our direction and said, "Come over here, let's see who we have."

Mama began to push me to the front of the room, but my feet froze to the floor. She put her hand on my back and prodded me toward Miss Harms's desk. "This is my little girl, and she is so excited about coming to school."

I looked up at Mama, scared to death that God was going to send down one of his lightning bolts and strike her dead for telling such a lie.

Lizard Lady squinted her beady eyes in my direction. "And what is your name?"

I dropped my head and whispered, "Bones." A chorus of giggles rose from the classroom. One stern look from her lizard eyes and the room fell silent.

"Bones, well now, that is a curious name for a little girl."

"Yes, ma'am, but it's the only name I got." I decided there and then that I would not reveal my true name to this lizard-faced woman.

In one swift movement she stood up, placed a cold hand on my shoulder, propelled me toward an empty desk, and said in Mama's direction, "We'll be just fine." Her voice sounded sweet as corn syrup, but the hand on my shoulder felt like a stream of ice water flowing down my back. I did not have a good feeling about this.

I sat down, folded my arms across my chest, and stared at the wooden desktop. When the recess bell rang, Miss Harms made us stand in two lines, boys in one, girls in the other. As we marched out to the playground, I saw Little Man standing by the monkey bars. He walked up to me and asked, "How you doin' so far?"

"I hate school, I want to go home."

"It's only your first day, it'll get better. I gotta go now. The boys are starting up a baseball game."

"Can I play?"

"I don't think so." Little Man lowered his voice. "Leastways, not in a dress." He started to walk away, then turned back and pointed across the playground to Skeeter Reems, who was standing with a group of older boys. "You see Skeeter and them boys over yonder? They ain't never up to no good. You stay clear of 'em, you hear me?"

"Yeah, I hear you."

Little Man looked at me like he had something more to say. But he pressed his lips together and slowly walked away.

A small group of girls walked over and stood by me. One of them girls, in a frilly dress, stepped forward and spoke to me. Her voice sounded like a kitten mewing. "My name is Betty Jean Davis. And what's yours again?"

"Bones."

"Bones . . . what kind of name is that? Were you born in a graveyard?" The other girls held their hands to their mouths and giggled.

"No, I wasn't, but I could put you in one."

"Oh my, aren't you just so tough. But let me tell you something, Bones. My daddy is a lawyer. He is the county prosecutor."

She squinted in my direction. "You do know what the county prosecutor is, don't you?"

I had no idea what she was talking about, but I sure wasn't gonna let her know that. I'd ask someone soon as I got a chance. I replied, "Course I know what that is! I'm not dumb, you know."

Betty Jean continued. "We own a swimming pool and we have one of the very first televisions, ever. And if you even so much as touch me, my daddy knows every policeman in town and he will have your mama and daddy arrested and put in jail."

Betty Jean placed her chubby hands on her waist, signaling for her butterfly girlfriends to stand beside her. They reminded me of butterflies 'cause they fluttered around her like she was some kind of special flower or something. Her eyes squinted nearly shut as she said, "I know who you are. You live out in the swamps with your half-breed daddy. You shouldn't even be going to this school." With that, she and her gang of friends giggled and walked away.

The rest of my day did not get any better. Neither, for that matter, did the entire year of school. I ended up spending a huge amount of time standing in the corner or on my tiptoes with my nose stuck in a circle drawn on the blackboard. It was a happy occasion when I passed first grade and moved on to a different teacher.

I shook my head as if waking from a nightmare. As I scurried past that room and all those memories, I could only hope that what Little Man said about my new teacher was true.

school

When I entered the classroom, it was jumble of fresh-scrubbed bodies and new clothes. My fifth-grade teacher, Miss Watts, was as big as the side of a barn and had two front teeth like a rabbit's. Her soft brown eyes sparkled with excitement as she walked around the classroom and handed each of her new students a home-baked cupcake.

The first part of the morning was spent introducing ourselves and telling what we had done over the summer. There was one unfortunate event: Betty Jean Davis sat directly across from me. She was the first to stand up and tell about her family vacation to Atlanta, Georgia. When she finished, she turned her prissy face toward me and squeaked, "And I heard that some people went to jail over the summer."

As usual, Betty Jean's little flock of friends, the butterfly girls, giggled at her every comment. From the first day I met her on the playground, I knew she was no butterfly. She was just a mean little wasp disguised as a butterfly. Anyone who was not included in her select group of friends had felt her sting.

The first recess bell of the year rang, and we all shoved our way out to the playground. The Reems boys, along with a couple of other mean-spirited friends, had already surrounded a skinny little boy with protruding ears and thick glasses. It was a new year, and they were in search of fresh food. Of course, they had their return victims to feed on at leisure. There was Fat Polly, who sat alone in the lunchroom and was always the last to be picked for any game. I had had Polly in my classroom for two years and still didn't know the color of her eyes. They were always cast down. There was Popeye Sullivan, who rode our school bus. Every morning he stood alone on the side of U.S. 1. Popeye's right eye stuck out of its socket and stared, vacant and unseeing, like a dead mullet's. There was Fish-Face Freddy, a chubby little boy who wore faded overalls and had no shoes. And Chicken Legs, a little girl in ragged dresses, her legs so skinny and covered with scars they looked like old gnawed chicken bones.

As I walked past Betty Jean and her group of butterfly girls, I heard her talking to a small girl dressed in a clean, freshly ironed flour-sack dress. "My goodness, isn't that a *nice* dress you're wearing. I bet it looked better when it was full of flour." The butterfly girls covered their mouths and giggled.

The little girl hung her head in silent shame. I stepped up to her side and said, "Those are really nice roses on your dress. I think a friend of mine has one just like it." Turning to Betty Jean, I said, "Nice dress you're wearing, too."

She twirled around and made an elaborate little curtsy.

"Why, thank you, Bones. This year my mama took me to Atlanta, Georgia, to buy school clothes. Sometimes I even go shopping in Miami."

"Well, isn't that special, Betty Jean. I bet that dress looked better hanging on a rack."

Betty Jean's eyes narrowed. The barbed tongue came out. "How's the swamp, Bones? Eat any good possum soup lately?" The butterfly girls giggled and fluttered in closer.

"No, Betty Jean, I don't eat possum. They're actually very nice little creatures. Nothing I would want to eat."

Sensing bigger prey close by, Skeeter and Smokey Reems, along with their no-account friends, left the little boy with protruding ears and sauntered over. They swaggered up to me and Skeeter said, "Well, hey, Bones, I heard your jailbird daddy went and killed a man and is going to prison for a long time."

Between the laughter and snickers I replied, "My daddy is not a jailbird. And you don't know what happened."

One of the other boys piped up. "Well, I know what I read in the newspaper. And I know what I hear folks talking about."

I stepped forward and clenched my fists. "You better take them words back."

I felt a hand wrap firmly around my shoulder. A familiar voice said, "Hey, so what y'all talking about? Bird huntin'?"

I turned and looked straight into the brown eyes of Little Man.

Skeeter and Smokey Reems slowly backed up. None of them wanted to scrap with Little Man—he stood a full head above every one of them. Someone mumbled, "Yeah, bird huntin'."

Little Man put his hand on the back of my neck, turned me around, and pushed me in front of him.

"Gol-durn it, Bones, I told you not to go scrappin'. Especially with them boys."

"Well, what was I supposed to do, just let 'em call my daddy names?"

"It's just names. I don't want to be takin' on all them boys."

"The two of us together could lick 'em."

"That ain't what I want to do. Now you go on back to class. I'll see you on the bus."

On the bus ride home I said quietly to Little Man, "I'm really scared for Nolay. I don't know what to think anymore. You know that day we took the train to the movies and we saw Sheriff LeRoy at the place where Peckerhead got run over?"

"Course I do. What of it?"

"Well, the sheriff was holding a red handkerchief just like the one Nolay always wears when he's fishing and airboatin'."

"That don't mean nothing. There's hundreds of red handkerchiefs around."

"But Nolay's *isn't* around. I've looked everywhere for it. It's nowhere to be found. And the sheriff keeps saying they have evidence against Nolay. There's been two murders close by us, and Nolay had run-ins with both those men."

"Bones, you gotta stop thinkin' like that. That's your daddy you're talkin' about."

"I know that, and it scares me, but my mind won't stop thinking about it."

The next morning, when I walked into the classroom, a piece of paper with a cutout cartoon pasted on top was lying on my desk. The cartoon was of a blackbird, and printed on top was *jailbird*. The next morning there was a picture of a chair with the words *electric* written over it. But the worst one was on the third day. It was a picture of a piece of bacon.

Betty Jean pranced into the room and stopped by my desk. "That's what they do to murderers in Florida, they send them to the electric chair. And they fry just like a piece of bacon. I should know. You do remember my daddy is the prosecuting attorney for Brevard County? And that is just where he is going to send your daddy."

"Shut your mouth, Betty Jean, before I punch you in your fat nose!"

"If you do that, you'll be joining your daddy in jail."

That afternoon as we rode home on the bus, I showed the pictures to Little Man. I had been too ashamed to show him before. He looked at them and said, "Where did these come from?"

"Who else but Betty Jean Davis? Every morning there's one sittin' on top of my desk. When I look at it, her and her friends all start giggling." I turned away from Little Man, blinking back my tears. Swallowing hard, I said, "She is so mean, I nearly hate her. And all she does is talk about how she has a television and a swimming pool, and how her daddy is so important. If you ain't part of her special group, she treats you like a clod of dirt. I swear, I just want to poke her right in her big nose."

"You don't want to be doing that, Bones; it'll only make things worse."

"Well, I want to do something. I'd like to put a snake down her dress. Not a bad snake, just one that would scare her half to death."

Little Man turned to me and smiled. "Now, that there gives me an idea. Maybe you should give Betty Jean a little present."

"A present? What kind of present?"

"You got any leftover wrapping paper and ribbon?"

"I think so. Mama usually keeps some in her cedar chest."

"You bring some tomorrow, and I'll bring you a little gift for Betty Jean."

"What kind of present are you thinking of?"

Little Man winked. "I got one that lives by the front door of the chicken coop."

Friday morning on the bus, Little Man handed me a small box. "You got the wrapping paper and ribbon?"

"Yep, right here."

"Make sure nobody sees you." Then, in a whisper, he said, "This here is what I want you to do."

I followed Little Man's instructions to the letter. Like Nolay had said, Little Man was one bright boy.

That afternoon, when everyone returned to class after

recess, a small package sat on Betty Jean's desk. It was wrapped in white paper with a pink ribbon. There was a note written in red crayon: "From your secret admirer."

Betty Jean picked up the little box, placed it next to her ear, and shook it. The butterfly girls fluttered around, twittering, "Open it, open it. Who's your secret admirer? What's inside?"

Betty Jean sat down at her desk and, with exaggerated prissiness, began to untie the pink bow. She leaned her face in as she slowly lifted the cover. A gigantic black and yellow spider leaped out of the box and onto her elbow. It ran up her arm, across her horrified face, and onto her springy brown curls.

The room filled with shrieks and screams. One of the butterfly girls fell down, and two others trampled her. Betty Jean sat at her desk, stomped her feet, and screamed hysterically. By the time Miss Watts reached her, the spider had scurried down Betty Jean's back and dashed toward an open window and freedom.

Betty Jean sobbed uncontrollably as Miss Watts led her out of the classroom.

At the end of the day, as I was leaving the classroom, Miss Watts called me over to her desk.

"Bones, would you know anything about that spider today?"

"Yes, ma'am, that's what we call a garden spider, or a writing spider. You know, like in the story *Charlotte's Web*. They make big pretty webs. But they don't bite."

"Do you have any idea how it got in that box and onto Betty Jean's desk?"

"I reckon, like the note said, it was from a secret admirer."

"I guess you're right, Bones. Let's hope her secret admirer doesn't give her any more gifts. I'll see you on Monday."

"Yes, ma'am."

On the bus ride home, Little Man made me tell him the story over and over. Each time he laughed harder and said, "I wish I coulda seen it. She was blubberin' in front of everyone? I wish I coulda seen it."

"Well, I don't know. Maybe it was sort of a mean thing to do. I didn't think it would scare her that bad."

"What are you talking about, Bones? You feel sorry for Betty Jean? She deserved even worse. That girl ain't never done one good thing for anybody. Don't go feeling sorry for someone like that."

"Well, I reckon so. Maybe after this, she won't be so mean."

As I was about to get off the bus at my stop, I turned and said, "Thanks, Little Man. . . ."

He crinkled up his freckled face and replied, "Aw, it wadn't nothing. I'll see you tomorrow, Bones."

reality

That evening I was helping Nolay tie up the airboat after one of his trips to the swamps. He still wasn't wearing his red handkerchief; he had a blue one tied around his mop of black curls.

He got out of the airboat and pointed to a stand of reeds. "Bones, can you see that little bittern over there?"

A small brown-speckled bird walked cautiously through the reeds. Nolay threw a pebble in the bird's direction. It immediately pointed its beak in the air and stood as still as a stick. It all but vanished as its little brown body blended in with the reeds.

I looked at Nolay. "You know, I been thinking. Maybe if things don't work out—I mean, you know, it could turn out to be bad for you. Bad for all of us. Maybe we could just move into the Everglades. We could go where nobody would ever find us. We could disappear into the swamps, just like that little bittern did."

Nolay stopped what he was doing. "Bones, do you think I killed those two men?"

"No, sir, I'm not saying that. I just don't want you to go back to jail. I don't want Mama to be sad. I just want us to live together and for things to be the way they were before all this happened."

"Bones, I wish things were different, too, but they ain't."

"Nolay, what happened to your red handkerchief, the one you used to always wear?"

"Lost it out fishing one night. Why you ask?"

"Just wondering is all."

"Bones, I know it's a confusin' time right now. It's confusin' for me, too. All we can do is be patient and see what ol' LeRoy comes up with."

"I don't know about Sheriff LeRoy, he's so big and clumsy. He just don't seem to be very smart. And he moves slower than pond water."

"Now, Bones, don't go faulting LeRoy 'cause he's big. And being slow don't mean he ain't smart. Pond water can fool ya. It can be smooth and still on the top, but you don't know what all is goin' on underneath. Still waters run deep."

Nolay put his arm around my shoulders. "Come on, Bones, we best be getting back to the house. Your mama will have supper ready."

At the dinner table as the conversation circled around things like court, lawyers, and Sheriff LeRoy's investigation, I asked Nolay, "What if Sheriff LeRoy don't come through? What will happen to you? Will you go to prison forever?"

"Bones, I ain't gonna beat around the bush with you, I'm gonna be truthful. Now, I'm trusting in LeRoy that he's gonna come through with some solid evidence, 'cause I ain't done nothing wrong, but if things don't work out, I could end up in prison, or even worse, sittin' in the electric chair."

Like a slap upside my head, I realized that Betty Jean could be right. Just the sound of the words *electric chair* felt like someone pouring ice water down my back.

Mama's eyes snapped over in Nolay's direction. "Nolay, for heaven's sake, don't talk like that. You don't need to make things worse for Bones. It's hard enough for any of us to understand."

"I ain't tryin' to scare Bones. That ain't my intention. But I don't want to hide the truth from her, either."

Mama looked over at me. "Bones, right now we have to trust in the Lord and pray that LeRoy will find the right answers."

"Yes, ma'am, I will try harder to do that."

I sat at the table and tried to picture LeRoy's big clumsy body working alongside the Lord to keep Nolay from being strapped into the electric chair. But the more I thought about it, the bigger that ugly old chair got, empty and waiting for someone to sit in it. How could someone think up something as mean as that to do to people? Then I thought of something that reminded me of mean, and that was those Reems boys.

"Mama, do you know what happened to Martha and Ruthie? Since school started they haven't showed up for one day."

"Why, no, I don't, Bones. This is the first I've heard of it. Why didn't you mention it before?"

"I just had so many other things on my mind, I forgot."

"Well, of course, that's understandable. Maybe you and I can go pay them a visit tomorrow."

"Are you sure, Mama? Remember Sheriff LeRoy told No-lay to stay clear of the Reems. I just thought you might have heard something."

"Don't worry about that. I am not your daddy, and I am not going out to see any of the Reems men. I am going out to see Miss Alvie."

Nolay looked at Mama. "I don't know, Honey Girl. You might want to stay clear of that family."

"I just want to know what's happening with Alvie and her kids."

"Promise me you'll be extra careful. And don't be getting into no arguments with them brothers. I don't want to have to come out there myself."

"I will be very careful. It's the neighborly thing to do, and I will be doing it. The sheriff said you had to stay away, not me."

Mama picked up her fork, took a bite of food, and that was the end of the conversation.

Saturday morning, soon as I walked into the kitchen, Mama said, "We're going out to the Reemses."

"Mama, are you sure?"

"I am not going to get into trouble. Now, get your chores done and let's get going."

As soon as we pulled into the decrepit yard, the pack of half-starved dogs came to greet us, but not the dirty-faced little boys. Mama looked around and said, "Something is not right out here." The house stood dark and foreboding. Old Ma Reems sat in her rocking chair chewing on her wad of tobacco and staring out into nothing.

Mama gave a neighborly toot on the horn, but the house remained silent. Finally the screen door squeaked open and Whackerstacker and Fats, his eldest boy, ambled out onto Willy's front porch. I squirmed in my seat and whispered, "Mama, maybe we should just go and come back some other time."

"No, we are here now. I am not afraid of that mean old man. And I don't want you to be, either."

The two of them swaggered down the steps and up to Mama's window. Whackerstacker spat out a long stream of black tobacco juice and said, "What y'all doin' here?"

"I came to give my regards to Miss Alvie. Do you know where she is?"

Whackerstacker hooked his thumbs in the tops of his ratty overalls and glanced into the back of the pickup. Seeing the box he said, "Looks like you come to my house bringin' more of your dag-blasted chairtee."

"I'm afraid you're mistaken, Mr. Reems. That is not charity; God provides some people with an abundance to share. Now, do you know where Miss Alvie and the children are?"

"Yeah, I know where they are. I done sent her and all them brats packin' back where they come from. I put 'em on the Greyhound bus with one-way tickets back to her mammy and pappy."

Mama sat in silence; I felt the air thicken in the cab of the truck. She looked directly into Whackerstacker's bloated face and spoke almost in a whisper. "Why, you heartless old dog. You put that poor woman and those poor children out of her own house! They were your brother's children!"

"Ain't her house. That there is my family house. My land. Not her'n. Them two girls ain't no blood of mine. Ain't my cause to take care of 'em. That's her blood."

"You old skunk, that poor woman was married to your brother. She had three children with him and another one on the way. She was slave to him and your mother for all these years. She deserved better; she deserved to stay here for the rest of her life. She deserved to be treated decently."

"Ain't none of your bizzness what I do. Now you get off my land before I send my boy here for my shotgun."

I grabbed Mama's arm. "Let's go. Remember what Nolay said."

Mama slowly and deliberately turned the ignition key; the old truck engine sputtered to life. She put her head out the window and said, "You cockroach-brained slug. One day I will look down from heaven and watch you roasting on a spit."

She jammed the truck into first gear, shoved down on the accelerator, and did a sliding U-turn out of the desolate yard. I looked back to see Whackerstacker and Fats standing in a cloud of grimy dust.

Mama drove over the bumpy dirt roads so fast I had to hold on with both hands to keep from banging my head on the roof. I kept my mouth shut so if slipped I wouldn't bite my tongue off.

That night at supper, I finally got up the nerve to ask, "Mama, what did ol' Whackerstacker mean about the girls not being his blood?"

Mama gave a sly glance in Nolay's direction. "I guess if you're old enough to ask the question, you're old enough to understand." She took a sip of her ice tea. "Martha and Ruthie are Miss Alvie's baby sisters. Old Peckerhead Willy met her family one time when he was in South Florida selling moonshine or some such shenanigans. Alvie's family were dirt-poor migrant farmers."

Mama stopped and took a deep breath. "Her parents gave—or maybe I should say sold—Alvie, along with her two younger sisters, to Peckerhead. As far as I know, the agreement was that the girls, along with any children Alvie had with Peckerhead, could live in that house for as long as they wanted or needed to.

"Those two little boys, Tim and Tom, and the baby, Teddy, and the one she was about to give birth to were Peckerhead's children. They were Whackerstacker's true blood kin." She shook her head. "And now that heartless old man has sent her and all those poor children back to another dirt hole."

I stared at Mama in disbelief. "That's why the girls look so different from the boys. That's why they were treated so badly." A picture floated across my mind of Martha and Ruthie standing in the yard with the Reems boys. "They really were cranes living in a pigpen."

Like a big rock, the full meaning of what Mama had said dropped on top of me. My eyes darted back and forth between

Nolay and Mama. "They sold their own kids? People can't be sold. You can't just buy and sell people. Can you?"

Nolay was the first to reply. "It wadn't that long ago, Bones. Surely you've read up on slavery in school. Colored people were passed around like old used-up rags. It shouldn't of happened then. And it sure shouldn't be happening now. But I guess in certain ways it does go on."

"But they sold their own kids. How can anyone do something like that?"

"Desperation. Ignorance. Being so poor you can't put food on the table. I don't know, Bones. I ain't gonna judge nobody else's actions, no matter how wrong they may seem to be."

"Why didn't y'all tell me this before? I would have been nicer to them." I hung my head. "I could have been nicer to them."

I looked across the table and met Mama's soft gaze. "Bones," she said, "just be nice to everyone. Treat people the way you want to be treated and you'll never live to regret it."

That night as I lay in bed, I pictured Martha and Ruthie, the bruises on their legs, the secondhand clothes they wore. The sad, blank look that lived in their eyes. I squeezed my eyes shut and tried to erase the pictures. But they wouldn't go away; they just hovered there in my bedroom.

shadows

It was mid-September and already a family of whooping cranes had returned to nest in the swamps. Every evening they flew over our house, their mournful cries announcing the end of the day and the coming of darkness.

Sunday after me and Mama returned from church, I was in the kitchen helping her knead some dough for our supper biscuits. "Mama, right before the sun sets, me and the dogs are going out to see if we can find the whooping cranes. Mr. Speed told me that just when it starts to get dark and they think nobody can see them, they do a magical dance with each other. He said it is just enchanting."

"Bones, I would rather you didn't go out in the swamps, especially by yourself."

"I won't be by myself; I'll have the dogs with me. And I'm not going in the swamps, just to the edge where the cranes come and nest. You know Silver won't let anything happen to me."

"Well, I guess it's all right as long as the dogs are with you.

And don't be too long, get back here before dark. And be real careful. Watch out for snakes."

"Don't worry, Mama, I will. And Mama, did you know that Florida has over forty-seven different kinds of snakes?"

"Forty-seven? I'm guessing you heard that from Mr. Speed."

"Yes, ma'am, I did. He told me that out of all them different kinds of snakes, the smartest one is the cottonmouth moccasin. He said when the babies are born, they have a little yellow tip on their tail and they use it like a fishin' worm. They wiggle it around and bait bugs and stuff to come close so they can eat 'em. And he said the rattlesnake is the best mama. She goes back to the same nestin' hole every year to have her babies, and she is a kind and loving mother."

"He said a rattlesnake is a kind, loving mother?" Mama smiled. "I do wonder where that man gets all his information."

"Well, sometimes he gets things a little mixed up and I have to listen real hard to try and understand. But I think he always knows what he's saying, even if we don't. Me and Little Man think he has a special connection to God."

"That could be, Bones, that could very well be."

Right at dusk the three cranes flew over our house. I whistled for the dogs, and we set out on our journey. At first we followed the well-worn path that led to the small landing where Nolay kept the airboat. From there we veered off and followed along the edge of the swamp. On one side were huge stands of cattails and saw grass; on the other was a field of tangled, twisted scrub palmetto.

The dogs ran ahead and sniffed their way along the trail. Before long we came to a wide stand of cypress trees that grew along the edge of the swamp. The trees stood tall and forlorn, like old forgotten soldiers, their trunks bent and gnarled from a lifetime in swamp water. I knew the cranes nested somewhere in this area.

I stopped to listen for the whooping cranes' melodious song. All I heard was the wind playing with the dry grass and leaves. That was when I saw Silver crouched down on her haunches, the hairs along her back raised straight up in the air like a rooster's tail. Paddlefoot and Mr. Jones stood still as statues; the three of them stared straight ahead.

I peered into the misty stand of cypress trees and thought I saw the shadow of something or someone move. From inside the darkness, something stared back at me; it stopped and waited for me to move closer. The air filled with a stale, sour odor. I stood as though my feet were frozen to the ground. The shadow shivered and moved forward. I turned, yelled for the dogs, and began running as fast as I could back toward our house.

Behind me I heard feet thrashing through the dry undergrowth. From the corner of my eye I saw Silver loping protectively by my side. Suddenly Paddlefoot veered in front of me and the two of us tumbled down. I rolled over and fell into a thick tangle of palmetto roots. The razor-sharp palm branches scraped and cut my bare arms.

Silver came to me where I lay on the ground. She faced

behind me, growled, and bared her teeth. Too terrified to look back, I jumped to my feet and raced forward. My heart pounded like a drum inside my chest.

Me and the three dogs hit the yard running. Through the window I could see Mama in the kitchen cooking supper. I ran inside and collapsed at the kitchen table, wide-eyed and breathless.

She turned and looked at me. "Bones, what on earth is wrong with you? My goodness, look at your arms. What happened? I'll get some kerosene and iodine to put on those cuts."

Mama left me panting at the kitchen table. She walked back in with a rag dipped in kerosene and a small bottle of iodine. She began to wash my cuts. "Bones, what happened out there?"

"Me and the dogs went out to find the whooping cranes, to watch 'em dance. But I ran into Soap Sally."

"Soap Sally! Bones, you know very well there is no such thing as Soap Sally."

"Yes, there is, Mama, I seen her."

"You saw her."

"Yes, ma'am, I saw her. She was out there waitin' on me."

"No, Bones, I was correcting your English. You did not *seen* her, you *saw* her. But you did not see her. There is no such thing."

"There is too. I've been out to her house before, with you and Nolay."

"What are you talking about, Bones? Whose house?"

"Miss Eunice's. There's something she keeps in that ol'

shed by the side of her house. And it has a strange smell. The same one I've smelled out in the swamps when I've met up with Soap Sally."

Mama finished cleaning my cuts, stood up, and leaned against the kitchen counter. She crossed her arms. "That is absolute nonsense. You are ten years old and letting your imagination run away with you. You can't possibly be talking about Miss Eunice."

"Mama, I'm telling you there's something out there! And it's got the same smell as I've smelled out at that house."

"Bones, that is nonsense. It can't be Miss Eunice, she's an old woman. How on earth could she walk from her house all the way out to where you think you saw her?"

"'Cause she's a witch, that's why. You've heard the stories Nolay tells about Soap Sally."

"Yes, I have. And that is exactly what they are, stories. Bones, for goodness' sake, do you believe every story your father tells you?"

"Mama, why would Nolay lie to me about such a thing?"

"He's not lying. It's just the way he is. He's just having fun with you. Or at least he thinks he is. I think it's time for him to set some things straight. Bones, I don't want you going back out in those woods alone."

"Do you think she's after me?"

"No, I do not think Miss Eunice or Soap Sally is after you! There have been two murders in this area. I don't know who is out there. I don't want you going out by yourself again. Do you understand?"

"Yes, ma'am."

• • •

Monday morning on our bus ride to school I told Little Man about my encounter with Soap Sally. "Me and the dogs were just about ten feet away from her. I swear."

"I don't know, Bones. I mean, I've heard that story about Sally all my life, too, but I ain't never seen her."

"Well, let me ask you this—you've been out to Miss Eunice's house, haven't you?"

"Course I have. She loves when my mama drops off some of her famous guava jam."

"You know that ol' shed next to the house? Have you ever seen anything strange moving around by it, or smelled something funny-like around there?"

Little Man quietly pondered that for a while; then he said, "I might of heard something, and come to think of it, I have smelled something peculiar around that area."

"See, that's what I'm sayin'. I think there's something livin' inside there. Something that can move around a lot faster than an old woman."

"Still, I ain't never seen Soap Sally or an ol' witch running around."

"Well, like Nolay says, everyone believes in the devil and nobody has seen him, so why not a witch?"

Little Man rolled his eyes. "Good Lord, Bones. Where do you come up with some of this stuff?"

"Nolay told me. Why would he lie to me?"

When I looked over at Little Man, that question mark was sitting between his eyes.

illusions

Early Saturday morning Mama gently nudged me awake. When I walked in the kitchen, Nolay was sitting at the table. Mama had a small flour sack filled with canned fruits and vegetables. Without a look in my direction, she said, "Bones, eat some breakfast, feed the animals, and let Ikibob out of the coop. You and your daddy are going on a visit."

I looked at Nolay. "Where are we going?"

"Out to drop some stuff off to a nice old lady."

"Are we goin' to Soap Sally's house?"

"We are going out to visit with Miss Eunice."

I finished my chores, went in my room, and got my .22 rifle. I filled the cartridge case with ten bullets and dumped a couple extra in the pocket of my flannel shirt. Nolay was waiting for me in the truck. Nonchalantly, I placed the gun in the front seat between the two of us.

"Bones, why are you bringing a gun?"

"I ain't goin' out to that house without a gun. And you

never know what we might run into along the way. You know, snakes and things."

Nolay shook his head. "I don't think we'll be running into anything that you will be needing your gun for, but you can bring it anyways."

My gun would come in handy, but not for shooting snakes.

There were only two ways out to that isolated house, by airboat across the swamp or driving up a long winding dirt road that ran by the edge of the swamp. As Nolay slowly navigated us over the bumpy one-lane road, I asked, "Why are we going out here?"

"Because you and me need to get some things straightened out."

I folded my arms across my chest. If anything did happen, at least I had my gun with me.

The dirt road came to an abrupt end as we pulled into a yard so tiny our truck nearly filled the entire space. Nolay parked a few feet away from the front porch of a very small wooden house.

The house and yard sat under the branches of a massive banyan tree. Like a monstrous green umbrella, the tree stretched out and flooded the area in a gray gloom. A thick blanket of dry brown leaves covered the roof of the house and spilled into the yard.

On the left side of the house sat the old shed. I kept my eyes on it, but so far nothing was moving around by it.

One side of the little house rested like a child's toy against the enormous tree trunk. On the other side, and for as far as I could see behind it, an assortment of mounds bulged up through the blanket of leaves. A little wooden cross was stuck on top of each mound. At the corner of the house, a huge black pot sat perched on a ring of stones.

I pointed. "That's a graveyard! It's bigger than the house! And there's the big black pot! Turn around, we gotta get out of here!"

Nolay held my gaze for a moment, then without a word calmly tooted the horn, opened the door, and got out. He carried Mama's flour sack and walked through the gloom toward the house. His steps crackled across the blanket of dry leaves.

The screen door opened and a short, stooped figure shuffled out. A black shawl concealed its face and hung down over its lower body. From the truck I squinted into the dimness to see if I recognized it. It looked like the same figure, the same form I had seen lurking in the swamp's shadows, waiting to snatch me up and boil my body into soap.

From the front porch Nolay called out to me. "Bones, come over here. Now."

I stepped out of the truck and held my rifle in the crook of my arm as I slowly walked to the house. Cautiously, I stepped up onto the small porch. My heart pounded so hard I thought it would pop out of my chest. I stood in the presence of an ancient, twisted being.

It turned, and I looked into the wizened face of an old woman. Her cloudy round eyes sat deep between a furrowed brow and a hooked nose. My body stiffened as I watched her thin lips open and expose a toothless mouth.

Then she spoke. "Why, hello, chile." Her voice rang in my ears, soft and tinkling, like little Christmas bells.

I stepped back and almost fell off the porch. I heard Nolay say, "Bones, say hello to Miss Eunice."

I mumbled, "Hello, Miss Eunice."

The soft, childish voice continued. "Why, chile, I cannot believe you have growed up so much. These ol' eyes cain't remember the last time they saw you."

Looking down, she noticed my gun. "Chile, is that a gun you're totin'?"

"Yes, ma'am."

"What on earth for?"

"We might run into a snake or something."

"A snake. My lands, a snake ain't gonna hurt you unless you hurt it first. Have you ever seen a snake strap on a gun and go huntin' down people?" The old woman wagged her head and giggled. "Don't you believe the good Lord has punished snakes enough by making 'em crawl on their bellies and eat dust? Guns is made for hurtin', and we got enough of that goin' on in this world with out any more hep." She looked at Nolay and said, "Just listen to me carryin' on, I done forgot my manners. Y'all come on inside and set a spell."

She turned and shuffled inside the house. I looked down at my rifle, quietly leaned it on the porch, and followed Nolay inside.

The aroma of smoke and musty roses filled the small, sparsely furnished room. On one side was a kitchen table with two straight-back chairs. A vase filled with roses sat on top of a crocheted doily turned yellow with age. At one end of the table was a place setting with a dinner plate, knife, fork, and a glass.

On the other side of the room, a patchwork quilt was draped over a stuffed chair. A tiny oval table stood next to it. On top of the table sat a kerosene lamp and a large Bible, its cover worn thin from use.

The old woman tottered in from another room, carrying another straight-back chair. She placed it by the table and said, "Y'all sit down. Make yourselves comfortable."

Nolay said, "Now, Miss Eunice, I could have got that chair for you. You just tell me if I can be of help."

Miss Eunice looked at Nolay. "Now, I might be old and feeble, but I ain't hepless yet. I can still do my own washin'."

Nolay shook his head and laughed. "Yes, ma'am, I sure will remember that."

The old woman sat down and pulled the shawl from around her head. Her thin silver-white hair was pulled back in a loose bun at the nape of her neck. She reached over and picked up the dinner plate sitting in front of me. "Now, chile, don't pay no attention to this. It's just the foolishness of a old woman. I keep it there in memory of my Herman. He's done been gone to be with the Lord, nigh on twenty years." She held the plate delicately in her wrinkled hands. "It does hep with the loneliness. Sometimes I feel like he's right here, sittin' down eatin' supper with me."

I took a deep breath. "Miss Eunice, what is that big black pot in your yard used for?"

"Why, that was my Herman's cook pot. He used to boil up some of the best sorghum syrup in the whole county. We had a right good patch of sugarcane, but since he's gone, I cain't tend it, and the bush has took it over."

"And is that a graveyard in back of your house?"

"It sure is. That's my animals. Over the years, me and my Herman, along with the hep of the good Lord, was able to heal up a lot of hurt and wounded animals. The ones that didn't make it, well, at least we provided 'em with a decent burial."

"Those are animals? That's an animal graveyard? You heal animals?"

"Oh yes, chile. But not much anymore. Just gettin' too aged to do much of anything anymore. 'Bout all I can do is tend my rose garden out back." She reached forward with her knobby, crooked fingers and gently caressed the vase full of roses. "I do admire roses. The good Lord has put some lovely things on the earth for us to enjoy."

I looked around the room and noticed crocheted pictures hanging along the worn wooden walls. Strings of yarn had been painstakingly woven into birds and praying hands and flowers and suns. "Miss Eunice, do you make those?"

"I useta could, chile, but not anymore. Cain't hardly see with my cateracts. And these ol' hands is too stiff with the room-a-tism."

"Miss Eunice, you live here all alone? Don't you have any children?"

Nolay broke in. "Bones, mind your manners. Don't be so rude, you've done nothing but ask Miss Eunice one question after another."

Miss Eunice giggled. "Now, Nolay, she ain't rude a-tall. She can ask all the questions she wants. To hear the voice of a chile is like a sweet song to these ol' ears."

She turned back to me. "The good Lord gave me and my Herman three babies, but he took 'em right back again. When I get up to the Kingdom and I'm reunited with my family, I'm gonna sit down and have a little talk with the Lord. I'm gonna ask 'im, 'Lord, won't you make a new commandment? Won't you make it a rule that no one can die before the age of thirty? Everybody should have a chance to enjoy this glorious world for at least thirty years. We shouldn't be buryin' childrun'.'"

Miss Eunice closed her eyes and clasped her hands together on top of the table, as if in prayer. The room filled with her silence and memories.

Quietly, I said, "Miss Eunice, have you lived in this house all your life?"

Miss Eunice opened her eyes, tilted her head toward me, and said, "Nearly 'bout, chile. I come here with my Herman as a sixteen-year-old bride. That's over sixty years ago. You see that big ol' tree out yonder? Me and my Herman planted it the first week we started our life together in this house. It was our weddin' present to each other. Why, chile, when we put it in the ground, that tree wadn't much bigger than you. And look at it now. Just like my life with Herman, the good Lord done turned it into a pure thing of beauty and joy. Pretty soon it'll swaller up this little ol' house. But I'll be in the Kingdom before then."

Miss Eunice laid a knobby hand across her chest. "Land sakes, listen to me, chattering on like a squirrel. So good to have comp-nee I done forgot my manners again. Let me get y'all a glass of cold tea to drink. I ain't got no ice, 'cause I ain't got no 'lectric. But the water from the well is mighty refreshin'."

I watched the frail, stooped body of Miss Eunice hobble off and disappear into the tiny kitchen.

As I sat at this lonely old woman's table, the reality of my fear and confusion mingled and washed over me like dirty dishwater. I sat in her straight-back chair, drenched in shame. Tears welled up in my eyes and I turned toward Nolay. He looked at me with a clear steady gaze, then leaned forward and whispered, "I bet Miss Eunice would appreciate some help with the tea. Why don't you go help her, Bones?"

Together Miss Eunice and I brought in three glasses of tea and a small plate filled with sliced-up corn pone. As we sat down I asked her about some of the animals she'd raised.

"My lando, chile, there's been so many, this ol' brain can't remember 'em all."

"Tell me about the ones you can remember."

"Well, there have been squirrels, foxes, opossums, rabbits, and just about every kind of bird you can think of. My Herman, he was real good with birds, knew just what to do for 'em."

"I raise animals, too. Right now I have a wild pig named Pearl and a raccoon named Nippy."

"A wild pig! Well, I never did have one of those. But I had a whole family of raccoons. Someone shot the mama and just left her layin' there. Herman found her with five little kits hangin' on to her dead body. Said it was about the saddest thing he ever did see. He brought all five of 'em home and we raised 'em up till they was big enough to go out on their own."

"That's sort of like what happened to Nippy. Her mama got run over by a car. My best friend's daddy, Mr. Cotton, found her alongside the highway. He brought her out to me 'cause he knows I love animals. She was so little I had to feed her with a baby bottle for the first couple weeks."

"Land sakes, chile, me and you got a lot in common."

For the next couple of hours we sat at Miss Eunice's table sipping tea, munching on cold corn pone, and talking about animals. Her cloudy white eyes glistened with memories.

All too soon, Nolay cut in. "Bones, it's getting late. We best be heading home. We can always come back and visit another time."

As the three of us stood on the small porch, Miss Eunice told me, "I sure hope I get to meet Pearl one day. I never did have me a pet wild pig. She sure sounds like a fine critter."

"I hope so, too, Miss Eunice. I'll try to bring her out one day; she loves to ride in the back of the truck."

"Well, I sure 'preciate y'all stopping by."

"Thank you, Miss Eunice, it's been a pure pleasure to meet you."

I picked up my rifle. As my hand wrapped around the cold steel barrel, my memory was jolted back to the reason I had brought it. Me and Nolay walked out into the yard. The magnificent old tree had erased the gloominess and replaced it with cool, peaceful shade. We walked across the spongy golden blanket of leaves and got in the truck. Miss Eunice stood on her porch and waved a frail hand high in the air as we drove away.

On our ride home I asked, "Nolay, why did you tell me stories about Miss Eunice? You know, about her being a witch or Soap Sally."

"Bones, I never told you no such stories about Miss Eunice. Soap Sally is an old swamp legend that's been passed around for generations."

"What about last time? We went out to her house on the airboat, and you came back and told me she was cooking up something in that big ol' pot in her front yard."

"She *was* cooking up something—she was boiling her clothes in it." Nolay looked over at me. "Good Lord, Bones, you sure got some things mixed up."

"But when you were tellin' me those Soap Sally stories, I thought you were talking about Miss Eunice."

"I had no idea you were thinkin' I was talkin' about ol' Miss Eunice. That would have been a harmful thing for me to do."

"Well, it was harmful. I thought she was a mean ol' witch and she's just a nice old lady, a lonely old lady. I brought my rifle out here thinking I might have to shoot her. That was a terrible thing for me to be thinking."

"Bones, you know I would never do anything to hurt you. I was just funnin' with you, that's all."

Funnin' with me? Nolay's words circled around me. Why would Nolay think it was fun to make me think there was a scary old witch living out in the swamps? I had always believed everything he told me. "Nolay, do you remember when I was little and you told me I was a boy but lightning struck me and turned me into a girl? You said if I could kiss the back of my elbow I would turn back into a boy. I nearly broke my arm trying to do that. Why do you tell me such stories?"

Nolay didn't reply. It was like my question had stunned us into silence. I couldn't ever remember a time when Nolay didn't have an answer.

Finally I turned and said, "If there's no such thing as Soap Sally, what did I see out in the woods?"

"I don't know, Bones; sometimes our imagination has a way of playing tricks on us. Then again, there are a lot of things living in the swamps. I'm sure there are things out there that we haven't met yet. I wish I had better answers for you, but I don't."

I folded my arms across my chest and gazed out the window. Sitting in the truck cab with my daddy by my side, I felt like I didn't have the sense God gave a piece of rope. How could I have been so stupid?

All the way home, Nolay's stories bounced and rolled around inside my head like a handful of marbles, each one hurting a little more than the last.

waiting

Sunday, Mama got a calling, and we ended up sitting for a few hours at the Bethany Baptist Church listening to Preacher Jenkins lecture on the wonders of being saved by the Holy Ghost. Along with about half of the congregation, I almost dozed off a couple of times, only to be rudely awakened by the preacher banging his Bible on the pulpit. He did this periodically, not only to make a point but to ensure everyone in church was wide awake and receiving his message.

Afterward, while Mama was talking with some of the ladies, I had a chance to tell Little Man about meeting Miss Eunice. "You were right, Little Man, she's just a nice old lady. I can't believe what I was thinking. But I could swear there was something out in that shed a couple of times. And I plumb forgot to ask Miss Eunice about it, I got so involved hearing her stories and all."

"Like I told you before, Bones, just 'cause you heard or smelled something don't mean it had to be a witch."

"But why did Nolay tell me such a thing?"

"It ain't all that bad. Mr. Nolay is just like that, he didn't mean no harm. Everybody gets fooled sometimes."

"Well, I sure did get fooled. But I can guarantee you it won't happen again."

Mama walked over and said, "Come on, Bones, we need to get back home."

On the ride home Mama said, "Bones, I hope you're not mad at your daddy for telling you that story about Soap Sally. I honestly think he had no idea you really believed him or thought he was talking about Miss Eunice."

"She's a nice old lady and we could have been friends all this time instead of me thinking she was an evil witch. How could I have been so stupid to believe something like that?"

"You're not stupid. Your daddy can be pretty convincing sometimes, but I think he's learned a good lesson. He didn't realize how much you believed his stories. I'm sure he understands now."

"I'm not mad, I just don't know what to believe anymore."

Monday when I got home from school, I changed out of my dress and slipped on my favorite dungarees. I grabbed the wishbone that I had got at Little Man's house. I had polished it to a sheen and tied a piece of blue ribbon around the top. I went in the kitchen and placed the wishbone on the table and showed it to Mama. "I'm going to give this to Mr. Speed for a present. We won't pull it apart and break it; that way the two of us can wish on it together for a lot of different things. Maybe if we wish hard enough, all our wishes will come true."

"That's nice, Bones. I know he will appreciate it."

"Can I go down and give it to him now?"

"Of course you can."

I walked as fast as I could to the Last Chance. I couldn't wait to tell Mr. Speed all about my visit with Miss Eunice.

But when I turned the corner to the store, Mr. Speed's bench was empty. I went inside and found Norbert, Mr. Ball's brother, behind the counter. "Hey, Mr. Norbert, do you know where Mr. Speed is?"

"Well, Bones, all I know, he's having a bad spell and his mama and daddy took him up to Gainesville to the veterans hospital."

"Is he sick? Is he gonna be all right?"

"Bones, I cain't say. All I know is they asked me and the missus to come watch the store till they get back. But I'm sure he'll be fine."

When I got back to our house, Nolay was busy out in the yard loading boxes into the back of the truck. I followed him back and forth from the house to the truck, asking him question after question. "Do you think Mr. Speed'll be all right? What is a veterans hospital? What kind of hospital did they take him to?"

Beads of sweat stood out on Nolay's forehead as he loaded up the boxes. He answered impatiently. "A veterans hospital is where they take people that have served in the military. Bones, you know Speed got injured in the war."

"I know that. But what are they gonna do with him up there?"

"Now, that I don't know. Maybe he's just there for a checkup. Ain't nothing gonna happen to ol' Speed. Not much worse could happen to 'em than already has. Don't worry; he'll be back sittin' on his bench before you know it."

"You promise? You promise he'll be back soon?"

"I promise. Now grab that box over there and help me load up the truck."

"Yes, sir, Nolay. I just got to run in and put this wishbone in a safe place. I'll be right back." I ran to my room and placed the wishbone in a special place on top of my dresser.

Tuesday morning when I got on the school bus and sat down next to Little Man, I said, "Did you know that Mr. Speed went to the veterans hospital?"

"How do you know?"

"Because Mr. Norbert is taking care of the store. I hope he's just there for a checkup or something."

"Yeah, me too. I'm sure he'll be back soon."

"I hope you're right."

And that night at supper I asked, "Has anyone heard any more about Mr. Speed? Will he be home soon?"

Mama answered, "Nothing yet. But Bones, he's in a very good hospital. They will take good care of him."

I turned to Nolay. "Has the sheriff got back to you about all his investigating? It's been weeks. Shouldn't he have found out something by now?"

Nolay answered, "Bones, you sure are full of questions lately. I'm sure he's doin' the best he can. Like he said, we just gotta be patient."

"But Nolay, has he ever had something this big to solve before? Maybe we need some help. You know, someone a little faster."

"You got any suggestions on someone faster?"

"No, sir, it's just I ain't sure about Sheriff LeRoy."

"Ain't nothing wrong with LeRoy. He'll do just fine."

"I sure hope so."

But I had serious doubts about the sheriff's po-lease work and his investigations. I was beginning to think he was even slower than pond water, if that was possible.

The next morning when I woke up, my throat felt like someone had been in there scraping it with sandpaper. I could hardly swallow, and my head felt like someone was inside banging it with a hammer.

Mama walked into my bedroom, took one look at me, and said, "Oh, my goodness. You do not look well." She sat down beside me and laid her hand on my forehead. "Bones, you are burning up."

"I don't feel good, Mama. I just want to stay in bed." I rolled over and snuggled up with my teddy bear. Mama and Nolay had given him to me for my birthday when I was one year old, and I had had him on my bed ever since.

Mama went and got her thermometer and stuck it under my tongue. When she pulled it out, she said, "Oh my, one hundred and two." Then she said, "Bones, you stay right here, I am going to get your daddy."

Mama didn't have to tell me to stay, because it took all the strength I had just to roll over on my side. When Mama returned, not only did she have Nolay with her, she also had a piece of cut-up flannel and her trusty jar of Vicks VapoRub. She rolled me over, unbuttoned my pajama top, and proceeded to rub my chest and throat with Vicks. As the menthol seeped into my skin, its strong smell snaked its way up my nose. As much as I disliked Vicks VapoRub, it did have somewhat of a soothing effect.

I slept through most of the day. Late afternoon after Mama took my temperature, she called Nolay into my room. "Good Lord, look at this, it's one hundred and three!"

Nolay replied, "I'll go down to the Last Chance and call for Doc Hayes to come out here soon as he can."

Mama left the room and came back in carrying a small jar filled with a golden yellow liquid. I knew what that was, and if I could have, I would have jumped up and run away into the swamps. She sat down on the side of the bed. "Now, Bones, you just relax and open your mouth so I can swab this on your throat."

The flaming sour taste of kerosene mixed with sugar slid around my mouth and down my throat. This was another of Mama's trusty cure-alls. But if it actually cured anything, it was only because it made you want to get well faster.

Mama rubbed my chest with more Vicks and wrapped me

up like a mummy. All that night when I woke up, either Mama or Nolay would be sitting in a chair by my bed.

That evening, Doc Hayes came in my room. I had only seen him one other time, years ago, when I was sick with the mumps, but he still looked just the same. And it looked like he had on exactly the same clothes. I had no idea how old Doc Hayes was, but he had to be older than dirt, because there was not one patch of skin on his body that was not wrinkled. A pair of little round glasses stuck out on the end of his pink pickle nose. I had serious doubts that he could actually see anything past that huge nose.

He opened his little black bag and began taking out instruments. He took my temperature, listened to my heart, and performed some more doctor stuff. "She's got a mighty bad case of tonsillitis Keep the Vicks on 'er so it won't go down in 'er lungs and turn into pneumonia. I'll give her a shot of penicillin and be back next week."

For the next nine days, I stayed in bed drifting in and out of sleep. Mama rubbed Vicks on my body and swabbed my aching throat with the sugary kerosene. She would wake me up and give me one of her concoctions to drink and say, "Bones, this will help you sleep." Or, "Bones, this will lower the fever." She had a never-ending supply of drinks and cure-alls, and she and Nolay continued to take turns sitting with me.

One time Miss Melba was there. She reached out and

placed a cool hand on my arm. "Bones, we're having a prayer vigil at church for you. You'll be well soon."

Another time, I woke up to find Little Man standing there. "Hey, Bones, I hope you'll be better soon."

"Me too." My voice came out sounding like a croak.

The days and nights ran into each other and became so twisted together I couldn't tell one from the other. I would toss and turn and wake up in a cold sweat. Someone would be there with a soft hand or a cold washcloth to lay on my forehead or rub across my face.

I would wake up and ask anyone that could hear, "Did the sheriff come by?"

"No, Bones, not yet."

"Is Mr. Speed back home?"

"No, Bones, he's still gone."

Strange dreams mingled with nightmares and wandered around inside my sleep. I saw me and Mr. Speed running down a road filled with tiny shining stars. He kept pointing at them and saying, "Look, it's shining, it's shining." The scars on his head were gone and a full smile spread across his face. There was Martha and Ruthie holding their little kittens and Sheriff LeRoy standing in a pond watching that dead man's leg hopping around in the swamp, looking for the rest of its body. I chased after Nolay's red bandanna as it drifted out over the swamps like a little kite. I would wake up in a cold sweat only to drift back into a restless sleep.

On Friday morning I woke up, and my stomach announced

that it was hungry. My throat was still sore, but at least I could swallow again. I was able to walk into the kitchen and eat some breakfast and eat again at noon dinner. That night I got out of bed, took a steaming-hot shower, and had supper with Mama and Nolay.

Mama looked across the table at me. "Bones, it is so good to have you back here with us. I can't tell you how worried we were."

Nolay agreed. "Yep, it's been mighty quiet around here without our little chatterbox."

"I'm glad to be feeling good, too. It is not fun being sick."

I turned to Nolay. "Has the sheriff come by? Have you heard from him?"

"Not yet, Bones. But soon as he has some information, he'll be stopping by."

"But it's been so long."

"Bones, it's only been a month. I know that can seem like a long time, especially at ten years old. But just be patient. LeRoy will be by soon enough."

"And what about Mr. Speed, has there been any news? When is he coming back?"

Mama replied, "Bones, every time I go to the Last Chance, Mr. Norbert tells us that as far as he knows, everything is all right. Remember, no news is good news."

"Maybe so, but I sure wish I would hear something."

Saturday morning was my first complete day up and out of bed. When I walked outside, I felt the sunshine wrap around and hug me. I spent most of the day playing with the animals and drinking up the fresh air and sunshine. All the while I was sick, Little Man had been stopping by to drop off my schoolwork. It took most of Sunday for me to catch up on everything. But at least that way I wouldn't be behind when I got back to class.

I had been sick in bed so long that I was actually looking forward to school.

angels

Monday morning I was up and ready to go. On the bus ride to school, Little Man brought me up to date on everything I had missed for nearly the past two weeks. And from the sounds of it, I had not missed much.

When I walked into the classroom and handed Miss Watts all my schoolwork, she said, "Why, Bones, I am so proud of you. Not everyone could catch up on this much missed work. I'm glad you are back with us. Everyone missed you." She looked out over the classroom. "Isn't that right, class?"

Everyone answered in unison, "Yes, ma'am, Miss Watts."

I looked down at my shoes and mumbled, "Thank you, ma'am, I'm glad to be back, too."

I turned and walked to my desk, and my eyes bumped straight into Betty Jean Davis. I was almost glad to see her until she stuck her pointed pink tongue out at me.

When I got home that afternoon, Nolay and Mama were sitting on the living room couch. Mama told me, "Bones, go change out of your school clothes. Then come in here. We have something to talk to you about."

I was curious but quickly ran to my room, took off my dress, and slipped into my dungarees. I went into the living room and sat in Mama's childhood rocking chair. There was a mistiness floating around Mama's face. When Nolay looked at me, his eyes were the dull blue of a rain cloud.

He took a deep breath. "Bones, I got something to tell you. And I wish I didn't, but I gotta tell you. This morning Mr. Speed passed away. He died."

I cocked my head. "Nolay, are you lying to me?"

"No, Bones, I ain't lying."

"Are you telling me a tale, then?"

"Bones, I ain't lying. I ain't telling you a tale. I sure wish I was. But I ain't. His mama and daddy sent word this morning."

I slowly stood up and looked at both of them. Nolay's blue eyes stared down at the floor, but Mama's green ones looked straight at me, all soft and shimmering, like the surface of a lake.

"Well, I don't believe you. I don't believe a word you're saying. Mr. Speed is coming home. You promised. You promised he would be back home soon. I should have known better. All you do is lie to me."

Nolay raised his head and looked at me. I could see that my words had cut into him like little daggers.

I walked to my room. Nippy was asleep in Pearl's old box in the corner. Now that autumn was on us, she slept most of the day and prowled most of the night. I picked her up and lay down on my bed. I hugged her warm furry body close to me. She looked at me with glassy black eyes and placed her little humanlike hands on my face. Safe in my arms, she began to purr like a contented kitten.

A crushing feeling wrapped around me like a snake, till I could hardly breathe. Right then and there, I decided to build a protective cocoon. I would build it just like I had watched the caterpillars do. I would start at my feet, spinning and twisting, strand by strand, right up over my head. It would be so strong that nothing could get inside. Not sadness, not memories, nothing painful. It would be invisible, and it would keep me safe.

The next afternoon, Mama was taking a platter of food over to Mr. Speed's house. "Bones, would you like to come with me?"

"No, ma'am, I don't want to go over there."

"You know, it might be good if you visited with Mr. and Mrs. Ball. Sometimes it helps being with people who feel the same as you do."

"I don't want to go. I don't want go over there."

"I know your heart is broken, Bones. I wish I could make it all go away, but I can't."

The rest of the week, Little Man and I sat on the school bus together, not saying a word. Our grief and unspoken words piled up like two ragged mountains with a deep valley running between them. Before I got off the bus on Friday, he said, "I'll see you tomorrow at the funeral, Bones."

Saturday morning Mama came in my room. "You can wear your dungarees if you want."

"Yes, ma'am."

"Bones, I know you are suffering. We all are. I wish you would talk about it."

"I don't have anything to say."

When we drove up to Bethany Baptist Church, we could hardly find parking. At the front door we were bathed in the rich sounds of church hymns. Before I entered I took a deep breath and squeezed my arms around my chest to make sure nothing could seep through my cocoon. I walked in between Nolay and Mama. Little Man sat with his family in one of the pews. We glanced at each other. His face was flushed, like he had been at the beach all day, and his big brown eyes were rimmed with red.

Sitting at the end of that same pew was the huge body of Sheriff LeRoy. He had his uniform on, but his Stetson sat in his lap.

The morning sun peeked through the small stained-glass windows, scattering broken rainbows across the room. A bronze-colored coffin surrounded by big bouquets of flowers stretched out in front of Preacher Jenkins's podium. Like a giant pried-open clam, the coffin stood half open.

As we walked down the aisle, Mama slipped her hand in mine. I stood beside the coffin and poked my head up through my cocoon and looked inside. The top half of Mr. Speed rested on a puffy white cloud of cloth; he looked like he was taking a nap. His head was turned in such a way that it didn't look lopsided anymore.

He was dressed in a fancy green army uniform. Brass buttons ran down the front, and two bright medals were pinned on the left pocket. A hat with a rim as shiny as a black mirror rested on his chest.

My eyes swept over his face, but I didn't recognize him. It wasn't Mr. Speed. It didn't even look like him. The body laying in all that whiteness looked like a little girl's doll. The skin was dull and waxy. It wasn't real, wasn't alive. This was nobody I knew.

I felt Mama squeeze my hand. Nolay placed his arm around my shoulders and gently turned me around. As we walked away, I saw Mr. Speed's mama and daddy sitting in the front pew. I looked at their faces and saw that they had built cocoons, too.

I looked to the back of the church, where the beautiful music was coming from. One side of the church was filled with colored people. Dressed in their Sunday finest, they sat in chairs and stood along the walls. Like reeds blowing in a gentle breeze, their bodies swayed together as they sang and hummed hymns. Their voices floated out and filled the room with an unbearable sadness.

Nolay led us to a pew and I sat between him and Mama. Before long, Preacher Jenkins took his place at the podium and started to speak. "Brothers and sisters, we are gathered here today to remember our beloved son. . . ."

That was all I heard. I closed my eyes and pulled deep inside myself. My mind wandered back to the Last Chance, to a time when me and Mr. Speed sat together on the bench. His lopsided head wobbled back and forth as he told me, "They done made a camera that can take a picture without film; it's called a Po-lee-roid. Yes, sir, a Po-lee-roid."

"How can that be?" I said. "Where does the picture come from?"

"Pops right out the front on a little piece of paper, a little piece of paper."

I laughed. "Now, that sure does sound interesting. I wish I could see one of those."

A woman began to wail and I jolted back into my body sitting on the hard wooden pew at the funeral service. The sound, like that of a wounded animal, ripped through my cocoon. It grew and groaned up from a deep, dark place. A bottomless black pond filled with memories, a place where I did not want to go.

The wailing continued. I squeezed my eyes shut and let the hymns the colored people were singing fill my ears. Colored people didn't attend white churches—they had their own—but I reckon Preacher Jenkins allowed them here today to honor Mr. Speed, and I sure was glad. Their voices blended and moved through the room like a soothing current of water.

I felt Nolay's hand squeeze mine. When I looked up, the coffin, draped in an American flag, was being carried down the aisle by four men in green Army uniforms. Everyone got up and walked outside. We stood and silently watched as they slid the coffin into the back of a black hearse.

Sheriff LeRoy's car was parked in front of the hearse. He opened the door, squeezed inside, put his flashing red light on, and led the way. We all got in our cars and snaked along behind the hearse. I couldn't stop my mind from thinking about why Sheriff LeRoy was here and not out doing his po-lease work. Why was no one in his rightful place? LeRoy should have been out hunting murderers, and Mr. Speed should have been sitting on his bench, not lying in a box.

Two chairs were in front of the grave site so Mr. Speed's mama and daddy had a place to sit. We walked up and stood behind them.

The coffin was placed over a dark gaping mouth dug in the earth. Two soldiers lifted the flag off the coffin and carefully folded it into a perfect triangle.

One of the soldiers walked up to Mr. Speed's mama and handed it to her, as gentle as though it were a newborn baby. She held it in both hands and clutched it to her heart. Mr. Speed's daddy put his arms around her and the two of them curled into each other's grief.

As I watched them, I realized something. That flag, folded in a triangle, was all that was left of their only child and one of my best friends.

The sound of a bugle broke the quietness. Its sad, beautiful notes felt like the fluttering of angel wings. The wings brushed and beat against the sides of my cocoon, trying to find a way inside. I threw my arms around Nolay and buried my face in his side.

On the ride back home, Mama wrapped her arm around me and kept saying, "It will be okay, Bones, it will be okay."

But it wasn't okay; my body felt like I had swallowed a rock and it was stuck in my heart.

When we reached home, I went to my room, strapped on my Roy Roger pistols, grabbed my .22, and tucked a sleepy Nippy under my arm. Nolay and Mama were in the kitchen. Nolay looked at me and asked, "Goin' someplace?"

"Yes, sir, I'm leavin', and I don't know when I'll be back."

Mama said, "Bones, you can't run away from your feelings. Just sit down and we can talk about it."

"Mama, I don't want to talk about anything. I just want to go away and never come back."

Nolay looked at Mama, then back at me. "Got anyplace in mind?"

"I don't know. A secret place. I'm taking Nippy and Pearl with me. And Harry can come along if he wants."

"How long you reckon you'll be gone?"

"I don't know. But I know one thing: I ain't never goin' to the Last Chance again. Never."

"Well, I hope you won't be gone too long, 'cause me and Mama sure would be lonesome without you."

"I don't care. I might never be back again."

Outside I found Pearl resting under her favorite tree. Nippy finally woke up enough so I could put her on the ground. Harry pranced alongside Pearl as we walked toward the opposite side of the swamp. At the edge of the scrub pines lived a majestic old cedar tree. Nolay told me that his daddy had planted it when Nolay was just a little boy.

Like a green mountain, the top of the tree stretched toward the sky. Its heavy limbs cascaded down, almost touching the ground. Under its fragrant branches, a smooth carpet of soft gray moss covered the earth. It was my secret place.

I crawled in and curled up against the huge solid trunk. Pearl grunted her little pig sounds and plopped down beside me. Nippy and Harry scrambled around, looking for something to eat. The soft shade folded around me and I drifted off to sleep.

I woke up to the wet noses of Paddlefoot, Silver, and Mr. Jones against my face. They wagged their tails and tripped over my legs. Mr. Jones stepped on Pearl. She let out a squeal, stood up, and head-butted him in the side. Through all the commotion, I thought I heard Mama's voice outside.

"Bones, are you in there?"

"Yes, ma'am."

"Is it all right if I come inside?"

"Yes, ma'am."

Mama crawled under the branches and leaned up against the trunk beside me.

"How did you know where I was?" I said.

"The dogs always know where you are. I just followed them." She looked around and took a deep breath. "This is a magical place, isn't it?"

She reached over, wrapped both arms around me, and pulled me close to her, and just like that, the thin walls of my cocoon unraveled and spilled around me like useless threads. My body began to shake as the tears poured out. Mama squeezed me tight as I sobbed, "It ain't fair. It just ain't fair.

God is so mean; I'm so mad at him. And I'm so mad at Nolay. He lied to me; he told me nothing would happen to Mr. Speed. He promised he would be back home soon. He promised and now Mr. Speed's dead and buried in a hole in the ground. And I won't ever see him again."

Mama gently rocked me back and forth. "Bones, I know you are hurt and angry. I know you want to blame someone. But you can't blame your daddy. He didn't cause anything to happen to Mr. Speed. You can't blame God; you can't blame anybody."

"But why did God take Mr. Speed away? He never hurt anybody. He was my friend."

Mama reached inside her pants pocket, pulled out a small white handkerchief, and gently wiped the tears from my face.

"And Mama, if God took Mr. Speed away, is he going to take Nolay away, too? Is he going to let him be put in the electric chair?"

"Shhh, Bones, don't talk like that. Don't think like that. God is good. You have to trust that all this will work out."

"But why did he take Mr. Speed?"

"I don't know why, Bones. All I know is that sometimes God sends special people to the earth. They bring joy and happiness to everyone around them, and then God calls them back home."

"You mean sort of like an angel?"

"I guess you could call it that."

"Mama, do you think Mr. Speed was an angel here on earth?"

"I think Mr. Speed was a very special person. He made our world a happier place to live in."

"I miss him. I wish God would have let him stay here with us."

"I know you miss him. I wish he could have stayed here with us, too."

Mama hugged me close to her warm body. She hummed a lullaby that she used to sing to me when I was a baby. I felt her breath going in and out; I listened to the soft, steady rhythm of her heart.

As we sat under the soothing shelter and breathed in the tree's fragrant scent, its huge limbs creaked and moaned with a life all their own.

I looked up at Mama's face. "Do you think I'll see Mr. Speed again, up in heaven?"

"Yes, I do, Bones; I do believe you will see him again."

"I hope so."

Pearl got up and waddled over to my side. She stuck her snout close to my face and began to snort and snuffle. "Mama, you know what, it's getting late. Maybe we should start heading back home. Pearl's telling me she's mighty hungry."

"That sounds like a good idea, Bones. Your daddy and I would just be too lonesome without you. And my goodness, what would all these animals do if you left them?" I did not say a word, because there just wasn't an answer to a question like that.

I was ready to go back home; I just wasn't ready for our next visitor.

po-lease work

Me and Mama didn't go to church on Sunday, and I sure was glad, because I didn't want to go back there anytime soon. All day I kept wanting to go down to the Last Chance and sit with Mr. Speed so I could feel better. But I would never be able to do that again.

For the next couple of days, when me and Little Man rode the school bus, I looked out the window as we passed the Last Chance. Mr. Speed's bench sat empty, like an abandoned island.

One afternoon on our ride back home, I looked out to see two men sitting on the bench. "Look, Little Man, someone's sitting on Mr. Speed's bench. They shouldn't be doing that."

"Bones, Mr. Speed ain't here no more. Ain't no reason why someone else can't sit there. I don't think he'd mind at all."

"It just don't seem right."

"You know what? I think you and me should go sit there one day. I think Mr. Speed would like that."

"You really think so?"

"Yep, I sure do."

"I'll have to think about that."

Wednesday evening we were just sitting down for supper in a kitchen filled with flickering kerosene lights and the aroma of fried chicken, when the dogs began to bark. Two smoky headlight beams sliced through the night, coming up our driveway.

I got up from the table and said, "I'll go see who it is."

From our living room I peered out into the darkness, and what I saw sitting in our driveway nearly took my breath away. It wasn't Ironhead or Mr. Cotton, it was Sheriff LeRoy in his patrol car. What was he doing here at this time of night? All I could think of was he was here to take Nolay away. I turned and ran back into the kitchen. I rushed up to Nolay and in a whisper said, "Nolay, it's Sheriff LeRoy, you got to run away! Quick, you got to run out to the swamps and hide! I'll go tell him you're not here. You got—"

Nolay turned and placed both hands on my shoulders. "Bones, what are you talking about? Have you gone crazy?"

"Nolay, he's come to get you! He's going to take you away! He's going to take you back to jail! He's got evidence! He's got—"

Nolay tightened his grip on my shoulders. "Bones, you get ahold of yourself. That's foolish talk." He pointed to my chair. "You get over there and sit down. I'll go let LeRoy in. I ain't running away from any man."

Nolay got up and went outside. I sat down and looked at Mama. Her gaze stretched across the table and rested on me.

"I know you are scared, but you have to believe your daddy is innocent."

"I'm trying. I just don't want him to die, Mama. I just don't want him to be gone forever, like Mr. Speed."

A few minutes later, Nolay and Sheriff LeRoy strolled into the kitchen. The sheriff took his oversized Stetson off and held it in both hands. "Evening, Miss Lori."

"Good evening, LeRoy. We were just sitting down for supper. Come join us."

"Thank you, ma'am. I ain't hungry, but I would appreciate a glass of that sweet tea, if it ain't a bother."

"No bother at all, LeRoy. Sit down and make yourself comfortable."

Sheriff LeRoy eased his bulky frame into one of the chairs at the end of the table. His massive body nearly filled the entire back wall of our kitchen. Carefully he placed his Stetson on the floor. Like an old dog looking for a comfortable spot, he twisted and turned until his body finally settled into the too-small chair.

Mama placed a big glass of honey-colored tea in front of him and asked, "So, what brings you out here this evening?"

Slowly and deliberately, LeRoy crossed his huge arms, took a deep breath, and said, "Well, ma'am, like I said before, I had some ideas, and I wanted to do some investigatin', so I took a little trip down to Dade County." LeRoy stopped and took a sip of tea. He looked at the glass, and a wide smile broke out on his face. "That sure is good tea, Miss Lori."

"Thank you, LeRoy." Mama picked up her fork and poked at a piece of chicken.

"Now, when I first got down there, them city po-lease didn't want to give me the time of day, treated me like I was dumb as a stick. But me being a sheriff and all, they couldn't refuse to hep with my investigation." LeRoy eyed the pile of golden fried chicken sitting in the middle of the table. "That chicken sure does smell good, Miss Lori."

"Let me fix you a plate, LeRoy." Mama put several pieces of chicken on a plate. "Would you like some mashed potatoes?"

"Well, yes, ma'am, I wouldn't mind a little bit."

"And how about some butter beans and a biscuit to go with that?"

"Well, if it ain't too much trouble."

"No trouble at all." Mama placed the heaping plate of food in front of LeRoy and sat back down.

Silently, LeRoy munched on a drumstick. The room filled with the clinking of LeRoy's fork scraping across his plate. Nolay's and Mama's forks were hanging in midair.

Nolay cleared his throat and asked, "So, LeRoy, how did that investigation of yours go?"

LeRoy put his drumstick down, slowly wiped his mouth with a napkin, and said, "Well, like I said, them city boys treated me like a dumb kid, but they had to hep me. So first off, I wanted to know a little more about that fella Fowler they found up here dead. Him and that other fella, Decker, were partners, and I wanted to know what they were up to."

Sheriff LeRoy picked up the drumstick and gnawed it clean to the bone. He finished his mashed potatoes and butter beans, wiped his plate with the biscuit, and contentedly leaned back in the small chair. "That sure was good, Miss Lori. I ain't had home-cooked food like that since my mama passed away."

"I'm glad you enjoyed it, LeRoy." Patiently, Mama pushed a butter bean around in circles on her plate. "Do continue with your story."

"Yes, ma'am. Now, where was I? Oh yeah, it turns out that Fowler and Decker were in cahoots with each other, buying and selling land. They'd buy up a piece real cheap, then run a advertisement in a paper up north somewhere, saying it was waterfront property or some such nonsense. Had 'em quite a business going on." LeRoy stopped and took a long swig of his tea. He smacked his lips together and slowly continued his story.

"Well, sir, after a little investigatin' on my part, I come to find out that Fowler—that's the dead guy—that his wife had took out a fifty-thousand-dollar life insurance policy on her husband not two weeks before he went missin'. Now, that struck me as peculiar. When I told one of those city detectives about it, he felt the same way."

Nolay and Mama both put their forks down and leaned in toward Sheriff LeRoy.

Nolay said, "So then what happened?"

LeRoy drained his glass and set it down. Mama picked up the pitcher of tea and refilled his glass.

"Thank you, Miss Lori. Well, after what me and this detective found out, seemed like the attention of the rest of those city po-lease perked up." He stared at the plate mounded with brown-topped biscuits. "Miss Lori, if it ain't a bother, I sure would like another one a them biscuits. Besides my mama's, that is about the softest biscuit I have ever had."

Mama jumped like she had just been stung by a bee. "Of course, LeRoy, have all you want." She pushed the plate in front of him. "And here, have some more tea." She grabbed the pitcher and poured tea into LeRoy's nearly full glass. The golden liquid flowed over the top, ran down the sides, and sent little rivulets across the table and over the side. "Oh, my goodness, I am so sorry, LeRoy."

Me and Nolay sat there as still as stones.

Mama shot a glance in our direction, snatched a dish towel, and began wiping up the tea. "LeRoy, I'm not sure I understand exactly what you just said. Does this mean the Dade County police suspect the wife of killing her husband?"

"Not exactly. Being that she wadn't up here to actually commit the crime, she would have had to have someone else do it for her. Now, I don't think she knew anybody in these parts well enough to ask 'em to do something like that. About the closest person to her husband would have been his partner, Mister Decker."

LeRoy picked up a biscuit and stared at it as though he had been hypnotized by a carnival magician.

I sneaked a quick look at Nolay. He spread both hands on the table and said, "LeRoy, exactly what does all this mean? Do they suspect the wife or the partner, whatever his name is?"

LeRoy took his eyes off the biscuit long enough to say, "Decker, his name is Decker." Then he cleared his throat and continued. "Well, I ain't sure if the wife or Decker is considered a suspect, but it does mean that they will be investigatin' that possibility."

LeRoy chomped that biscuit in half. "Now, we all know that them two Yankees were here on your land and out back by the swamp with the Reems brothers. What I need is some solid evidence that links them together where that body was found. That is what I need, some solid evidence."

The sheriff consumed the rest of the biscuit and leaned back in his chair. "And Nolay, I want to make one thing crystal clear: that you are still the number-one prime suspect. Ain't nothing been cleared up. So you stick close by." The words "You are the number-one prime suspect" fell out of Sheriff LeRoy's mouth, dropped down on top of our kitchen table, and lay there like a dead fish.

Sheriff LeRoy got up from his chair, then sat back down. "There is one more thing. About that situation with Peckerhead Willy. First off, that occurred in my jurisdiction, so it don't concern them Dade County po-lease. I have come up with some evidence. There were footprints left at the scene. Appears there was some sort of commotion went on. One of 'em was barefoot. I have a pretty good idea where that barefoot one come from and where it went back to."

A thick silence filled the room. I watched as Nolay cocked his chin and said, "LeRoy, I know you take your work seriously, but I'm gonna ask you to leave that ol' boy alone. Charlie ain't capable of hurtin' nobody."

"I know what you're saying, but I got my job to do. I need

to ask a few questions is all. I have come up with some evidence, and there was more than one person involved."

"You think Charlie saw something or was involved in some way?"

"Not sure which, but I aim to find out. And Nolay, while we're on the subject, where were you the night that incident happened?"

"Out fishing."

"You can confirm that?"

"If need be."

Me and Mama exchanged a quick glance.

Nolay continued, "Could you tell me when you think you might be goin' over there to talk to Charlie?"

LeRoy closed his eyes, as if the answer were written on the inside of his eyelids. "I got some po-lease work to do. I ain't gonna be back for a couple of days. I'll be stopping by then. I can let you know beforehand if you want. You sure you want to be there?"

"I'm sure, LeRoy. And thanks again for all you're doin'."

"Just doin' my job." LeRoy picked up his Stetson and placed it squarely on his thick head. "I best be getting on my way now." His massive body squeaked and jingled as he twisted out of the small chair. "Miss Lori, I sure do thank you for the food. Y'all have a good night."

"You're welcome, LeRoy, and you have a good night, too."

Nolay got up and walked LeRoy out to his car.

I looked at Mama. "I reckon it's a good thing he wasn't hungry."

"Don't be rude, Bones." Then she shook her head and began to laugh. "My goodness, if he had been hungry he might have taken the food right off our plates! I must admit, LeRoy is an interesting man."

Me and Mama looked at each other across the table. "Mama, you know Ironhead said Nolay wasn't fishing with him that night. When you asked him about it, he said he was up in Jacksonville. Why did he tell the sheriff he was out fishing?"

"Hush, we'll talk about this another time."

Nolay walked back in. He stood in the middle of the kitchen, put his hands in his pockets, and said, "Well, am I right or am I right? Bones, what do you think? Ol' LeRoy might be slow as pond water, but it looks like he's stirrin' it up a little bit."

"Yes, sir, I reckon he's doing something, I'm just not quite sure what. All I know is it sure took him long enough to spill out that story."

Nolay shook his head. "You're right about that, LeRoy does take the long road when he's explainin' something. But by and by he gets to his destination."

"I just wish he could be quicker finding some 'solid evidence.' Whatever that means."

After me and Mama finished with the dishes, we went in the living room. Nolay had built a big fire in the fireplace. The room filled with the warm aroma of burning pine. Nolay was sitting on the couch. "Bones, Lori, y'all come on over here and sit down."

Nolay put one arm around me and the other around

Mama. We watched silently as blue and yellow tongues of flames leaped up and chased each other around the pine logs.

Mama was first to break the silence. "Nolay, what do you think all this means? Some of it makes perfect sense, and then LeRoy says you are still the prime suspect."

"Lori, at least LeRoy is investigatin'. I have a feeling he's sniffing out something. And I tell you what, I don't mind being the prime suspect for the time being, as long as I don't have to go back to jail. I think LeRoy is doing the best he can to see that that don't happen."

Nolay squeezed me and said, "Bones, how big is that baby rooster of Ikibob's?"

"It's gettin' to be a pretty good size. Big enough that Ikibob is starting to peck after it. You know how he is about another rooster being in his yard, even if it is his own son."

"How about tomorrow when you come home from school, me and you go pay Charlie a visit? I think we need to give him a little present."

cracked eggs

Thursday morning soon as I sat down next to Little Man on the school bus, I told him about the sheriff's visit. "I mean, I know he's doing something, but it seems like he could be doing more. I just wish he would hurry up."

"Bones, he's moving about as fast as he can. You gotta be patient."

"But he's so confusing. I mean, is he trying help Nolay with evidence or put him in jail with evidence?"

"The sheriff don't want no harm to come to Mr. Nolay."

"I hope you're right."

"Now, that part about the Yankee man's partner sounds right promising, but that part about Mr. Charlie sounds like a concern."

"I can't imagine Mr. Charlie hurting anyone, not even one of the Reems brothers."

"It don't sound right. I think the truth will uncover itself."

"Me and Nolay are going out to go visit Mr. Charlie today after school. I'll let you know what we find out."

"I sure am curious."

After school, I could hardly wait to jump off that school bus and run home. I went straight to my room and changed clothes. Nolay was outside chopping some firewood.

"Nolay, are you ready? I'll go get the little rooster."

"Let me finish up here and I'll meet you at the truck."

I went to the chicken coop and picked up the baby rooster. As I walked out with him under my arm, Ikibob cocked his big head and glared coldly in our direction. "Ikibob," I said, "you don't have to look at him so mean. You have not been very nice to him lately. I'm taking him to a place where he'll be loved and cared for, just like you are here." Ikibob blinked his stone-yellow eyes at me, shook his floppy red cockscomb, and strutted out into the yard.

Nolay and I got in the truck and headed to Charlie's. I clutched the young rooster close to my body to keep him calm. We rode along in silence; the truck tires crunched on top of dry sand, sending up little gray dust devils.

Nolay turned down the guava-tree tunnel to Charlie's house. As we pulled into the yard, the brown carpet of chickens split apart like a giant zipper.

Soon as Nolay tooted the horn, the screen door squeaked open and Charlie, dressed in his usual faded overalls, stepped out on the porch.

Nolay and I got out of the truck and walked up to the porch. Charlie's round, plump face broke into a huge grin as he recognized us. "Well, howdy, Nolay, Miz Bones. What brings y'all out this side?"

Nolay leaned up against the porch railing. "Howdy, Charlie. Me and Bones just stopped by to bring you a little present."

"A present? For me? Why, lordy now, y'all just come on up here and sit for a spell." Charlie gently picked up a fat brown hen sitting in a rickety cane chair and set her on the floor. "This here is Lorraine. She ain't nestin', she's just relaxin'." Charlie brushed off the chair's seat. "Miz Bones, you just sit yourself down right here. Nolay, you want me to get you a chair?"

"Naw, Charlie, I'm fine right here. Thank ya."

Charlie limped over to his well-used rocking chair and sat down. I walked over to him and held out the young rooster. "Mr. Charlie, this is one of Ikibob's babies. I know you been wanting one for a long time."

Charlie's eyes glistened with happiness. He carefully wrapped his thick hands around the rooster and held him up in front of his face. "Lordy, look at this fella, ain't he beautiful?" He sat the rooster in his lap and stroked its smooth feathers as though it were a puppy. "Thank you, Bones, thank you. This here is about the best present I ever did get in my whole life."

I sat down in my chair. Charlie continued to admire the little rooster. "I think he looks just like his daddy, don't you?"

"Yes, sir, I reckon he does. And from the looks of his size, I think he's gonna be just about as big."

Charlie nodded in agreement, the rows of fat under his neck jiggling in harmony. "I'm gonna name him Sonny. Sonny-Boy. And he's gonna stay in the house with me until he gets big enough to be boss of this here yard."

I looked out at the sea of chickens as they scratched, pecked, and clucked in the yard. "Mr. Charlie, do you have a name for every one of those chickens?"

"Well now, I do have to admit, there might be a few that I didn't get around to naming. But named or not, every one of 'em is special."

"I was wondering about something. What happens when they . . . you know . . . when they grow old and stuff?"

"You mean when they die? Well, of course that does happen. And when it does, I got a pit around the back of the house. I place 'em in there, real respectful like; sometimes I say a little prayer, then I cover 'em up with leaves and manure. I ain't never be able to eat any of 'em. Just their aigs. They're more like my friends and family. I could never bring myself to hurt one of 'em."

"You bury them in manure?"

"Now, Miz Bones, I know that might sound right strange. But what I do is just like my granddaddy taught me. Every day I rake up all the chicken droppins' in my yard and put 'em in that pit, along with any of my birds that has passed on. Before you know it, the good Lord melts it all down and turns it into the best fertilizer a person could use." Charlie reached down and repositioned the rooster in his ample lap. "Farmers come from all over to buy my fertilizer. I feel like my birds being mixed in with it, it's like giving 'em a chance to be part of life again. That's something my granddaddy passed on to me before he went to heaven."

Nolay placed his foot on one of the steps and leaned in toward the two of us. "Charlie, I been curious about something. You remember when we stopped by a couple months ago and ol' Peckerhead was here?"

Charlie looked down at the floor. "Yeah, I remember."

"Was he over here just visiting?"

"Yeah, he was just visiting."

"You sure about that, Charlie? 'Cause ol' Peckerhead didn't seem the neighborly type to just stop by for a visit."

Charlie kept his eyes down as he gently stroked the rooster in his lap.

Nolay said, "Charlie, what was ol' Peckerhead up to? Was he over here pestering you about something?"

Charlie looked up at Nolay. Wrinkles of concern crept across his pudgy face. "He had a paper. He said I had to sign it, that if I didn't, he'd burn my house down."

"What kind of paper?"

"It was a paper to try and make me sell this here land. He wanted my land. Told me I didn't need it. I could take the money and go live in a trailer somewhere." Charlie looked out over his yard full of chickens. "What would I do with all of 'em? If I didn't have this land, what would happen to 'em? They cain't live in no trailer."

"Charlie, this is your land, free and clear. You've lived here nearly all your life and cain't nobody take it away from you. Ol' Peckerhead was just trying to scare you and pull a fast one." Nolay leaned closer. "Charlie, the night Peckerhead got run over by that freight train, do you know anything about that?"

A flicker of fear crossed Charlie's face; he pressed his lips together and shook his head back and forth. Ripples of fat ran down his neck and disappeared into his overalls.

"Charlie, I'm here as your friend. Did you see something? Is there something you need to tell me?"

Charlie slowly looked up at Nolay again. "I did see something, but I cain't talk about it."

Nolay looked down at Charlie's bare feet. "Charlie, Sheriff LeRoy is coming out here to talk to you."

"Oh Lordy, I don't want to talk to him. I have done something bad." Charlie looked at me with a face as sad as an old hound dog's.

"Miz Bones, you done come and give me this fine rooster, and I just don't deserve it." Charlie's voice squeaked as he continued. "I sure am sorry. I know what I done was wrong. I shoulda told the sheriff what I seen. But I just couldn't, I just couldn't." He hung his huge head and softly said, "I ain't no better than a cracked aig. Ain't no good for nothin'. Just an ol' cracked aig."

Nolay shook his head. "Now, Charlie, I don't want you to be feelin' that way. I'm sure you had your reasons. I'm gonna set it up so I'll be around when the sheriff comes out here. We'll talk it out and set everything straight. You hear me, Charlie? We'll work everything out."

Nolay looked at me. "Bones, we best be headin' back now."

As I got up to leave, Charlie said to me, "Miz Bones, if you don't want me to keep this here rooster, you can have 'im back."

"Why, no, sir, Mr. Charlie, that's your rooster. And I know Sonny-Boy is gonna be mighty happy living here with you."

"Thank ya, Miz Bones. I sure am proud to have 'im."

"And Mr. Charlie, you ain't no cracked egg. You're just about the finest Humpty Dumpty I could ever imagine."

Charlie looked at me and laughed, his round belly jiggling like Jell-O under his overalls. "Why, thank you, Miz Bones, I sure will take that as a compliment."

As Nolay slowly pulled the truck out of the front yard, I looked out the window. Charlie sat in his old rocking chair, the little rooster perched contentedly in his lap.

On the way home I asked Nolay, "Do you think Mr. Charlie was involved in killing ol' Peckerhead?"

"Naw, I don't think that."

"Do you think he saw something he shouldn't have?"

"It appears that way."

"Nolay, if you knew who killed Peckerhead, would you let Mr. Charlie go to jail or the electric chair?"

Nolay glanced at me. "What kind of fool question is that?"

"Well, if you know he didn't do it but maybe you know who did do it . . . well . . . I don't know."

Nolay shook his head. "Bones, I don't know, either. If I knew who killed that ol' scallywag, I'd tell the sheriff. All I know is that old man don't deserve nothing harmful to come to him. I've known Charlie all my life, knew him when his grandparents were still alive. Ain't never heard Charlie say a mean word against anyone."

"Yes, sir, I feel the same way." I turned and looked out the window. My reflection stared back at me. Questions were bubbling up in my mind like a shook-up bottle of Coca-Cola. Who did Charlie see out there? Why didn't he want to tell us? Would he tell Sheriff LeRoy?

the tea party

Friday morning on the bus ride to school I filled Little Man in on the visit with Mr. Charlie. "I swear, Little Man, Mr. Charlie was almost shaking with fear when he told Nolay about Peckerhead coming over and threatening him."

"But why would ol' Peckerhead want to scare Mr. Charlie off his land?"

"Probably because those Reems brothers wanted to sell it. Like those Yankee men wanted to try and buy up our land."

"Still don't make much sense if you ask me."

"Little Man, not much of anything is making sense anymore. Sometimes I feel like I'm on some kind of roller-coaster ride. Everything just goes up and down. You never know what's going to happen next."

Little Man had that question mark sitting in the middle of his forehead when he looked at me. But he did nod in agreement.

• • •

Saturday morning when I woke up I looked over at the wishbone with the blue ribbon tied around it, still lying on top of my dresser. I picked it up and took it in the kitchen. Mama had just sat down with a cup of coffee and a Lucky Strike.

"Mama, you remember I made this for Mr. Speed? I was going to give it to him for a present. Do you think it would be all right if I gave it to his mama and daddy?"

Mama tilted her head. "I think that is a wonderful idea. I'm sure they would appreciate it."

I walked to the Last Chance. As usual, Mr. Ball stood behind the front counter. I went up and placed the shiny turkey bone on the counter. "Mr. Ball, I made this for Mr. Speed as a present, and, well, I thought you and Miss Evelyn might like it. It was going to be something we could wish on together."

Mr. Ball leaned on the counter with both elbows and picked up the wishbone. It was the first time I had seen him since the funeral. Dark half-circles sat below his deep-set eyes. "Why, thank you, Bones. I know Speed would have enjoyed this." He continued to look at the bone as if it were speaking to him. Then he said, "Bones, let's me and you take it over and give it to his mama."

I followed Mr. Ball to the little room where Miss Evelyn spent most of her time when she was in the store.

A long, thin lightbulb attached to the top of the ceiling bathed the small room in a harsh glare. On one side sat a desk stacked with papers, a bulky adding machine, and a typewriter. On the opposite side a tall rectangular filing cabinet stood like a tin soldier.

When we entered the room, Miss Evelyn swiveled around

on her chair, a look of surprise on her face. Mr. Ball walked over and held the wishbone out to her. "Evelyn, little Bones here made this for Speed, as a gift. And now she wants to give it to you and me. Wasn't that thoughtful?"

Miss Evelyn cautiously reached for the wishbone, as though it might be a hot coal. I noticed her face had the same tired look as Mama's when Nolay was in jail, only more so. She held the little bone in her hand and ran her fingers across the blue ribbon. I saw her eyes begin to glisten.

I looked up at Mr. Ball, but his face was blank as a biscuit. I turned back to Miss Evelyn. "I sure am sorry if I made you sad. I just thought . . . well, I'm not sure what, but I guess I thought you might like it."

Miss Evelyn blinked, as if seeing me for the first time. She said, "Why, Bones, you haven't made me sad at all. This is a lovely gift, and I appreciate you bringing it to us. I know Speed would have loved it."

"Yes, ma'am, I think Mr. Speed would have liked it too. He used to talk to me a lot about how to make your wishes come true. I figured we weren't going to break it apart, we were just going to use it to make wishes on. He always had the wisest things to say. I think of him pretty much every day."

"I'm sure you do, Bones," Miss Evelyn said softly. "Of course you do, just like we do." She looked up at me, a thin smile on her lips. "Bones, I think I need a little break from work. If you have time, would you like to come home with me? I have something I want to share with you."

"To your home?"

"Why, yes, it's just round back."

"Yes, ma'am, I know. I think I have time to do that."

The Ball house was located behind the Last Chance. It was a large white house, with a front porch and windows all around. An even whiter picket fence stood guard around the entire property. I could see the front of the house when I passed by on U.S. 1 and the side of it when I turned up the county road and headed home, but that was all I had ever seen.

Miss Evelyn straightened up some papers on her desk, swiveled around, and stood up. Her rusty-brown hair was swirled on top of her head, and she stood a full bun taller than Mr. Ball. She draped her arm around my shoulders. The two of us walked out of her little office room, past Mr. Ball, through familiar aisles packed with fishing and hunting supplies. There was a door with a sign painted above it in black letters: *Private No Entry*. She pushed the door open and we stepped out onto a narrow sidewalk that ran along the white picket fence.

We passed through a gate and followed a line of square stepping-stones to a set of stairs. Miss Evelyn walked up them and opened the screen door for me. "This is actually the back door to our kitchen, but coming from the store, it's easier to enter this way."

I was dazzled by the brightness. The floor, as well as the countertop, was covered in lemon-yellow linoleum. On one side of the counter stood a white enamel stove; on the other side, past a huge double sink, was a white enamel refrigerator. Cabinets with glass doors lined the walls. In the middle of the room was a table covered with a white tablecloth with embroidered yellow flowers.

She led me through the kitchen, down a small hallway, and out into the living room. A large brown rug edged with green flowers and twisted vines sat on top of a glossy wooden floor. Curtains with the same design as the rug hung at the front window.

A small table with a radio on top sat between two overstuffed chairs facing a matching couch. A larger table sat in front of the couch. Framed pictures nearly covered the walls, and hanging above the fireplace mantel was a huge mirror with gold edges. Across the room, by the front door, stood a magnificent black piano. On top of the piano was a photograph of a young soldier, a small wooden box, and, in a glass case, the triangular flag.

I stopped in the doorway. Miss Evelyn allowed me to stand and drink in the strange beauty of this room. She placed a gentle hand on my shoulder. "Bones, have you ever played a piano?"

"Piano? No, ma'am, I never have. Do you play?"

"Yes, I do. Actually, when I was younger I went to college and studied music in hopes of one day becoming a music teacher. But sometimes life has a way of leading us down roads we never knew existed."

I pointed toward the photograph on the piano. "Is that Mr. Speed?"

"Why, yes, it is. Would you like a closer look?"

We crossed the glossy floor and stood in front of the piano. Miss Evelyn stood tall and elegant, like women I had seen in movies. She placed my wishbone between the photograph and the small wooden box. When I looked closer, I saw that the two medals that had been pinned to Mr. Speed's uniform were sitting in the little box.

Miss Evelyn picked up the photograph and held it out to me. "He was such a handsome young man, and so proud to march off to fight for his country."

I pointed to the small wooden box. "What are those medals, Miss Evelyn?"

She replaced the photograph and picked up the box. "This one is a Purple Heart, for when he was wounded in battle. And this one is a Silver Star. He was awarded this for bravery under enemy fire."

"Bravery under enemy fire . . . you mean he was a war hero? Like John Wayne?"

Miss Evelyn looked at me and smiled. "Oh yes, Aaron was a hero. He saved a lot of people's lives by sacrificing his own."

"Aaron?"

"Yes, that was his name, although most people called him Speed." As the memory settled in, a smile spread across her face. "As a young boy, he could run like the wind."

"I have heard the story about how fast he could run, but I never knew Aaron was his name. I never knew he was a real war hero."

"Oh, Bones, he would blush if he heard you say that."

Miss Evelyn's hand drifted absently to the piano, and she lifted the lid. Like rows of white teeth, the keys grinned up at us. As her slender fingers walked across the keys, the sound reached out and surrounded me like bees kissing flowers in the springtime. She turned to me and said, "Bones, would you like a cup of tea?"

"A cup of hot tea? I ain't never—I mean, I have never had hot tea."

"Well, let's go to the kitchen and fix a lovely pot of tea. When I was a little girl growing up in New York, my mother and I shared many lovely tea parties together."

I followed Miss Evelyn back into her lemon-yellow kitchen. She stopped by the table and said, "Bones, have a seat while I make us a pot of tea."

I sat down and watched as she put a kettle of water on the stove and placed two delicate white cups on the table. I felt like I was at the movies. After she filled our cups with tea, she sat down across from me and said, "Bones, I am so glad you stopped by. This brings back some very fond memories."

I watched real close as Miss Evelyn gently held her cup handle between two fingers. I tried to copy her just right.

"Yes, ma'am, I am too. And, Miss Evelyn, you said you grew up in New York. Were you born there?"

"Why, yes, Bones, you didn't know that?"

"No, ma'am. But if you're from New York, that would make you a Yankee, and that would make Mr. Speed half a Yankee." Once the words were out of my mouth I wanted to grab them and stuff them back in. "Sorry, Miss Evelyn, I didn't mean for it to sound like that."

Miss Evelyn closed her eyes and laughed out loud. When she opened them again, I noticed they were the same soft brown sprinkled with gold flakes as Mr. Speed's. She placed a hand on my arm and said, "Thank you, Bones, I haven't laughed since . . . well, I haven't laughed in a while, and it certainly feels good to know that I still can."

"If you're from New York, Miss Evelyn, how did you get here?"

"One winter, on a whim, a friend and I decided to come to sunny Florida for a week's vacation. Our car broke down along the highway, not far from here, and Mr. Ball came to our rescue. He was young and handsome and had a voice as sweet as honey. I guess you could say I was smitten by his country charm."

"Did you just stay here and never go back to New York again?"

"Oh no, it took Mr. Ball a full year to convince me to move to this wild land. Being raised in the city, I was scared to death of the bugs and snakes and sounds of the night. But after I moved here, I was quickly overwhelmed by this land's beauty and magic, and most of all, its lovely people." She looked at me with a twinkle in her eye. "And although I am a Yankee, these generous inhabitants accepted and welcomed me into their midst."

I had never heard anyone speak the way Miss Evelyn did, so elegant-like, except in movies.

After we finished our cup of tea, Miss Evelyn asked if I would like to see Mr. Speed's room. She stood up and led me into one of the bedrooms. The room smelled familiar, almost like the inside of Mama's cedar chest. A four-poster single bed sat in the middle of the room. Two sides of the walls were lined, from floor to ceiling, with shelves overflowing with books.

Miss Evelyn sat on the edge of the bed and patted a place next to her. A long dark brown dresser stood across from the bed. On top of the dresser were a wooden car, a yo-yo, a pocketknife, and, perched at the end, the green baseball cap that me and Little Man had given Mr. Speed last Christmas.

I looked around at the volumes of books. "The only time I've ever seen this many books in one place was in the school library. Mr. Speed sure must have loved to read."

"He was nearly born with a book in his hand. I do believe he read something every day of his life. Of course, after his injury, he couldn't keep his focus on the words, so his father and I read to him."

We sat for a few moments in silence, each of us absorbed in our own thoughts of Mr. Speed. Then Miss Evelyn continued. "Before he went away, he told us when he came back from the war, he was going to go to college and become a teacher. He said he didn't want to follow in his daddy's footsteps and run the Last Chance. He wanted to be a schoolteacher and teach children about the wonders of the world."

"He wanted to be a teacher?"

"That was his dream."

"Miss Evelyn, you know what? I think his dream came true. Every time I talked with Mr. Speed I learned something new, and Little Man says the same thing. I do believe he really was a teacher."

Miss Evelyn bit down on her lip. "Thank you, Bones. It

means so much for me to hear that. Aaron loved his visits with you and Little Man." She pointed to a row of books. "You see those? They are all about the history and nature of Florida. Nearly every night, his father or I would read him something about Florida so he could share it with you."

"Really? He would study on things so he could share them with me?"

"Oh yes, Bones, he so looked forward to your visits. You were very special to him."

"I didn't know that. If I had known that, I would have come to visit him more."

"You did just fine. He could remember all the details about Florida that we read to him, but he had a difficult time with other information. At times it was very frustrating for him."

"Yes, ma'am, sometimes I had to listen real hard to what he was telling me. But he knew just about everything there was to know about Florida. I learned so much from him. And he was just a pure comfort to be around."

Miss Evelyn smoothed the front of her skirt with both hands and slowly stood up. "I should get back to the store soon. Mr. Ball will be wondering if we disappeared."

She stepped up to the brown dresser and picked up a small framed photograph. It was of a young soldier in uniform, standing straight and proud. "Aaron would have so loved your wishbone gift. I know he would have wanted you to have this in return." She handed me the photograph. "Bones, this is from Aaron . . . Mr. Speed, to you. It was taken just before he got on the ship to leave."

I stood up. "Thank you kindly, Miss Evelyn," I whispered.

Miss Evelyn walked me through the living room and to the front door. "Bones, I have so enjoyed our visit. I do hope you will come back. Maybe next time we can play a few tunes on the piano together."

"Yes, ma'am, I would like that. I enjoyed it, too, especially the tea party. Maybe I can come back next week."

"That would be lovely. You are welcome anytime."

I walked out the gate and strolled along the picket fence. I stopped and looked back at the white house. I thought I saw the silhouette of Miss Evelyn still standing behind the screen door. That house didn't look so big or mysterious anymore; I now knew it was full of wonder and the presence of Mr. Speed.

discoveries

I clutched the picture of Mr. Speed and raced the entire way home. Mama was in the back room pumping her foot up and down on her treadle sewing machine. I ran in and held the photograph in front of her. "Mama, this is Mr. Speed when he was in the army. Miss Evelyn gave it to me. The two of us went to her house, the big white one, and had a tea party with her Chinese tea set."

Mama looked at me and raised an eyebrow, a crooked little smile on her face. "A china tea set?"

"Yes, ma'am, she said it was from China."

"A china tea set?"

"Yes, ma'am, that's what I said, it's from China."

"Bones, it's not from China. It's a type of very fine dishes called china."

"Well, anyway, we had a tea party, and Miss Evelyn is so nice and elegant. She looks like Maureen O'Hara. Don't you think so, Mama?"

"Bones, it sounds like you had a wonderful time with Miss

Evelyn. Why don't you wait until supper, when your daddy is home, to tell us all about your visit."

"Yes, ma'am. I just hope I can wait."

I ran into my room, then turned around and ran back out. "Mama, can I go over and see Little Man? I want to show him this picture and tell him all about Miss Evelyn."

"That sounds like a good idea. Because you're going to be jumping around like a flea until suppertime." Mama stopped pedaling on the sewing machine and looked at me. "Bones, stay on the road. Don't take any shortcuts into the swamp. You hear?"

"Yes, ma'am, I will. And I'll be back way before dark. I promise."

I clutched my picture of Mr. Speed and ran the whole way to Little Man's house. When I arrived I ran up the steps. As usual the front door was open. I looked inside and saw Miss Melba standing at the kitchen counter making biscuits.

"Miss Melba," I gasped, "look at this, it's a picture of Mr. Speed when he was in the army."

Miss Melba's hands were covered almost up to her elbows in fine white flour dust. She kept her hands in the biscuit bowl and leaned back for a closer look at the picture.

"My goodness, he was such a handsome young man. Where did you get his picture?"

"Miss Evelyn gave it to me. I went to her house today, and we had a tea party together. It's the first time I ever spent any time with her. She's a real nice lady."

"Yes, she is. I'm so sorry for her loss. Speed was their only child. He was a smart young man with a bright future."

"Did you know him when he was younger?"

"Oh yes. Cotton and I are quite a bit older, but I do have fond memories of him as a young boy. Along with your daddy, we all pretty much grew up here together."

I stood in the warm familiar kitchen in front of Miss Melba and felt dumber than a doorknob. How could I not have remembered all of this? Of course they grew up together, just like me and Little Man were doing right now!

I finally caught my breath and asked, "Do you know where Little Man is? I want to show him this picture, too."

"He's out back at the pigpen."

"Thanks, Miss Melba, I'll see you later."

I ran back down the steps. When I got to the pigpen, Little Man had just closed the gate and was walking back to the house.

"Little Man, look at this, it's a picture of Mr. Speed in the army."

Before he could say a word, I told Little Man all about my tea party with Miss Evelyn.

On our walk back to his house, I said, "While I was with Miss Evelyn I forgot about our troubles for a while. Now I'm back to worrying again. What if Mr. Charlie did see something. What if he saw Nolay out there?"

"Gol-durn, Bones, that's your daddy you're talkin' about. You think he killed ol' Peckerhead and that Yankee man, too?"

"No. I mean, I don't want to think like that. But there's so much stuff piling up in my mind. Where's his red hand-kerchief? How did his knife get out in the swamps where that man's body was found? And the night Peckerhead died Nolay was supposed to be fishing with Ironhead, but now he says he was up in Jacksonville."

"I still say you got to have faith in the Lord, you got to trust Sheriff LeRoy, and most of all you got to believe in your daddy."

"I hope you're right, Little Man. I'm doing the best I can."

"Besides, there ain't much we can do about it. We just got to wait and see what uncovers itself."

When we reached Little Man's house, I said, "I best be getting back home. Mama don't want me out at dark. And come to think of it, I don't much want to be out at dark, either. I'll see you tomorrow."

I pretty much ran the whole way back home. I knew there was no such thing as Soap Sally trying to get me, but there was for sure something out there.

When I got home, I went to my room and placed the picture of Mr. Speed on my dresser in a special place where I would see it first thing every morning.

Darkness had just slipped in when Nolay pulled into the driveway and walked in the house. I helped Mama put supper on the table, and we all sat down. Before Nolay could take his first bite, I said, "I went to visit Miss Evelyn today, and she invited me inside her house. We had a tea party, with real tea cups from China—I mean, china cups. She has a piano and she knows how to play it. And she's a Yankee from New York. Did you know that, Nolay, that she's a Yankee and she went to college in New York? And—"

Nolay held up both hands. "Whoa, whoa, pull in them

reins a minute. You're talking so fast I can hardly understand you."

"Sorry, Nolay, I'm just so excited and I learned so much. Did you know Miss Evelyn was a Yankee? And that Mr. Speed is half a Yankee, and that he's a war hero, like John Wayne?"

"Well, of course I did. You didn't know all that? How long you known Miss Evelyn?"

"I guess my whole life. But she's always been sort of quiet-like, and she spends most of her time in that little room in back of the store. I don't think I ever heard her say more than a dozen words before."

"I've known her as far back as I can remember, and Miss Evelyn is a mighty fine person. What difference does it make that she's from New York?"

"You told me all Yankees were bad, that they came here to steal our land and change our way of life. But Miss Evelyn don't seem to be bad at all. She walks around all elegant, like a movie star. And she looks like Maureen O'Hara, when she played in *Miracle on 34th Street*. And Mama thinks so, too, don't you, Mama?"

Mama nodded. "She does resemble Maureen O'Hara."

Nolay's face crinkled in thought. "Bones, I don't recall telling you that all Yankees are bad." He glanced across at Mama. "Honey Girl, did you ever hear me say such a thing?"

"Never heard you say all Yankees were bad, but you have definitely said some unflattering things about Yankees in general."

"I might have had a few choice words concerning some Yankees . . . or outsiders I've run across. But you can't say they are all bad; that would be like saying everybody from Florida is a dumb cracker. And like I've told you before, I'm proud to be a cracker, but I sure ain't dumb." Nolay munched thoughtfully on a piece of corn bread. "Bones, the world is sorta like a big ol' pot of vegetable soup. A potato don't taste like a onion, a green bean don't taste like corn. Each one of 'em has their own look and flavor. But when you mix 'em all up together, they make a mighty fine-tasting soup. That's sorta how it is. Every one of us is different, but we can still be mixed up together. You understand what I'm sayin'?"

"Yes, sir, I reckon I do."

"It's just that you can't go judgin' people by what they look like or where they come from. That ain't important. What's important is what's inside, their flavor, what comes out of 'em." He cocked his head and said, "Life is full of surprises, that's what keeps it interesting. You take ol' Chicken Charlie. Did you know that he don't come from around here?"

"Mr. Charlie? He wasn't born here? Is he a Yankee, too?"

"Nope, he's more what you could call a foreigner, comes from a different country altogether, Germany."

"Germany? Mr. Charlie is a German? Didn't we fight them in the war? Aren't they bad people?"

"Now, there you go again. Not all Germans are bad people, not all of 'em wanted to fight a war. Actually, they had to fight in two wars. The way I heard it, when the first war was going on in Germany, it was pretty hard on a lot of people. If you were different or didn't agree with what the government said, they just killed you or locked you up. Charlie's mama and daddy were both killed. Somehow or other, Charlie's granddaddy and grandma got on a ship and came to America. I wadn't even born yet when they moved over here."

"They came all the way from Germany to live here?"

"I don't know about coming intentional to live here, they were just lookin' for somewhere new and peaceful to live. Sometimes life has a way of putting you in the place you need to be. Had something to do with their religion. They were Jewish."

"Mr. Charlie is a Jew, like Jesus was?"

"Something like that, but I don't think he remembers he's one. Charlie's body grew up to be a man, but his mind stayed behind as a child."

"How did Charlie come to live where he is now?"

"The way I heard it, my daddy showed 'em that little guava grove and told 'em they could clean a spot out and stay as long as they wanted. Well, before you knew it, them people had carved out a nice little space in them guavas and built 'em a little house. They were hardworkin' people, and eventually my daddy took them down to the courthouse with what money they had and got 'em a legal deed to the land." Nolay took a deep sigh, looked down at his plate, and said, "Charlie ain't never done nothing bad to nobody, and I'm gonna see to it that nothing bad comes to him. It makes me madder than a hornet that ol' Peckerhead was trying to pull a fast one on that old man."

Nolay looked over at me. "Charlie don't quite understand

what a land deed is, but I'm gonna make sure nothing happens to his land."

I sat at the supper table and let all this information seep into me. I felt like a cup filled to the brim and spilling out over the edges. Maybe I didn't really know any of our neighbors or even my own family.

smoke

The month of October was quickly chasing itself to an end. The dryness of autumn had stumbled in and hung fully sweet and heavy in the air. The days were shorter and the swamp was almost completely covered in a golden-brown cloak. Huge flocks of squawking ducks darkened the sky as they flew over our house on their way to Lake Okeechobee and the Everglades. Some would stop and rest in our swamp for a couple of days.

Old Snaggletooth's gator hole shrank to a small bog. Her babies had grown to the size of giant brown lizards. A whole new generation of baby gators scampered around the murky waters of their birthplace. Snaggletooth was always close by, her huge body floating just under the water's surface, her eyes sticking up like two periscopes. She was constantly on guard for animals in search of a drink or a quick meal of one of her children.

At night, the air filled with the growls, screeches, and

snarls of hungry animals roaming the dried-up swamp looking for food and water.

Sunday morning after breakfast and our chores, Nolay announced, "'Bout time we went and chopped us a new batch of firewood. It's gonna start gettin' chilly in the evenin's."

We went outside and climbed into Nolay's swamp buggy. Mama brought a little straw basket filled with food and sat it on the floor between her feet.

The buggy consisted of nothing more than an old car frame with bloated tires and seats at the front and back. Nolay turned the key, and the engine coughed and rumbled to life. We headed out toward the sandy patch of longleaf and slash pine.

It was like riding a carnival roller coaster. The buggy's huge tires rolled easily over the tangled mass of palmetto roots. We sloshed through a couple of small bogs and finally entered an area filled with the cool, pungent scent of pine. Nolay stopped and surveyed the area for any dead pine logs laying around. They had to be just the right size for cutting and fitting into our fireplace. He nodded. "Looks like a perfect one, right over yonder." He sat down, shifted the buggy's gears, and started forward.

I looked back. Something strange caught my eye: thick gray clouds of smoke snaking up through the clear blue sky. I pointed and exclaimed, "Nolay, looky yonder, what is that?"

Nolay stopped the buggy and stood up in the seat for a better look. "That's a mighty big fire. And it's over by the Reemses', and Charlie's place. This don't look good. Y'all hang on, we're gettin' over there."

Nolay turned the buggy around, and we bounced back over the palmetto roots. When we reached the county marl road, he gunned the engine, and we raced toward Charlie's place. The swamp buggy's bloated tires sent up plumes of yellow dust so thick they blotted out the blue sky behind us.

Nolay slammed on the brakes when he spotted Blue's old pickup truck parked on the side of the road. You couldn't miss that truck, because it had so many different colors of paint over patches of rust that it looked like a multicolored leopard. Blue and a gang of colored men stood as if paralyzed by the thick gray smoke.

"What's goin' on, Blue?"

"I don't know, Mista Nolay. We just looked up and seen this here fire. The wind is blowin' it directly toward Mr. Charlie's. I done sent some of the womenfolk over to hep him however they can. I done sent Jackson back to the house to get our diggin' tools. We goin' to start choppin' a firebreak between here and Mr. Charlie's."

"Sounds like you got it under control, Blue. I'm gonna check on Charlie, and I'll be right back to help y'all."

"Yes, suh, Mista Nolay."

Nolay drove up Charlie's road and pulled into the front yard. When he turned off the swamp buggy's noisy engine, we were surrounded by an eerie silence. On one side of the yard the chickens had bunched together like a giant discarded feather duster. They clucked quietly among themselves. The sound of burning trees crackled through the air. A few live sparks and pieces of black cinder floated softly to the ground.

Charlie and several colored women came around from the

back of the house; each carried a bucket of water. Charlie's huge body waddled from side to side as he limped toward us. Water sloshed out of the buckets and painted the legs of his faded overalls in streaks of bright blue. "Nolay, Nolay," he cried, "they gonna burn my house down. They gonna burn up my chickens."

Nolay got out of the swamp buggy. "Everything's gonna be all right, Charlie. You just keep dousing any sparks and as much of your house as you can with that water. Blue and his gang are already cutting a firebreak." Nolay turned to me and Mama. "Lori, get down to the Last Chance, put a call out to both the volunteer fire stations. Then round up the neighbors. We'll need every hand we can get."

Mama slid over to the driver's seat, and I jumped in front with her. When we reached the Last Chance, she left the buggy's engine on. She ran inside and told Mr. Ball and the other folks there what had happened. She ran back outside, got behind the steering wheel, and shifted gears, and off we went. Over the rumbling of the engine, she said, "Mr. Ball is going to call the fire stations."

Soon as we pulled into Little Man's front yard, I saw him and his two brothers out in their little sugarcane patch. I jumped out and ran over to them. "There's a fire over by Mr. Charlie's, and we need help!"

The three of them immediately started for the buggy. As they ran past the house, Earl and Ethan grabbed a couple of shovels and machetes. Little Man already had a hoe in his hand. Miss Melba came to the front door to see what all the fuss was about. "Miss Melba," I said, "there's a fire at Mr. Charlie's, and we need all the help we can get."

She wiped her hands on her apron. "I'll go tell Cotton, and we'll be right over."

By the time we arrived back at the fire, there was an assortment of cars and trucks parked along the road. A black and white human chain of men, women, and children stretched out over the scrub brush. Together, they cut, slashed, and chopped through the thick vegetation. The firebreak looked like a giant snail had crawled over the dense vegetation.

Earl, Ethan, and Little Man jumped out of the back of the buggy and joined up with the rest of the people. Mama said, "I hope the fire trucks will reach here in time."

No sooner had she said those words than we heard the mournful wail of a siren. The ancient Grant volunteer fire truck came lumbering up the road. Ironhead sat in the driver's seat, and as he got closer, he reached up and began to clang the bell that hung by the driver's door. He drove the old truck out onto the firebreak. Several men came up and began to uncoil the hose at the back of the truck. Ironhead cranked open a wheel that released water into the hose. Like a limp gray snake, it sprang to life and sprayed a stream of water toward the orange tongues of fire.

Sheriff LeRoy arrived with red lights flashing and sirens screeching. He jumped out of his car and headed straight in to help with the hose. The air filled with the hiss and sizzle of water fighting fire. Patches of gray smoke began turning into thick black clouds. Like a hungry old toad, the clouds gobbled up the clear blue sky. For several hours we all worked to bring the fire under control. Me and Little Man used our shovels to spread a thin layer of sand over the smoldering coals. Finally, the fire began to dwindle and admit defeat.

Me and Mama followed Nolay back to the buggy. Our clothes were drenched in sweat. Small leaves and black cinders clung to our bodies like leeches. "Honey Girl," Nolay said, "you and Bones stay here; I got something I need to do."

Mama crossed her arms and said, "And what would that be?"

"I'm goin' out to the Reemses'."

"Nolay, I don't think that is a wise thing for you to do."

"I ain't thinkin' wise right now, I'm thinkin' about what I need to do."

Mama got in the front seat. "Then I am going with you."

I jumped in the back. "I'm going, too."

"I ain't got time to argue with you two hardheads." Without another word, Nolay got in, and we drove off toward the Reemses'. We pulled into the dirt yard and saw the three boys and Whackerstacker standing under a dismal little tree. If the Reemses were good at anything, it was wasting time. Nolay parked in front of them.

Whackerstacker said, "What you doin' on my property?"

Nolay eased out of the buggy and stood in front of them. "What in tarnation were you doin'? You tryin' to burn that old man out?"

"You dumb Indian, you get off my property," Whackerstacker said.

As quick as the strike of a rattlesnake, Nolay's fist shot forward and connected with Whackerstacker's face. Whackerstacker grabbed his nose with both hands and sagged to his knees. Nolay quietly said, "That would be Mister Indian to you."

Whackerstacker recovered and picked up a shovel and swung it toward Nolay. Nolay jerked his head back. The tip of the shovel slashed across the side of his head. He staggered and fell to the ground. The three boys—Fats, Skeeter, and Smokey—moved in and began to kick Nolay.

Without thinking, I leaped from the backseat and onto Skeeter's back. I wrapped my arms around his thick neck and bit down on his right ear. Skeeter screamed and began wheeling around like a dog chasing its tail. I saw Whackerstacker with the shovel held high in the air.

The crack of a gunshot pierced the air. A silence fell over us; everyone stood still as sticks, then, as if in slow motion, turned in the direction of the sound. Mama stood on the front seat of the buggy, her little pearl-handled .32 revolver in her hand. It was pointed skyward. She slowly brought it down level with Whackerstacker's eyes.

Whackerstacker glared at her, dropped the shovel, and stepped backward. I let go of Skeeter's ear, loosened my grip, and slid off his back. Just as my feet touched the ground, a car slid to a stop behind the buggy. The door flew open, and the huge body of Sheriff LeRoy uncurled from the front seat.

I ran to Nolay and kneeled down. He pushed his body up with his hands and rose to his knees. A thin red gash cut across his right temple and into his curly black hair. Blood trickled down the side of his face, along his neck, and over his chest. Speechless, I stared into his eyes. He looked back and said, "Bones, you all right?"

"Yes, sir, I'm fine. How about you?"

"I'm fine." He started to unbutton his shirt. "Now, look at this, these buzzards done messed up my shirt." He took his shirt off, wadded it up, and pressed it against his head. He placed his other hand on my shoulder. "Let's get going."

Sheriff LeRoy jingled over to us. "You all right, Nolay?"

"Never been better, LeRoy."

Whackerstacker pointed a finger at Nolay. "Arrest him, Sheriff. He come on my property and threatened me and my kids. He attacked us. Look what he done to my boy here." Fats stood next to his father, two small streams of blood oozing out of his nostrils.

Mama stood still as a park statue on the buggy seat, her pistol pointed directly at Whackerstacker.

LeRoy turned toward her and said calmly, "Miss Lori, I sure would appreciate it if you would put that gun down."

Mama looked at him, then at the gun, as if it were the first time she had seen it. Without a word, she sat down and slipped the gun back inside her little straw basket.

LeRoy swung around and gave his full attention to us and the Reemses. "Well now, from what I saw when I first drove up, there must be two sides to this story. And I aim to get to both of 'em." LeRoy strolled over to where the shovel lay in the dirt. He reached down and gingerly picked it up with two fingers. He asked Whackerstacker, "This yours?"

"Yeah, it's mine."

"I gotta take it in for evidence. I'll bring it back when I'm finished."

"What you takin' my shovel in for, Sheriff? It cain't talk."

"That's right, Joe, I'm gonna arrest your shovel. When I'm through interrogatin' it, I'll bring it back." LeRoy walked over to Nolay. "You might want to have a doctor look at that."

"It would take a lot more than these dumb buzzards to send me to a doctor."

"Now, Nolay, I want you to get in your buggy and go home. I don't want to see you over here again."

"LeRoy, if you don't mind, I'm gonna stop by and check on Charlie first."

"Fair enough, I'm headed back there myself. When I looked around at Charlie's place and saw your buggy gone, I figured this was where I'd find you. Thought I'd better get here before you got yourself into deeper trouble." LeRoy looked closer at the cut on Nolay's head. "Looks like I got here just in time."

LeRoy turned to the Reemses. "You fellas stay clear of Charlie. If I see or hear of you being close to his house, I'll put every one of you behind bars. You understand?"

Whackerstacker smirked. "Yeah, we understand."

LeRoy stood and watched as me and Nolay got in the buggy with Mama. He strolled over, leaned up against the buggy's frame, and folded his arms across his chest. "Just to let you know, I'll be stopping by tomorrow afternoon to pay a visit with Charlie."

Nolay said, "Thanks, LeRoy, I 'preciate you lettin' me know."

We rode along in silence until Nolay glanced over at Mama. "Honey Girl, since when did you start totin' a gun when we go firewood chopping?"

Mama smiled and said, "You never know when you might come across a snake."

When we arrived back at Charlie's, the once-raging fire had been defeated. Blue and his crew were still shoveling sand and dirt over the few small smoldering patches of coals. Earl, Ethan, and Little Man were helping Ironhead clean up his fire truck and re-coil the hose.

Nolay drove into Charlie's front yard. A few of the guava trees on one side of the house were scorched, but other than that there was no damage done to Charlie's place. Mr. Charlie was sitting in his rocking chair with Sonny-Boy Rooster in his lap. When he saw us, he got up, tucked Sonny-Boy under his arm, and waddled over to the buggy. "Nolay, that nearly scared me to death. I'm scared they gonna come back and kill all my chickens. Me and my chickens ain't never done nothing bad to the Reemses. Why are they doing this?"

"Charlie, it ain't nothing that you've done, they're just dang mean people. Now, the sheriff has warned them not to come near you. Everybody's gonna be watching out for you real close."

Mr. Charlie stood by the side of our buggy, gently strok-ing Sonny-Boy's head. Like a father admiring his children,

Mr. Charlie looked out over his yard full of chickens. A look of love and concern swept over his pudgy face. "I just thank the Lord that none of 'em was hurt. I don't know what I would do without 'em."

"Charlie, ain't nothing gonna happen to you or your chickens," Nolay said.

Mr. Charlie and his chickens were safe now. But for how long?

confessions

Monday's morning light was just a thread on the horizon when I heard Nolay drive away in the truck.

As I waited for the school bus to arrive, an idea was fluttering around my head like a bumblebee. When I got on and sat down next to Little Man, I said, "That sure was something yesterday, wasn't it?"

"It was mighty scary for Mr. Charlie."

"And it was a awful mean thing for the Reemses to do."

"How do you know the Reemses started that fire?"

"Little Man, I told you what Mr. Charlie said about Peckerhead coming out and threatening to burn his house down. And that was just what his brother was trying to do."

"I reckon you're right. I'm just glad everyone pulled together and stopped that fire from doing any real damage."

I turned and glanced at the back of the bus. Skeeter Reems wasn't even looking in our direction; he was looking out the window making like I didn't exist. There was a bright red semicircle around the top of his ear. I had left a good impression on him.

"Little Man, I have an idea. How 'bout after school you and me go giggin' down at the river? And we can keep a lookout for Nolay and the sheriff. They're going out to Charlie's today. I sure am curious as to what Mr. Charlie saw that night."

"I don't know, Bones, that sounds sorta like snooping on someone's business."

"It's not snooping. I just want to know what's going on. Especially concerning Nolay."

"I guess you're right. Sounds good to me. I'll hurry up and get my chores done and be over at your house."

I was outside feeding Pearl and Harry when I saw Little Man stroll up our driveway with a croker sack tied around his waist and his four-prong gig.

He reached into the croker sack, pulled out a mason jar full of thick brown liquid, and handed it to me. "Give this to your mama; it's some fresh-squeezed sorghum syrup."

In a few minutes I returned with my gig and fish stringer.

Me and Little Man walked down the sandy road, across the railroad tracks, past the Last Chance. We crossed U.S. 1 and climbed down the familiar trail to the Indian River. The tea-brown water stretched out in front of us, the afternoon sun glistening over its flat surface. We tied our fish stringers to our pant loops, rolled our pant legs up, and stepped to the water. Little Man pointed to several areas where the surface rippled with bubbles. "The mullet are already feeding. You go around that way, and I'll go this way."

I silently slipped my feet into the warm, brackish water. Like gritty peanut butter, the sandy bottom squished up between my toes. The mullet were so busy feeding they weren't aware of us until we plunged our gigs into the midst of them. We moved from feeding frenzy to feeding frenzy. Before long, our stringers were full; we had enough for our families and some to share.

We dropped both stringers inside Little Man's croker sack, climbed up the riverbank, and headed toward the Last Chance.

We walked up to the front entry, where Mr. Speed's bench sat blank and empty. I stood and looked at it. My chest felt like a big hand was squeezing it. Little Man placed the croker sack by the front steps and said, "Bones, let's go in and see if we can sell some of these."

We walked inside. The familiar silhouette of Mr. Ball stood behind the counter. Those dark half-circles still sat under his eyes. I looked toward the back of the store, to Miss Evelyn's little room, but she wasn't there. It was as empty as Mr. Speed's bench.

"Howdy, kids," Mr. Ball said. "Been down to the river?"

Little Man answered, "Yes, sir, and we had a mighty bountiful day."

"Well, if you got some extras, bring 'em on in. Folks are always looking for fresh fish."

Mr. Ball paid us two dollars and fifty cents for five of our fish and threw in two RC Colas and a moon pie for each of us. As we went outside, I watched as Little Man walked over to

Mr. Speed's bench and sat down. He looked at me. "Come on, Bones."

I walked over and slowly sank down beside him. I scooted back; my feet dangled over the edge. We silently munched our moon pies and sipped our RCs. I looked across U.S. 1 at the Indian River, stretching out like a brown blanket for as far as I could see. More to myself than to Little Man, I said, "I reckon this is how he looked out at the world every day. Waitin' for someone to come by so he could talk to 'em. I sure do miss him."

"Yeah, I miss 'im, too. He always had something good to talk about."

A gentle breeze fluttered by as me and Little Man sat silently on Mr. Speed's bench.

I looked up at the sound of car tires crunching on gravel to see Sheriff LeRoy turn onto the county road and drive past the Last Chance. I nudged Little Man. "Let's go. I bet the sheriff is going up to see Mr. Charlie. Nolay should be by any minute now."

Little Man grabbed the croker sack, and we walked toward the railroad tracks. Before long, Nolay pulled up beside us in the truck. "Where y'all been?"

Little Man held up the sackful of fish. "Down to the river, giggin' mullet."

"Looks like you had a good day. I can give y'all a ride home, but I got a stop to make first."

Little Man put the sack in the truck bed, and the two of us climbed in front with Nolay. He drove down the guava-tree tunnel to Charlie's house. As we pulled up, Sheriff LeRoy was just ambling up to Charlie's front porch. Charlie stood at his screen door, the little rooster clutched under his arm.

Nolay turned to us and said, "Y'all wait, I'll be back shortly."

I looked at Little Man. "We can't hear nothing from here. I bet if we climb up those guava trees we can hear what they're saying."

"We cain't do that, Bones, that wouldn't be right."

"Well, do you want to know what's going on or not? 'Cause I sure do. Nolay said wait, he didn't say where we had to wait."

Little Man rolled his big brown eyes. "I don't know, Bones, we sure could get in trouble."

Reluctantly, he opened the door, and we crawled out into the thick guava trees. The branches were so close together it was like climbing on a huge spiderweb. We reached the top, where we had a perfect view of the front porch. LeRoy sat across from Charlie in a little cane chair that looked like a child's toy under his enormous body. Nolay stood at the porch railing. Charlie sat in his rocking chair with Sonny-Boy Rooster nestled on his lap.

As we settled in, swarms of hungry mosquitoes swooped in and began to devour every patch of skin that was uncovered. Little Man looked at me and whispered, "We're gonna get eat up by these skeeters."

We watched as Nolay and the sheriff swiped and scratched at the mosquitoes. They swarmed around Charlie but never seemed to land on him.

The voice of Sheriff LeRoy drifted up to our perch. "Now,

Charlie, I ain't here to cause you no trouble. There's been a murder right here near your place, and if you can hep me with my investigation, I sure would appreciate it."

Seated in his old rocking chair, Charlie turned toward Nolay. Nolay nodded to Charlie and said, "It's all right, Charlie, ain't nothin' gonna happen to you. I done explained to the sheriff about the Reems brothers trying to make you sell your land."

Charlie cleared his throat and began, "Well, that evenin' you're asking about—that was the same day Nolay, Bones, and Little Man stopped by my house—I went out back to my outhouse and heard voices yellin' at each other. My curiosity got me and I snuck out down the trail to see what was goin' on. I seen them two Reems brothers over by the railroad tracks. They was both liquored up. Whackerstacker was yellin' about Peckerhead stealin' his liquor money. Peckerhead knocked his brother to the ground. When Whackerstacker stood up, he had a fair piece of tree branch in his hand and he started hittin' Peckerhead."

Charlie stopped, closed his eyes, and took in a deep breath. "Even after Peckerhead was down on the ground, he woodn't stop hittin' 'im. He beat 'im like he was a pile of old dirty clothes. His own brother. About then, Whackerstacker's oldest boy, Fats, come runnin' up and grabbed his daddy. The two of 'em talked for a while, then they drug ol' Peckerhead's body up to the railroad tracks and laid 'im across. They hid that tree branch up under some bushes."

Sheriff LeRoy leaned in closer. "What happened then, Charlie?"

"After they left, I snuck up to see if maybe he was still alive and I could hep 'im. But it was too late, he was already gone. So I turned around and hightailed it back home."

I looked over at Little Man and whispered, "Do you think he's telling the truth?"

"Course he's tellin' the truth! Mr. Charlie don't know how to lie!"

Sheriff LeRoy leaned in closer yet and said, "Did they know that you saw 'em?"

Charlie hung his head. "The next day, after the po-lease took away Peckerhead's body, Whackerstacker and two of his boys, Fats and Skeeter, come over here. He asked me did I see or hear anything last night." Charlie looked up at Nolay and continued. "Now, I was raised not to tell no lies, so I said, yeah, I seen a little, but I wouldn't tell nobody. Well, next thing I know, ol' Whackerstacker's sayin', 'Charlie, I'm gonna show you what would happen if you ever go tell anybody.'"

Charlie pointed to an old crate sitting by the side of his house. His voice cracked as he continued. "That there is where Lulu nested. She was just sittin' there on her aigs. Whackerstacker reached over, grabbed her by the neck, and wrung her head clean off. Throwed her body out in the yard. It was a-floppin' and a-twistin' in the dirt. Then he started pickin' up her aigs and smashin' 'em on the ground. After he smashed every one of 'em, he picked up her little crate and set it right in front of me. He told me, 'This here is a empty nest. Every one of 'em will look like this if you open your mouth.'

"That was about the worse sight I ever did see. Lulu was

just a sweet little ol' hen, never hurt nobody in her life. And there she was, floppin' around on the ground; blood flyin' everywhere. And her baby aigs smashed all over the floor. I just cain't get that picture outta my mind."

Sheriff LeRoy took off his oversized Stetson and held it with both hands in front of his knees. "That was a dang mean thing for him to do, Charlie. I cain't blame ya for not saying anything."

Charlie's shoulders slumped and he began to cry. Tears slid down his face like raindrops on a windowpane. "I know I done wrong by not comin' out and tellin' what I saw. But Whacker-stacker told me if I said one word, he and his boys would come back and kill every one of my chickens. Every one of 'em. And burn my house down, too."

Sheriff LeRoy reached inside his pocket and pulled out a red handkerchief. My breath caught in my throat as he held it out toward Charlie. Charlie looked at it, gently reached out, grasped it, and promptly blew his nose into it. "Thank ya, Sheriff."

As I watched Charlie blow his nose into Sheriff LeRoy's red handkerchief, my mind felt like a rainbow stripped of all its color, dull and gray. I slowly turned and looked at Little Man. His brown eyes glistened soft and lucid like a bottomless pool of water. As mine began to mist over, he looked away and whispered, "Ain't no reason to be sad. That there is happy news."

"But I was so stupid . . . I thought . . ."

"Hush, there's more."

Perched in the top of those guava trees like oversized bats, me and Little Man turned our attention back to Chicken Charlie's porch.

Nolay and LeRoy glanced at each other. LeRoy said, "Now, Charlie, what you said here ain't going any further than this here porch. I'm gonna do some investigatin'. In the meantime, I don't want you to be scared of them Reemses. I've already warned them, but if they come around here, you get down to the Last Chance and put a call in for me. You know how to use the telephone?"

"Yes, sir, Sheriff, I do. And if I need hep, Mr. or Mrs. Ball can hep me."

Sheriff LeRoy stood up and placed his Stetson back on. His massive frame filled the front entry of the porch. "Now, Charlie, you take it easy, and I'll be gettin' back in touch with you soon. Thank you for all your hep." He was nearly down the steps when he turned around. "Charlie, do you mind if I take that little ol' crate with me?"

"Lulu's crate? Why, no, Sheriff, you can have it if you want. Lulu won't never be needin' it again."

LeRoy placed one of his large hands under the crate, carried it out to his car, and placed it in the trunk.

Nolay nodded to Charlie and walked over to LeRoy's car. "What do you think, LeRoy?"

"I think I got some work to do. When I did my first investigation, I seen all them feet prints. Now I know who they belong to. I got to put all the pieces together. And Nolay, you stay away from them Reemses. I'll go out and pay them another visit and make it crystal clear they are not to come near Charlie or his place. This here is po-lease business, and I will take care of it."

The sheriff got in his car and Nolay began walking back to the truck.

Little Man turned to me. "We better get down before your daddy gets back to the truck."

We scrambled down and crawled back to the truck. Just as Little Man closed the door, Nolay opened the driver's side and slid in. He glanced at us with a twinkle in his eyes. On the ride to Little Man's house, the two of us scratched and rubbed the red welts that covered our face, hands, and feet. Nolay was doing the same thing.

Nolay cleared his throat and said, "You know, I seen the durndest thing back at ol' Charlie's. I thought I saw two monkeys sitting up in his guava trees."

Me and Little Man stared at each other.

"Did y'all hear everything?" Nolay said.

I answered. "Yes, sir, we heard everything. Sorry, Nolay, but we just couldn't help ourselves. Just like Mr. Charlie, our curiosity got the best of us."

"Well, you know what curiosity did to the cat. So let's get this straight. Not one word of this goes any further than the inside of this truck. You two understand that? This here is serious business. You heard what the Reemses said they would do to ol' Charlie."

I looked at Nolay. With my right index finger I made the sign of the cross over my chest. "I cross my heart and hope to die. I won't say a word."

Little Man made the same sign. "Cross my heart and hope to die, too."

Nolay pulled up in front of Little Man's house. As he got out of the truck, Little Man reached in back and got his croker sack and gig. He pulled out my stringer of fish and set them in back. "Thank ya for the ride, Mr. Nolay. Bones, I'll see you tomorrow."

I waved. "Okay, Little Man, see ya on the school bus."

As we drove home, I asked Nolay, "Are you gonna tell Mama?"

"Well, of course I'll tell your mother," he said. "I think it might help to ease her mind."

"Yes, sir, I reckon it will. It sure did ease my mind. I'm so relieved that you and Mr. Charlie weren't involved."

Nolay gave me a sideways glance. "Now, why would you think me or Charlie would have been involved in killin' Peckerhead?"

"I'm not real sure, I just got confused. I mean, with all the stuff the sheriff was saying about evidence and you not telling the truth about being out fishing that night with Ironhead."

"Well, sometimes things ain't the way they seem to be. Just 'cause I wasn't out fishing don't mean I was out killing someone."

Nolay took a deep breath and said, "To set things straight, that night I was supposed to be fishing with Ironhead, I was up in Jacksonville, delivering a load of moonshine. Not something I really care to share with you. I know it's against the law, but far as I'm concerned, it's a white man's law. The way

I look at it, I ain't hurtin' nobody and I'm puttin' food on my family's table."

Nolay looked at me. "Bones, now that you're growing up I can see how I got to change some of my ways. The last thing in the world I want to do is hurt you . . . or your mama. I'm closing down the still. I ain't gonna do that anymore. I aim to change my ways."

We rode along in silence as Nolay's words tumbled around inside the truck cab.

Finally I said, "I just got confused is all. I'm glad it's over with."

"It ain't over with yet. We still got a dead Yankee to deal with."

"Nolay, do you think Whackerstacker killed that Yankee man, too?"

"Naw, he's too dumb. It took a much smarter person to pull off something like that."

Nolay took another deep breath. "Bones, I hope I can win your trust back one day."

I turned and looked at him, but the rest of the ride home was spent in silence. As I looked out the window, all I could think of was Mr. Charlie's poor little old Lulu, flopping around in his yard without a head.

I wanted to trust Nolay with all my heart, but there was still a small worm of doubt wiggling around in my thoughts.

knuckles

Tuesday afternoon when I got off the school bus and started walking home, my thoughts closed in around me like a hot, sweaty hand. It had been ten days since Mr. Speed's funeral. I could still hear his words echoing in my mind. I felt like my heart had a hole in it. As I walked along our winding road, I absently kicked a small stone stuck in the sand. It dislodged and rolled to the side, and the sun glared down, sending sparkles racing across its top. I stopped and stared at it. Then it hit me like a bolt of lightning. "We live on the knuckle. It sparkles on the knuckle."

Mr. Speed had been trying to tell me something. I knew exactly what I had to do. I had to get out there. I ran the rest of the way home, changed my clothes, and went looking for Mama. I didn't want to lie to her, but this one time, I would have to. The truck was gone and so was Nolay, so I wouldn't have to lie to him, too. Mama would never let me go out in the swamps by myself, but I knew I had to do it.

I found Mama out by her garden. I put my right hand behind my back and crossed my fingers. "Mama, Little Man asked if I could come over to his house and help him fix his chicken coop. I'll take the dogs with me and we'll be back way before dark, if it's all right."

"That's fine, Bones, just stay on the road, and no shortcuts through the swamps."

"Yes, ma'am."

I turned around and walked away real fast before she could see the lie sitting on my face. The swamps was just where I was headed.

Me and the dogs walked down the road, turned off into the woods, then backtracked to the swamp. When I came to the water, I followed along its edge. I felt naked without my gun, but if I had taken it, Mama would have known I wasn't just going to Little Man's. At least I had the dogs with me. They ran ahead and I followed behind, hoping they were leading me along a safe way. Before long, we came to the mound where Silver had found that leg. She laid her ears back and walked very slowly beside it. I walked past it as fast as I could.

We walked for about another ten minutes. The water's edge began to curve; then it took a sharp turn into a shape just like a bent knuckle. Locals that used this river called this area Knuckle Bend. Growing up here, Mr. Speed would have known exactly where it was located. I stopped and looked out over the pockmarked swamp. Now that autumn was fully settled in, the swamp was drying up fast. There were large areas streaked with black cracked mud. Last summer most of this would have been underwater, especially after that big storm blew in.

I saw an area that had been dug out, almost directly across from where I was standing. That would be where Jakey Tom's hounds found that man's body and where the sheriff had it dug up.

I picked up a stick and began to brush over the dried mud. I told the dogs, "Y'all come over here and help me. I need your noses." They zigzagged around me, sniffing and smelling the dried earth. Mr. Speed's words echoed in my mind: "On the knuckle. Watch the knuckle." Finally, after I poked my stick round and brushed back and forth a heap of times, it hit something hard. I bent down and scratched some dirt off. And there it was, staring back at me: Sheriff LeRoy's solid evidence. It was crusted with mud, but when I cleaned off the top, it sparkled in the sun's rays.

I stood up and called to the dogs, "Come on, y'all, we gotta get back home fast as we can!" I raced the dogs back to our house.

When I got back to the house, I saw one of the happiest sights I had seen in a long time: Nolay's truck parked in the yard. I ran in the house and called out, "Nolay, Nolay, where are you?"

"Good Lord, Bones, I'm right here in the kitchen. What happened to you? Are you all right?"

I stood in the kitchen and stopped to get my breath. "Nolay, quick, we have to go find the sheriff! We need to get him out here!"

"And why on earth do we need to do that?"

"'Cause I found something. I found the sheriff's solid evidence that he's been looking for. We gotta get down to the Last Chance and call him!"

"Hold your horses, I just walked in."

"Nolay, we need him out here before it gets dark!"

"All right, all right, we'll drive down to the store. Go let your mama know."

I ran out and said, "Mama, me and Nolay are going down to the Last Chance. We'll be back soon."

Before she could answer or ask me a question, I ran back to the truck.

On the ride down, I told Nolay what I had found, but from the look on his face, I could tell he didn't believe it was all that important. "I hope this ain't a waste of time, Bones."

While Nolay went inside the store to use the phone, I sat down on Mr. Speed's bench. I looked over at the empty space where he should have been and said to myself, "Mr. Speed, I should have listened better to you. Thank you for making my wish come true."

Nolay came out and sat down beside me. "The sheriff is on his way, should be here in about a half hour. We'll meet him out by the top of our road."

"Thank you, Nolay. I surely hope he gets here before dark."

"Bones, I hope this is as important as you think it is, 'cause ol' LeRoy is making a special trip out here."

"Yes, sir, it is."

I looked over at Nolay filling up Mr. Speed's empty space, and that old bench almost felt comfortable again.

We drove out and waited for the sheriff to arrive. By the time he got there, the sun was just starting to paint shadows over the day. We got out of our truck and walked over to the sheriff's car. Nolay said, "Sorry to bother you like this, LeRoy, but Bones thinks she's found something of interest for you to look at."

"Well, then let's just go have a look. Y'all get inside and I'll drive you where you need to go."

I slid in the front seat and sat between the sheriff and Nolay. The sheriff looked down at me and said, "Where to, Miss Bones?"

"Out to the swamps, where you found that man's body."

"Fair enough, if that's where you want us to go."

I took a quick look around the inside of Sheriff LeRoy's car, and Little Man was right. There was enough stuff in here for someone to set up housekeeping.

The ride out to the edge of the swamp was a quiet one. The sheriff parked his car, and we got out. He reached back inside and pulled out a long black flashlight. "Better take this just in case."

As we walked along the water's edge, shades of night danced beside us. When we got to the place where the water bent into a knuckle, I walked over and pointed to the ground. The three of us squatted down. I picked up the same stick I had used the first time and dug up the dirt-encrusted object. It hung on the end of the stick like a dried-up dead snake. The sheriff cocked his large head to one side and said, "Well, I can see what it is, but why would it be so important?"

"Because, Sheriff, the last time I saw this, it was dangling from that Yankee man's arm. Not the dead one, but the live one."

"Well, I'll be dogged. Now, that sure could be something of interest."

"Yes, sir, that's what I was hoping."

The sheriff straightened his head and said, "Now, Miss Bones, how did you know to come out here looking for something like this?"

"It was Mr. Speed that told me. He kept trying to tell me to look by the knuckle, but it didn't come clear to me until today when I was walking home. He was talking about Knuckle Bend."

"Speed? How would he know something like this?"

"Because he sat on that bench every day. He heard everything people said. Some people thought he was dumb, so they didn't care what they said around him. But he wasn't dumb. Besides my daddy, he was just about the smartest person I ever did know."

"Well now, that could be a possibility."

Nolay stood up and said, "But how do we know it's the one that man was wearing?"

The sheriff and I stood up at the same time. I looked at Nolay, then back to the sheriff. "I know it is. I just know it."

The sheriff and Nolay glanced at each other over the top of my head.

Sheriff LeRoy answered, "Now, Miss Bones, I have to make positive sure of who it belonged to. I will have to do some further investigatin'. But I want you to know I appreciate you bringing me out here."

The sheriff knocked some of the crusty dirt off the object and stuck it in one of his oversized pants pockets. We turned around and started walking back to his car. By the time we reached it, he had his big flashlight switched on so we could follow its thin yellow eye of light as it cut through the darkness.

LeRoy drove us back to our truck. When we got out, Nolay said, "Thanks, LeRoy, for taking the time to come out here."

"No trouble at all. I'm just doin' my job. Y'all have a good evening."

By the time we reached home, Mama had nearly every lantern in the house lit. Before we could open the front door, she was standing there. "Where have you two been? I thought you were just going down to the Last Chance. I was nearly ready to come out looking for you."

Nolay looked back at me. "Sorry if we worried you. I thought Bones told you we might be gone for a while."

"She just said you were going down to the store, that's all. Y'all go wash up, supper is sitting on the stove."

When we were settled around the table, Mama asked, "So what took you so long?"

Nolay said, "We ended up meeting LeRoy and taking a walk out to the swamps."

"What on earth for?"

"Well, looks like Bones found something out there today that she thought the sheriff might be interested in."

And from the tone of his voice it was clear he did not think it was of any interest.

Mama put her fork down and looked straight at me. "You were out in the swamps today? By yourself? Didn't you tell me you were going over to Little Man's."

"Yes, ma'am, I know I told you a lie, but I just had to. I had to go out there and look."

"And it was worth lying about?"

"I'm sorry, Mama. I know it was wrong. But I kept hearing what Mr. Speed was trying to tell me and I had to go out there."

"Mr. Speed? Bones, I know how much you loved him and enjoyed being with him. And how much you miss him. But he's not with us any longer. And you are going to have to accept that. He's in heaven, he's at peace."

"Yes, ma'am." I knew better than to open my mouth, but Mr. Speed was at peace when he was right here on earth. He didn't have to go to heaven for that.

"I hope nothing will be so important again that you have to lie to me about it. You were told not to go out in those swamps, especially by yourself. Young lady, that was a silly and dangerous thing for you to have done."

"Yes, ma'am, sorry. I won't do anything like that again."

Mama was so upset with me that she didn't even ask what I had found in the swamps, and Nolay didn't tell her.

I sat at the kitchen table with my mama and daddy and felt dumber than dust.

gratitude

Wednesday morning when I got on the school bus and sat down next to Little Man, I didn't say a word about what I had done the day before. I was too ashamed to tell him I had lied to my mama and done a stupid, dangerous thing. I was not in the mood for sharing something like that.

All that day I felt like I had a little gray cloud hovering over my head. For that matter, the entire next week felt like that. One whole week had passed since I'd given Sheriff LeRoy his solid evidence, or at least what I thought was solid, and we had not heard one word from him. Not one word. I was beginning to feel like the sheriff was just a big puddle of water.

Thursday afternoon Little Man came home with me after school and helped me give Pearl a bath. We were out back when the dogs started barking and we heard the toot of a car horn from the front yard. We walked around front to find the hulking frame of Sheriff LeRoy leaning against his car.

I turned around so fast I bumped broadside into Little Man. Before I could speak a word, he put both his hands on my shoulders and said, "Let's go see what the sheriff is here for."

Just then, Nolay opened the door and walked out. "Howdy, LeRoy, what brings you out here today?"

"Well, if it ain't a bother, I got something I need to talk to y'all about. It's pretty important and I figure I should get it done with."

"Ain't no bother, LeRoy, come on in."

Little Man leaned over and whispered in my ear, "There ain't nothing to be scared about."

"I don't know, I hope you're right. We better get inside so we can find out."

Me and Little Man ran back and hosed Pearl off, then ran into the house.

Mama heard LeRoy's voice and came out to greet him in the living room. "Hello, LeRoy, how are you today?"

"Just fine, Miss Lori. I got something I need to talk to you folks about. Sorry to be bargin' in like this, but it's mighty important."

"It's all right, LeRoy, you just have a seat."

LeRoy squeezed into one of our living room chairs. He took his Stetson off and placed it on the floor.

"Would you like a cup of coffee? I just made a fresh pot." Mama kept a pot of coffee on nearly all day. She had told me one time, "A cup of coffee and a Lucky Strike is one of the little joys of life."

"Why, yes, ma'am, that would be fine, if it ain't too much trouble."

"No trouble at all."

Little Man and I made ourselves comfortable and as invisible as possible on the floor. Mama came in and placed the coffee on a little table in front of the sheriff, then sat next to Nolay on the couch.

LeRoy took a sip of coffee and opened a folder full of papers he held on his knees. "I been down in Miami since last Wednesday, just drove up this morning. You remember last time I told you about going down there? Well, this here is the results of the investigation."

Nolay and Mama watched silently as LeRoy shuffled through the papers. He took another sip of coffee. "Mighty fine coffee, Miss Lori."

"I'm glad you enjoy it, LeRoy." I could tell by the determined look on her face that Mama wasn't about to offer him any food to go along with it.

LeRoy raised his huge head and said, "First off, I reckon I got them city po-lease a little more interested in what them two fellas, Decker and Fowler, were up to. Me and this detective, we started to poke around in the neighborhood where Fowler lived. Come to find out the neighbors had plenty to say about the Fowlers. Seems Mr. Decker spent a lot of time over at the Fowlers' house when Mr. Fowler was away. I do believe Mr. Decker and Mr. Fowler's wife was having them a little go-around."

LeRoy stopped midsentence, glanced sideways at me and Little Man, and lowered his voice, as if we would not hear him sitting two feet away. "If you know where I'm gettin' to with that."

Nolay said, "Yeah, LeRoy, we understand what you're saying. So then what happened?"

"Appears they got a search warrant and went to Decker's house." LeRoy leaned back in his chair and looked around as if to make sure he had the full attention of everyone in the room. "Know what they found in his closet?"

Nolay shook his head. "No idea, LeRoy, what did they find?"

"They found a .38-caliber pistol, same kind of gun that was used to shoot Fowler. You will recall that when I found that man's body, there was a bullet hole in his head." LeRoy sipped his coffee. "Next thing they did was test that gun. Law enforcement has come a long way; they got ways of testing things out like that now. You know what they found?"

Nolay and Mama sat silently and stared at LeRoy.

"They found that that gun was the exact same one used in the killing."

LeRoy took another sip of his coffee. "Now we were startin' to get some evidence put together. But we still did not have anything solid that would put Decker in the same place where that murder took place." LeRoy stopped and looked in my direction. A smile played across his wide face. "That is, until Miss Bones here found that watch out in the swamps. After we cleaned it up, we saw an inscription on the back of it, to Decker from Fowler's wife. Sorta like a little love letter.

There wadn't no doubt who it belonged to or how it got out there. That pretty much sewed up the case."

Little Man whispered, "A watch?"

I turned to look at him. He had that question mark sitting right in the middle of his forehead.

Mama sat straight up. "A watch? What watch?"

Sheriff LeRoy replied, "Why, the one Miss Bones took me and Nolay out to the swamps to find. She said Speed had given her the directions, and by golly, there it was."

I could see by the look on Mama's face she was trying to sort out all this information. She said, "Bones, that's what you went out in the swamps to find?"

"Yes, ma'am. I know it was wrong to lie. But it was like all the things Mr. Speed was trying to tell me came together. And when I found that watch, I just knew it was the same one that Silver almost ripped off that man's arm the day the two of them came out to our house."

Mama sat quietly, blinking her eyes. Then she said, "LeRoy, what does all this mean?"

"Well, Miss Lori, it means they arrested Decker for the murder of his partner, Mr. Fowler. Seems Decker and Mr. Fowler's wife was planning on having them some fun with that fifty thousand dollars of insurance money."

Me and Little Man sat with our mouths open like two gulping fish. Nolay and Mama remained silent as stumps. I could almost see LeRoy's words hovering around their ears like bees.

Mama and Nolay turned to look at me. Nolay slapped his

knee and said, "Gol-durn, Bones! And here I thought that watch didn't mean anything. I sure was wrong this time."

Mama kept her eyes on me. "Your daddy and I certainly owe you an apology. Especially me. I should have paid better attention to what you were trying to do."

LeRoy shook his head. "I wish you could have seen the look on Decker's face when I walked into that interrogatin' room and laid that watch on the table. I thought he was gonna swallow his tongue. He looked at me and said, 'Where did you find this?'

"And I tolt him, 'In the swamps, pretty close to where you dropped off your partner's body.' He started ranting and raving about having paid those stupid Reems brothers good money to find it for 'im. Appears them Reems bothers was in cahoots with those Yankee real estate boys. They were gonna go around and hep 'em buy up property real cheap and sell it off for a profit." The sheriff let out a little laugh. "But I guess they weren't that stupid, 'cause they knew that area would be under water until winter came and the swamps dried up."

LeRoy stopped and took a sip of coffee. "That's why it was so easy for Miss Bones to find it." He looked in my direction and nodded in approval. Then he continued, "When they arrested Mrs. Fowler for being an accomplice to murder, she turned on Decker quicker than a squirrel a-hidin' a nut. Told them city po-lease how Decker killed her husband and dumped his body in the swamp. Being that the two of 'em had got into that confrontation with Nolay, Decker thought that would be the best place to dump the body." LeRoy took a sip of coffee. "I reckon he thought the gators would take care of the body and nothing would ever be found. He would just report his partner missin', and that would be the end of it. He didn't count on losing that watch."

LeRoy took another sip of coffee and continued. "Still ain't real clear on how the leg got separated from the body. Although when I found it, the body was pretty well chewed up. Could have been any number of swamp critter to do that. Got to admit, Decker was a smart Yankee, but not smart enough to get away with murder."

Nolay leaned forward. "LeRoy, does that mean I have been cleared of the charges?"

"It sure does. It means your name has been cleared. You are no longer a suspect. You are a free man."

The reality of Sheriff LeRoy's words spread inside me like drops of oil shimmering across the surface of water. I turned to Little Man. Words bubbled up and stuck in my throat. Before I could utter a sound, Little Man smiled and turned away.

Mama clasped both hands together as if in prayer. "Thank you, LeRoy. Thank you."

A flush of crimson crept steadily up LeRoy's long face. He hung his giant head and mumbled, "Just doin' my job, Miss Lori." He drained the rest of his coffee and set the cup down on the small table. "Now, the next situation is that one with ol' Peckerhead Willy. I knew who done it, 'cause ol' Charlie was brave enough to tell me. It was just a matter of figurin' out how to catch 'em, without causin' no harm to Charlie." LeRoy looked longingly at his empty coffee cup.

Mama said, "LeRoy, would you like some more coffee?"

"Yes, ma'am, if you got some more, that would be mighty fine."

As Mama got up and walked toward the kitchen, she hesitated, glanced at Nolay, and then said, "LeRoy, would you like some sausage biscuits with your coffee? I have some left over from breakfast."

"If it ain't no bother, Miss Lori, I sure would appreciate it."

"It's no bother, LeRoy. No bother at all."

LeRoy's eyes glazed over as Mama placed a heaping plate of biscuits stuffed with sausage patties on the table in front of him. Nolay looked at me and raised one of his eyebrows. A smile nudged at the corners of his mouth. We were in for a long, slow story. One that we were all anxious to hear.

LeRoy picked up a sausage biscuit, and in two chomps it disappeared into his huge mouth. "Miss Lori, that is a biscuit comparable to my mama's. Now, like I said before, law enforcement has come a long ways. For a couple of years, I been dabblin' in something called fingerprints. It's been around for a while, but being we ain't a very big po-lease force down here, it was harder to come by." LeRoy held up one of his massive hands and pointed to the fingertip. "You see all them little squiggly lines. Every person has their own special lines. Each time we touch something, we leave a little fingerprint trail behind us."

Me and Little Man held our hands out in front of us and compared fingertips.

LeRoy talked around another biscuit. "When Charlie told me about Whackerstacker using a branch as a weapon, I went out and found it. It was hid up under some bushes, so it still had some blood and hair on it and some usable prints. The next thing I got was that chicken crate over at Charlie's that Whackerstacker picked up. It had prints on it, too. And then there was the shovel he used to try and chop off Nolay's head."

The sheriff stopped for a biscuit break, then continued. "Now that I had the evidence, I needed to get it all up to Jacksonville, where they had the proper FBI equipment to document everything. Course there were other prints on everything, but turns out all of 'em had one print that matched up perfect. They was all from the same person: Whacker-stacker Joe Reems." LeRoy took a sip of coffee. "For your information, late yesterday afternoon, me and two Florida State po-lease men arrested Joe Reems for murder. He is now sittin' in the Titusville jail."

A smile spread across Nolay's face as he looked at the huge man scrunched up in one of our chairs. He stood up, walked over to the sheriff, and stuck out his hand. "I'll be durned, LeRoy, you have made me one happy man. I always knew you had it in you. You're an even better sheriff than your daddy was."

LeRoy hung his head and mumbled, "Well, I don't know about that. I'm just doin' my job."

"You done a dang good job. Let me ask you one thing. What about ol' Whackerstacker's boys? They're young, but they're still meaner than a pack of cornered weasels. You think they might try to hurt Charlie?"

"I don't think so, not after what just happened to their daddy." LeRoy shook his head and let out a little chuckle. "I do believe them state po-lease men put the fear of the devil in them boys. That oldest boy could have been arrested for being an accomplice. If he goes to jail with his daddy, them other two boys would end up in reform school. So I don't think they'll be causing any more harm to Charlie."

When the last biscuit was gone, LeRoy looked wistfully at the empty plate. He sat silently for a moment and then said, "I clean forgot about one more thing—the bail money. Soon as you can get up to the Titusville Courthouse, you can sign for it and it will be returned to you."

Mama said, "The bail money? But it doesn't belong to us."

"Why, sure it does, Miss Lori. Now that Nolay is cleared of all charges, that money is yours, free and clear. All you gotta do is go pick it up." He gathered up his folder of papers, picked up his Stetson, and placed it on his head. "I best be gettin' on now, it's been a long day. I just wanted to let you folks know the good news." He tipped his hat in Mama's direction. "Much obliged to you, Miss Lori, for the coffee and biscuits."

Mama looked up at the massive man standing in front of her; her eyes sparkled like dewdrops in the sun. "Thank you, LeRoy, for the best gift we have ever had."

Nolay stood up. "I'll walk you out to the car, LeRoy."

LeRoy jingled across the room and was just stooping to walk through our door when I jumped up and ran over to him. "Sheriff LeRoy?"

He turned and looked down at me. I stuck out my hand. His huge hand slowly stretched out and wrapped around mine, as soft and gentle as a dishcloth. "Sheriff, I just want to say thank you, and I want to tell you that I think you are a mighty fine sheriff."

"Why, thank you, Miss Bones, I 'preciate them kind words. I always try to do my best. And I want to thank you for your hep. Without that watch it woulda been a harder nut to crack. You are a mighty fine little detective."

"Thank you, Sheriff." I watched as the massive man ambled back out to his car, with Nolay by his side. I now had a lot of admiration for pond water and puddles.

When I turned around, Little Man was still sitting on the floor. The question mark was gone, and he was wearing a smile so big it nearly split his face in half. I went over and sat down beside him. "I'm glad you were right, Little Man. I can't believe my imagination got the best of me. I let my mind go to some places it never should have went." I looked down at my feet and said, "Little Man, are you mad at me?"

"Course I ain't mad at you. Why would I be? You didn't do nothing wrong. It ain't important that I was right. It's more important that what you were thinking was wrong. I'm just glad it all turned out this way."

The two of us sat on the floor and shared our silence. "Little Man, you know that hunting knife that I found that day out in the swamps?"

"Course I do."

"I'd like you to keep it for your own. It would just remind me of things I don't want to be reminded of."

Little Man let out a soft laugh and looked down at the floor. "Bones, I think you should have it. It can remind you of things you need to be reminded of and to never let your mind go wanderin' like that again. I'll bring it next time I'm out here."

Little Man was just about the best friend a person could ever have.

puzzles

Nolay walked back in the house and let out a hoot. He sauntered over, pulled Mama off the couch, and swung her around the room a couple of times. Me and Little Man busted out laughing.

Nolay put Mama down and stood in the middle of the living room. "Hallelujah! Ol' LeRoy pulled it off!" He looked straight at me. "Bones, I'm mighty proud of you. I'm proud of what you did."

"I'm just glad it all turned out for the good. But you know what, if it hadn't been for Mr. Speed, I never would have known to go looking for something out in the swamps. I guess we owe him a big thank-you."

"You're right about that, Bones. I wish he was here so I could shake his hand."

Nolay and Mama sat down on the sofa. "Bones, what do you think about that big old slow-movin' sheriff now?"

"I think he's about the smartest sheriff I ever did know."

"You know what I'm thinkin'? I'm thinkin' we should have us a celebration. What do you say, Honey Girl?"

"That's a fine idea. We certainly have a lot to celebrate."

"Tomorrow being Friday, I'm going out to invite everyone I know to come over here this Saturday. We're gonna have us a cookout and fellowship with each other. It ain't New Year's, but I think we just might break out some fireworks and shoot 'em off."

Nolay stood up so quick it looked like he had springs on his feet. "Come on, Little Man, I'll give you a ride home. I want to see if your daddy can come over tomorrow and help out settin' up some stuff."

That night at supper, Nolay and Mama looked like they were walking through sunshine instead of standing under a rain cloud. I felt like a chameleon that had just shed its old skin and was trying to get comfortable in its new one.

Later, our conversation centered on the return of the bail money. Three hundred dollars. What would we do with it?

Mama said, "It's just not right for us to keep that money. It should be returned to the people who gave it to us."

Nolay shook his head. "How do we know who gave us what? It was a gift. It would be durn embarrassing for us to return a gift. That would be like telling someone you don't like what they gave you."

"I don't know, Nolay. It just doesn't seem right for us to keep it. Maybe we should put it in the bank and save it to help other people in an emergency."

Nolay stopped eating and cocked his head sideways.

"Helping people, now, that is a mighty fine idea. How 'bout we use that money to buy six telephone poles, have 'em installed, and get hooked up to electricity?" He glanced over at me and winked. "We might even have enough left over to buy you a brand-new refrigerator."

Mama leveled her gaze at Nolay and said, "And just how would us having electricity and a refrigerator help other people?"

"Anytime someone needed some ice or something cold, we could help 'em out with it." He turned to me. "Bones, what do you think?"

"I reckon it's a great idea to have electricity and a refrigerator!"

"Now, see there, Honey Girl? Two out of three agree on it." Nolay reached over and placed his hand on Mama's. "I think our friends and neighbors would be danged happy for us to have electricity."

Mama just smiled and shook her head.

After supper Nolay opened up Mama's cedar chest to survey the assortment of firecrackers we had been accumulating over the past year. Every trip that Nolay took up to north Florida or Georgia, he came back home with fireworks. There were strings of firecrackers, Roman candles, cherry bombs, and bottle rockets.

Nolay stacked all the fireworks in neat little piles, stood up, and rocked back on his heels. "Yes, sir, we are gonna light up the sky Saturday night."

Mama walked in and said, "I was just thinking; I have a

bag of marshmallows that needs to be used up. Why don't you two go out and make a fire so we can roast a few?"

"Honey Girl, that sounds like a mighty fine idea. I'll get out there right now."

I followed Mama back into the kitchen and started to help her clear the table, but she said, "Bones, I can wash up. Why don't you grab our old beach blanket from the closet and go help Nolay? I'll be out in a few minutes with the marshmallows."

I went in my room and woke up Nippy. Now that winter was almost here, she slept most of the time. I held her warm sleepy body under my arm. As I grabbed the blanket, Mama called out, "Bones, be sure to rub on some DDT. There's some in the can right there by the door with a rag in it. The mosquitoes will be out on a night like this. And take some for your daddy, too. I'll put some on before I come out."

"Yes, ma'am, I will."

I opened the door, and Nippy and I walked out into the moonless night. It was like stepping into a bottle of black ink. I whistled, and Pearl, Harry, and the dogs ran to me. They led me to the small pile of wood that Nolay had just set on fire. He stirred the embers with a stick and watched as a cluster of cinders raced each other up into the darkness. He pointed to one side of the fire and said, "Bones, put the blanket down over there, out of the breeze, so the smoke don't make us cry."

We sat down; the fire came to life and bathed us in a warm orange glow. Paddlefoot and Mr. Jones curled up as close as they could to the blanket. Silver lay down on the other side;

like a small sphinx, she stared into the fire, her front paws crossed and resting on the blanket's edge. Pearl grunted as she plopped down and made herself comfortable in the back, away from the heat. Harry laid down behind Pearl and rested his head on her plump belly.

Nippy curled up on the blanket between us for a few minutes, then got up and stretched. She looked at me, then scurried toward the darkness. I called out to her; she stopped and looked back at me, then turned and melted into the night. I started to go after her. Nolay placed his hand on my arm. "Bones, you gotta let her go."

"But she might run away, and I don't want to lose her."

"She's a wild critter; you can't take the wildness away from her. You gotta let her go find that part of herself."

I stared out into the blackness. "Yes, sir, I will, but I don't want to."

Nolay placed his hand on my head and said, "Let's me and you lay down on the blanket and see who can count the most stars."

So me and Nolay lay down and looked up into the black sky.

"There must be a zillion stars up there. The angels are working hard tonight, pouring out all those bushel baskets of miracles." I pointed to a huge star that stood out from the rest. "Nolay, you see that star over yonder? I think that one belongs to Mr. Speed. I think he's up there with God, looking down on us right now."

"I'm sure he is, Bones. If I know Speed, he's busy helping the angels pour out all those miracles. He poured one down on us, that's for sure."

"Yes, sir, I think he did, too."

"Bones, the last three months has been a whirlwind learning lesson. I learned I got to take my actions a little more serious. I got you and your mama to look after. You can't stay a kid all your life. But you can still enjoy life like you're a kid. I intend to change some of my ways."

"Yes, sir, that makes sense. I intend to change some of mine, too, like keeping better track of my thoughts so they don't go wandering away someplace they shouldn't."

The dogs stirred as Mama walked up and joined us on the blanket. "It is such a beautiful night." She lit up a Lucky Strike.

Nolay and I sat up; he gave us each a sharpened stick. Mama opened the bag of marshmallows, releasing their sweet scent into the night air. Pearl grunted in anticipation. "Wait till I roast one," I told her. "You know you like the roasted ones better than the raw ones." Her shiny black eyes followed every move I made as I slid a sugary blob on the stick and held it over the fire. The flames licked up and turned the white ball into a glazed marble. "You know," I said, "life sure can be confusing. I mean, I've lived here all my life, but it seems like lately I'm meeting people I didn't even know. Or I knew 'em, but I didn't know who they really were."

Nolay looked over at me and smiled. "Bones, life can be as mysterious as one of them puzzles in a box. You know the kind with them little pieces you put together to make a picture?"

"Yes, sir, a jigsaw puzzle. I don't know why they're called that, but I've played with 'em at school."

"Well, the way I figure it, every one of us is just a puzzle being put together. Nearly 'bout everything we do is a little piece of us that gets stuck together to make up the whole picture of who we really are. You understand what I'm sayin'?"

"Yes, sir, I reckon I do."

Mama let out a little laugh. "Nolay, you do have a way with words."

I looked at Nolay and Mama and realized what huge pieces of my puzzle they were. Mama's piece nestled perfectly into its own snug little space, but Nolay's was like looking at the sun through a silver of broken glass, a mixture of soft jagged colors bending and blending, trying to mix together.

As the fire crackled and popped, I thought about how exciting Saturday night would be. We were going to light up the sky with fireworks. Little Man and everyone would be here, celebrating together.

Nolay looked over at me and Mama. "Next year this time we will be hooked up to electricity. Might even have us a television set. What do you think about that, Bones?"

"A television? Why, that would be about the grandest thing I could ever imagine!" But I wasn't going to count on that to happen anytime soon. Nolay was just having some fun. After all, I couldn't expect him to change overnight.

The darkness closed in around us and came alive with the familiar voices of frogs and crickets. Our little family sat on the blanket in a pool of amber light, roasting our marshmallows. Bullbats swooped down and gobbled up bugs on the edge of the fire's light. A white sliver of moon peeped over the horizon and smiled down at us sideways. Pearl nuzzled close to my leg and grunted in contentment. I reached down and scratched behind her bristled ears. "Nolay, do you think we could take Pearl out to visit Miss Eunice? You know how much Pearl loves to ride in the back of the truck, and I know Miss Eunice would enjoy meeting her."

Nolay smiled and nodded. "Of course we can, Bones. That sounds like a mighty fine idea."

the hunt

Friday when I got on the school bus, Little Man was still grinning from ear to ear.

I sat down next to him and said, "I am so happy all this is over with. I have to admit, Sheriff LeRoy sure knew what he was doing."

"Me too. I'm glad Mr. Nolay got his name cleared."

"I'm just happy my daddy is never going back to jail."

"Bones, after school today, why don't me and you go for a hunt out by the swamps? Now that everything has been cleared up, it's safe to go back out there. Maybe we can scare up something for the cookout."

"That sounds good to me. I'm sure Mama will let me go out there now."

On the school playground I walked up to Betty Jean Davis and said, "Did you hear about what happened with my daddy?"

"No, I did not. Did he get arrested again?"

"No, Betty Jean, he has been cleared of everything. He never did any of those things."

Betty Jean sniffed in some air and said, "I do not care. *You* and *your* family mean nothing to me."

I leaned in a little closer to her and whispered, "Betty Jean, you should start being nicer to people or your secret admirer might come crawling around in your bed when you're sleeping." Betty Jean's eyes bulged out. Her mouth puckered up like she had just taken a swig of vinegar. I turned and walked away before she could find her voice again.

After school I was outside with my rifle, all dressed for hunting. I heard Mr. Cotton's tractor coming up our driveway. Little Man was in the driver's seat. He wasn't old enough to have a driver's license, but sometimes his daddy let him drive the tractor because it wasn't a car.

I went out to meet him. He climbed down from the tractor, then turned around and picked up his double-barreled shotgun from the floor. It was his Christmas present from last year, but you would think he'd just got it. He dearly loved that gun. Little Man's face glowed with pride as he held it out in front of him. "Bones, is that about the prettiest thing you ever did see?"

"Little Man, you say that every time you touch that gun. C'mon, let's get going."

As we headed toward the swamps, the dogs started to follow us. "Bones," Little Man said, "turn your dogs around. None of 'em is hounds and they'll just scare everything away."

"They're good huntin' dogs, they won't scare anything away."

"They are not. Not a one of 'em has a drop of hound in 'em. Now tell 'em to stay back. You remember how bad they were last time they came in the swamps with us?"

"They were not bad. Silver was the one that found that Yankee man's leg."

"That was just luck on her side. Tell 'em to stay back."

I turned around and told the dogs to stay. The three of them sat in the yard and watched forlornly as I walked away with Little Man.

Me and Little Man walked along in silence. Tall stands of parched saw grass rustled in the cool evening breeze. A thin gray mist hovered over pockets of warm water. The only sound was our feet crunching along the tops of dry leaves.

Every few minutes, Little Man would stop and dramatically hold out one arm for me to stop, too. He would bend his head forward and search back and forth, like an Indian in the movies.

After he did this a couple of times, I couldn't stand it anymore. "What are you doing, Little Man? You're acting like you're Davy Crockett or something."

"I am not. I'm just huntin', that's all."

"Well, I ain't ever seen you hunt like that before."

"Well, now you have. Hush up, Bones, before you scare everything in the swamp away."

We continued to walk along in silence. The evening shadows had come alive, flickering over the thick undergrowth. Suddenly Little Man stopped and held me back with his arm. Only this time, he didn't do the Indian search thing with his head. He looked back at me and whispered, "You hear that?"

I cocked my head and strained my ears, but all I heard was the breeze as it brushed across the tops of the dry leaves.

Little Man squatted and pulled me down with him. He stared into a cluster of trees. "There's something in there."

The sound of his voice made the hair stand up on the back of my neck and along my arms. "Are you tryin' to scare me? There ain't nothing in there."

Little Man turned and looked at me. The brown of his eyes became one with the evening dusk; all I could see were two white circles in his face. "I'm sure there's something in there."

As I stared into the thicket, something moved. I watched as a murky form began to rise up from the shadows. At first it looked like somebody covered in an old brown blanket trying to scare us. Then it slowly moved forward, away from the shadows and out into the clearing. Two large golden eyes glinted in our direction.

Little Man's grip tightened on my arm. I looked at him and saw small silvery beads of sweat pop up across his forehead. "Bones, that is a gol-durn black bear."

I looked closer. The shadowy lump unfolded, and sure enough, it was a bear. It took a few hesitant steps in our direction and stopped. It raised its huge head and began to sniff the air. The bear was so close I could see white hairs around its jaw and eyes. A familiar musky smell drifted off its shaggy body and filled the air. It was the same smell I had smelled those other times out on the edge of the swamp.

Little Man let go of my arm. He eased his hand under the stock, slowly raised the gun, and pointed in the direction of the bear. His head leaned in against the stock; one eye squinted shut as he looked down the smooth metal barrel and aimed at the bear's chest. His finger wrapped around the trigger.

I reached over and placed my hand on the gun, right above the hammer. "Little Man, that's Sandy Claws. You can't kill Sandy Claws."

"That's a bear, a big black bear."

"That's Sandy Claws. If you kill her it would be like . . . like killing a story. I've heard stories about her all my life, and so have you. Sometimes I didn't think she was real, but there she is, right in front of us. She's real, and she's still alive."

Little Man turned, and we stared deeply into each other's eyes. Slowly his face softened as memories flooded in and overpowered the hunter. He moved his finger away from the trigger and lowered the gun.

We continued to stare at each other, a pungent smell surrounding us and drifting up our noses. We whispered at the same time, "Sandy Claws is Soap Sally!"

We watched as the old bear pointed her nose straight up and sniffed as if in search of some familiar scent. She dropped her massive head and slowly rocked back and forth. She looked sleepily in our direction. Her huge maw opened and yawned. Then she turned and ambled back into the thicket of trees, where her body once again blended into the shadows.

Little Man put his hand on my arm. "Wait till we know for sure she's gone."

For a few minutes we sat in silence, our ears filled with the rhythm of our own breathing.

"Okay, Bones, I think it's safe now."

We got up and walked over to where the bear had stood. We knelt down and reverently placed our hands in the prints she had left behind.

"I reckon it was a honor for us just to get to see her." Little Man stood up. "We better be heading back. I gotta get back home before dark, and that old tractor ain't got headlights."

As we walked side by side, I asked, "Do you think it's sorta sad that ol' Sandy Claws has to live all by herself? I mean, she don't have no friends or family. Do you think she's lonely?"

"I don't know about a bear being lonesome. I'd have to think on it. I reckon it could happen." Little Man shook his head. "I swear, Bones, you ask some of the dangest questions. But I do admit, it does get your mind a-wonderin'."

Back at the house, Little Man got on the tractor and started it up. As he rumbled off into the night, he yelled over the noise of the engine, "I'll see you tomorrow, Bones."

That evening at the dinner table I could hardly wait to tell Nolay and Mama.

"You'll never guess what happened to me and Little Man today when we went huntin'."

Nolay replied, "Y'all track something down or did something track you down?"

"Better than that, Nolay. We saw ol' Sandy Claws. She came out and stood right in front of us, clear as day."

"You sure about that, you really saw her? Your eyes wadn't playing tricks on you?"

"No, sir, it wasn't a trick, she was really there. She's real; she was so close I could see her eyes and even smell her. You remember those times I thought Soap Sally or something was after me? Well, it was Sandy Claws. I know it was her. I recognized the smell. She smells like an ol' wet rug or something. After she left, we went out and looked at her feet prints, and just like you always said, the claws were so big they dug right down into the sand."

"Well now, I am mighty glad to know that ol' bear is still alive. She's got somewhat of a legend around her. She must have woke up from her winter nap for a little break. And Bones, I know what you mean about that smell. I've smelled it myself." Nolay let out a little laugh. "Now, ain't that something . . . that ol' bear spying on us all these years!"

"Nolay, do you think she's lonely? Do you think she misses her kids and family?"

"Well, I reckon she could feel that way. No tellin' how far she roams up and down these woods lookin' for her kids, lookin' for a friend. I don't know if she quite understands that they're all dead and ain't ever coming back. But she must miss 'em."

"Did you ever shoot a bear?"

"Lord, no. Why would I go shoot something I didn't want

to eat? You don't go killin' something just 'cause you got a gun or something that's more powerful than it is. You name me one animal that kills just for the fun of it."

"Well, cats. I seen our cats kill a mouse or a bird and not eat it, just play with it."

"That's because they've been tamed and spoiled. They live with people that provide 'em with everything they need. Believe me, if they were out in the wild, they wouldn't play with their food. There ain't no need to kill something if there ain't a good purpose for it."

"Nolay, what about those people that kill animals to have them stuffed and hung up on their walls?"

"That's a shameful waste of life. That's one of the reasons we don't have any more black bear or panther or flocks of egrets and whooping cranes. Them fool Yankees." Nolay stopped, gathered up his thoughts, then continued, "Well . . . not only Yankees, but lots of greedy people came down here and slaughtered animals for their fur and feathers. Didn't even eat 'em. Just left their bodies to rot. They're killin' the swamps, stealin' the water, buying up the land. It just ain't right."

Mama said quietly, "Nolay, I think if you look back on what's happened, it wasn't just outsiders that did those things. It was also the people that lived here. The people that knew the ways of all those animals and how to hunt them. You can't just be blaming Yankees and outsiders."

"That's true, Honey Girl. But I do think I could put the blame on one thing and just about one thing only. Greed."

Nolay leaned forward and looked at me. "Bones, I will do whatever it takes to protect this land. To protect these swamps and our way of life. We done lost enough of it already, and I don't intend to lose any more. Or there won't be none left for you or anyone else. You understand, Bones?"

I looked at Nolay, his eyes bumping into mine like two clear blue ice cubes. "Yes, sir, I do understand."

fellowship

Saturday morning I was up before the first rays of light. I ran into Nolay and Mama's bedroom. "Y'all get up. It's Saturday!"

Nolay looked at me with one eye closed. "Good Lord, Bones, Ikibob ain't even crowed yet."

"That's 'cause he's just a rooster, and he don't know what day it is."

"All right, all right. I do have a lot of stuff to take care of."

At breakfast, Nolay told us all the things he had done the day before. "I went by the Fish House and told Ironhead, stopped by the Last Chance and put a call in to the Cat clan. Hopefully some of 'em will make it up here tomorrow. I didn't get to see everyone I wanted to, but I think the word will get out."

Mama said, "You must be expecting everyone we know to show up, because you brought home enough corn on the cob to feed the whole town. We'll have to use a washtub to boil it in."

"Don't worry, Honey Girl, I'm sure none of it will go to waste."

· · ·

We had just finished breakfast when we heard a car horn out-side. I ran to the window and saw Mr. Cotton's truck. Sitting in the back bed were Little Man, Earl, Ethan, and a jumble of sawhorses and boards. Nolay walked out and told Mr. Cotton, "The shadiest place will be over yonder under the mango tree." Mr. Cotton drove over to the tree, and the boys jumped out and started unloading the truck and setting up makeshift tables and benches.

When they finished, Little Man came over to me and said, "Mama's baking up some pies, cakes, and corn bread. She sure is makin' good use of that new oven. We gotta go back and get some more things, then we'll be over to help y'all with everything."

When they came back, they had not only Miss Melba but also just about every pot, pan, and plate they owned. All morning long, Mama's kitchen was bustling with activity.

The boys made a long rectangular fire out in the yard. Pots and washtubs were cleaned and stacked up, ready to be put to use. Me, Mama, and Miss Melba started carrying stuff out to the tables.

Late morning, our visitors began to arrive. First came Ironhead. I watched as his old blue pickup truck inched its way up the drive. Sitting next to him was Mr. Charlie. Iron-head drove up by the fire, the whole back of the truck stacked with fresh oysters in the shell.

Ironhead got out and huffed and puffed in our direction,

"It being November, this here is the first and best batch of oysters."

Mr. Charlie got out and wobbled over carrying a huge handmade basket. It was full of hard-boiled eggs. "I boiled 'em up myself this morning," Mr. Charlie said as he stood in the yard and looked around.

I walked up to him and took the basket. "Thank you, Mr. Charlie." I pointed toward the side of our house. "Looky over there."

His eyes followed the direction of my finger and came to rest on Ikibob Rooster standing in the shade with a couple of his hens. Mr. Charlie smiled and shook his head. "Now, that is one handsome fella. I know my Sonny-Boy's gonna be just like 'im."

Mama walked over and said, "It's been a while, Charlie. I am glad to see you out here again. And I must say your fertilizer grows some happy, healthy vegetables. Now you just come on over here and have a seat by us."

Nolay brought over a washtub. Ironhead helped him fill it with oysters and fresh ears of corn. The two of them put it the trunk of the Champion.

Nolay walked back over to where me and Mama were setting up plates and forks on the tables. He handed Mama a croker sack and said, "Lori, put some corn bread and one of them cakes in here. I'm gonna take all this over to Blue and Jackson's. Just 'cause they're colored don't mean they ain't part of this community. I figure they deserve to take part in our celebration just like everyone else."

As I watched Nolay walk back to the Champion, I felt a lump climb its way up my throat and a fine mist spread over my eyes. Like a warm breeze, Mama's arm wrapped around my shoulders. I looked back at her. "I am proud of him, too." She squeezed my arm. "Now come on, we have lots of work to do."

"Yes, ma'am." Nolay was one surprise after another.

Next came Mr. Ball and Miss Evelyn. Mr. Ball got out and opened the car door. Inside were three big blocks of ice and two cases of RC Colas! The boys took over a washtub and loaded it all inside. Miss Evelyn got out and stood by the car. I walked over to her and said, "Hey, Miss Evelyn."

She looked down and smiled. "Bones, you know I have never been out to your home before? It is just lovely. I'm so glad your daddy invited us. I need to get out of that office a little more often."

"Yes, ma'am, I'm glad y'all came, too."

Mama walked over and said, "Evelyn, it is so nice to see you. Come have a seat in the shade."

"Thank you, Lori, but it looks like you could use a few more hands. You know I'm pretty good at husking corn."

"That would be great. Come on over."

Next, a green pickup truck came nosing up the road. Uncle Bob Cat was in the driver's seat, and Uncle Tom was beside him. Sitting in the back was a jumble of brightly dressed women and kids. The Cat clan had arrived. They looked like a bunch of happy, colorful ants crawling out over the back of the truck.

I ran to meet them. We all hugged each other. The women

began carrying bags of food over to the table where Mama and Miss Melba were. I said to the kids, "Y'all come here and meet my best friend, Little Man. He's over by the fire pit. Then we can all go out back and meet Pearl and Harry."

Just as we were about to head out back, Jimmy Cat turned and pointed. "Looky there, what's that?" Coming up our driveway real slow was Sheriff LeRoy with his red lights flashing! He drove up and parked out front, opened the car door, and unfolded his huge body. He stood by the car, set his Stetson squarely on his head, and looked in our direction. Then he waved one of his long arms in the air, motioning us kids to come over. Everyone rushed to be first.

Sheriff LeRoy said, "Howdy, Miss Bones, Little Man. And who are all these fine-looking folks?"

I answered, "These are my cousins from the Everglades. They're from Nolay's family, the Cat clan."

"Well, I swear, it is a pleasure to meet everyone." He turned toward his car. "Would y'all like to see what all is inside a real po-lease car?"

I sure wanted to know what was inside that car, because I remembered plain as day what Little Man had told me about the time he rode with the sheriff out in the swamps to retrieve that Yankee man's leg.

For the next half hour, everyone hooted and hollered as the sheriff showed us his handcuffs, keys, billy club, and even how his police radio worked. He took his .357 Magnum out of its holster and let everyone rub their hands across the slick, shiny barrel. He reached inside the car and brought out a sawed-off shotgun that had been hanging on the backseat.

With both hands he cradled it as gentle as a baby and held it out for us to admire. Sheriff LeRoy cocked his head and looked straight at us. "Now, this is something I would use only in an emergency. If one ever did occur. And I can guarantee that if I had someone sittin' in the backseat, this little puppy would be ridin' in the front seat with me." This brought a burst of laughter from everyone.

I looked over and smiled at Little Man. He sure had been right about that car—Sherriff LeRoy was prepared for just about anything that could possibly happen.

We had just finished exploring the sheriff's car and were ready to start a furious game of tag when I looked down our road and saw the biggest surprise of the day driving toward us.

There was the Champion, its top down and Nolay behind the steering wheel. Sitting next to him was Miss Eunice. Nolay drove in and parked next to Ironhead's truck. I went over to the car. Nolay flashed one of his dazzling smiles. "I thought Miss Eunice might want to come over and meet Pearl sooner than later."

"Yes, sir. I think that was a fine idea, too."

I looked at Miss Eunice. Her old brown shawl covered her head. Her body was so bent she could hardly see over the dashboard. "Howdy, Miss Eunice."

Miss Eunice looked at me, her cloudy eyes searching for my face. She smiled and said, "Why, chile, this is about the grandest surprise I have had in many a year. I could hardly believe my ears when your daddy showed up and tolt me to get dressed up 'cause he was takin' me to a cookout."

"Yes, ma'am. I know what you mean. My daddy is full of surprises."

"And look at me riding in this here fancy car. Why, I feel like pure royalty."

Nolay opened the car door and got out. He walked over to Miss Eunice and opened her door. "Come on, Miss Eunice. Me and Bones is going to take you to get acquainted with Pearl and some of her friends."

Me and Nolay walked over to Pearl with Miss Eunice between us. I reached down and scratched Pearl behind her ears and said, "Miss Eunice, I would like you to meet Pearl."

Miss Eunice leaned in close, and Pearl, as if to show off how smart she was, stuck her snout under one of Miss Eunice's hands and let out a little snort. Miss Eunice giggled like a schoolgirl and started patting Pearl's snout. "Why, chile, that is about one of the sweetest animals I ever did meet."

"Thank you, Miss Eunice. She's quite the show-off, but she sure is special to me."

Miss Eunice squinted her cloudy eyes in my direction. "Now, next time you come to visit with me, I hope my special girl is around so you can meet her, too."

"You still have a special pet?"

"She actually ain't a pet, but she comes visitin' and I give what food I can. She comes out to that ol' shed at the side of my house. You might of heard of 'er, she's pert near a legend in these parts. She's an ol' black bear called Sandy Claws."

Miss Eunice's words nearly knocked me to the ground. Sandy Claws! That was what I had heard and smelled in that little shed! So, I wasn't so wrong after all, Soap Sally really had been there. I stood there, stunned speechless.

Nolay winked at me over Miss Eunice's head and said, "What do ya think, Bones, am I right or am I right? I said life ain't always the way it appears to be. Sometimes it can be puzzlin'. You got to take the time to fit all them little pieces together so you can see the whole picture."

"Yes, sir, I sure will remember that. And from now on I intend to do my po-lease work before making up my mind on something."

This started Nolay laughing, which got me to laughing too.

I could not wait to find Little Man and spill this bucket of beans to him! That question mark would sure enough be sittin' in the middle of his forehead.

I said, "Miss Eunice, I do hope I get to meet her. I bet she is just a pure wonder."

I stood there with Nolay, Miss Eunice, and Pearl, looking out over our yard. There were cars and trucks and friends and family strewn all over. Smoke curled up from the fire pit and the warm smell of roasting oysters and fresh corn on the cob floated in the air. It was just about the prettiest sight I ever did see.

And to top it all off, I knew there was an angel looking down on us, with a full smile spread across his face.

author's note

A bejeweled finger of land curved gracefully out into the majestic blue-green Atlantic Ocean. A flat, slender finger of land, young and untamed, still in the fragile process of growth. That was Florida, back in the late 1940s and 1950s. This novel was written as a tribute to that time and to the people that lived it.

Precious Bones is purely fiction, thought some of the characters and events are loosely based on a mixture of childhood memories. I am fortunate to have spent my childhood in the small East Coast community of Micco, Florida. Growing up there, surrounded by swamps, forests, and characters galore, was a fascinating experience. We lived in a time that was measured not by hours and minutes but by the events that made up a day.

A swamp is indeed a womb of the world, forever changing, hosting a myriad of plants, animals, reptiles, and birds. The changes of the seasons are announced by vivid colors and the noisy commotion of returning visitors. When a family of whooping cranes flew over our house in Micco and filled the stillness with their mournful cries, and the sky darkened with flocks of squawking, squabbling ducks, we knew the swamps would soon be wrapped in winter's dry jacket of brownness. When nights filled with the bellows of bull gators and the trees with a chorus of chirping birds, summers silvery rains would begin to pain the swamps a fusion of green and gold.

Our quaint community revolved around the Last Chance General Store and Gas Station. It served as our supermarket, post office, and gossip center. Besides Fisher's gas station, it was the only store within twenty-five miles in either direction on the two-lane highway U.S. 1.

The legend of Soap Sally ran deep and strong throughout the South. Parents were known to use it to keep unruly children in line. There were even occasions when an adult would actually dress up as a witch, fake nose and all, and scare the bee-dickens out of us kids. Without electricity and televisions, our entertainment was created mostly in our imaginations.

Of course, this story never would have been told without the memories created by my friends, who I actually thought of as family. The McLains: Nathan, Melba, Pat, Laverne, and Irvine; the Browns; the Tumblins—there were so many it would be impossible to name them all.

Sadly, the United States in the 1950s was still deeply mired in bigotry. Public places were strictly segregated. Until the Black Power movement in the late 1960s, African Americans were known as "colored people." Segregation was legally ended when the Civil Rights Act of 1964 was passed and became law, but there would sstill be decades of struggle to change people's hearts and minds.

Writing this story was a lot of work, but it brought me much joy. I hope it pays justice and honor to a time and place that no longer exist.

acknowledgments

It takes a lot of faith and teamwork to make a dream come true, and that is exactly what happened with this novel. I have so much to be thankful for and so many people to thank.

It all began with my wonderful agent, Catherine Drayton of Inkwell Management. Thank you for believing in this story and finding the exact team to understand and move it forward.

My amazing editor, Michelle Poploff, and her assistant, Rebecca Short, had the vision and patience to help me weave a small story into the tapestry it has now become. You ladies are great detectives, and a lot of fun to work with, too.

My writing coach and mentor, Barbara Rogan, took me under her wing and guided me through this incredible journey. Thank you for your steadfast encouragement and guidance.

My friends and family have touched my life and left indelible fingerprints. Without all those good, bad, and unforgettable memories, this story never would have come to life. Thank you.

Last but most important, I want to thank my husband, Stuart, for his enduring confidence in my talent and for instilling in me the belief that failure is not an option! Thank you for being in my life.

about the author

Mika Ashley-Hollinger was born and spent her childhood on the east coast of Florida. *Precious Bones* is her debut novel; she wrote it in tribute to a way of life that has all but disappeared. Mika lives with her husband and an assortment of endangered birds and wild chickens on a protected wetland in Hawai'i.